I0634724

Mrs. Goodman's First Murder

Ginny Fite

MILFORD
HOUSE

an imprint of Sunbury Press, Inc.
Mechanicsburg, PA USA

MILFORD HOUSE

an imprint of Sunbury Press, Inc.
Mechanicsburg, PA USA

NOTE: This is a work of fiction. Names, characters, places, and incidents either are the product of the author's imagination or are used fictitiously. While, as in all fiction, the literary perceptions and insights are shaped by experiences, any resemblance to actual persons, living or dead, events, or locales is entirely coincidental.

Copyright © 2025 by Ginny Fite.
Cover Copyright © 2025 by Sunbury Press, Inc.

Sunbury Press supports copyright. Copyright fuels creativity, encourages diverse voices, promotes free speech, and creates a vibrant culture. Thank you for buying an authorized edition of this book and for complying with copyright laws. Except for the quotation of short passages for the purpose of criticism and review, no part of this publication may be reproduced, scanned, or distributed in any form without permission. You are supporting writers and allowing Sunbury Press to continue to publish books for every reader. For information contact Sunbury Press, Inc., Subsidiary Rights Dept., PO Box 548, Boiling Springs, PA 17007 USA or legal@sunburypress.com.

For information about special discounts for bulk purchases, please contact Sunbury Press Orders Dept. at (855) 338-8359 or orders@sunburypress.com.

To request one of our authors for speaking engagements or book signings, please contact Sunbury Press Publicity Dept. at publicity@sunburypress.com.

FIRST MILFORD HOUSE PRESS EDITION: October 2025

Set in Adobe Garamond Pro | Interior design by Crystal Devine | Cover by Lawrence Knorr | Edited by Abigail Bunner.

Publisher's Cataloging-in-Publication Data
Names: Fite, Ginny, author.
Title: Mrs. Goodman's first murder / Ginny Fite.
Description: First trade paperback edition. | Mechanicsburg, PA : Milford House Press, 2025.
Summary: *Fargo* meets Miss Marple in *Mrs. Goodman's First Murder*, a darkly comic twist on the amateur sleuth genre set in a small town where no one is an angel, everyone has an agenda, and fate deals from the bottom of the deck.
Identifiers: ISBN : 979-8-88819-360-0 (paperback).
Subjects: FICTION / General | FICTION / Humorous / Dark Humor | FICTION / Mystery & Detective / Amateur Sleuth | FICTION / Mystery & Detective / Women Sleuths.

Designed in the USA
0 1 1 2 3 5 8 13 21 34 55

For the Love of Books!

For all of us who are not like the others.

ALSO BY
Ginny Fite

Santuary

Leave Everything You Know Behind

The Physics of Things

Possession

Blue Girl on a Night Dream Sea

No End of Bad

Lying, Cheating, and Occasionally Murder

No Good Deed Left Undone

Cromwell's Folly

Thoughts & Prayers (co-author)

)(

"Every murderer is probably somebody's old friend."

—Agathy Christie, *The Mysterious Affair at Styles*

)(

Chapter 1

UNSEEMLY noises rang out from the lobby, shocking Harmon Rutledge into lifting his gaze from the to-do list he was typing on his phone.

"This is a robbery!" a man shouted.

Rubber-soled shoes squeaked. The same voice ordered, "Everybody, down on the floor. Get down or we'll shoot."

The large lobby clock ticked off the seconds and a woman broke into sobs.

Harmon leaped from his leather executive chair and raced into the lobby to take command of the unfolding disaster, the heels of his black leather shoes hammering the marble floor.

"Enough," Harmon shouted, skidding to a stop in front of a short, masked man standing with his arms extended. "The police are on their way."

As if on cue, a white-haired patron sprinted across the floor and hurled herself at the tall, skinny man in a ski mask looming over the tellers' counter. Without saying a word, she whacked the robber in the head with her large bag, threw herself against him, knocking him to the floor, and sat on him.

Spurred to greater courage, Harmon pushed the shorter bandit to his knees, where he cowered, whimpering. They unmasked the robbers, and all the color drained from the brave woman's face as she gaped at the hooligan Harmon had restrained.

When city, county, and state police finally charged into the bank, barking orders and filling the space with their authority, Harmon buttoned his suit jacket and straightened his tie.

Three hours later, his Monday now shot and his face matching the color of his blazing red hair, Harmon escorted the county sheriff to the bank's main entrance and extended his hand in a cordial farewell. "Thank you, Sheriff, for restoring order to our little world." He resisted showing any other signs of deference.

"You did quite well for a bank vice president," the sheriff said.

Harmon quickly discarded the idea that she was mocking him. While he appeared to be the model of decorum, inside Harmon was steaming. His elegant, high-ceilinged bank with polished brass fittings and gleaming chandeliers had been saved not by the police but by a little old lady in sneakers.

The police had checked every cranny of the building for other ruffians, dusted for fingerprints, reviewed video surveillance, and interviewed everyone who'd been in the bank at the time of the failed robbery. To Harmon, they had done more to interrupt normal operations than the robbers, who had been subdued within ten minutes of their intrusion.

"What happens to those miscreants?" Harmon asked.

"Don't worry, sir," Sheriff Jo Hammersmith said, shaking Harmon's hand somewhat too firmly. "We've got 'em dead to rights. We'll make sure the culprits go away for a long time. These guys aren't going to rob any more banks."

Almost as tall as Harmon's six-foot, four inches, the sheriff compelled him to meet her ultramarine eyes. Her irises, ringed in a darker blue, accused him of something, although she said nothing of the kind.

Maybe constant suspicion was a result of her job, he thought. Everyone she met was guilty of something. Almost involuntarily, he cast his eyes down her figure. She was pregnant, a mildly repugnant fact he stored away in case that information might prove useful.

Hammersmith explained that although the bank was located in Charles Town, the 250-year-old West Virginia county seat where, to Harmon's mind, time had stood still, the state police would lead the probe of the bank robbery, assisted by the FBI, if necessary.

Harmon nodded. "We deserve to be protected by the highest authority." This arrangement made sense. In addition to the five thousand Charles Town residents, the federally insured bank served sixty-thousand people who resided in Jefferson County.

"There might be follow up interviews, but they'll notify you directly," Hammersmith said.

Just what he needed. More strangers blindly groping around in his business. Harmon couldn't imagine what additional evidence would be necessary to prosecute the two dodos who tried to rob his bank. They had been caught in the act on videotape. He didn't care who took the lead on locking up the devils. Someone needed to be held responsible for disturbing his peace.

"Arresting the robbers is a good start," he said as he waved goodbye to the sheriff.

Turning to his tellers, Harmon placed his hand on his heart and bowed his head in recognition of their calm comportment despite their fear of being killed during the robbery. They tittered, as they did whenever he thanked them, as if being acknowledged for their work were the last thing they expected.

Their giggles brightened an otherwise horrific day. Now he had to complete a hundred incident reports for corporate headquarters, the insurance company, federal government agencies, and God knew who else. Thank God the ruffians hadn't actually stolen anything. The management manual would tell him who he was supposed to notify first. He'd have to field calls from the board as soon as word of the robbery got out. His ordeal must be all over town by now. Any minute, his direct supervisor, the bank's regional vice president, would call. Harmon intended to use the emotion of the moment to press for hiring a full-time armed guard.

He marched into his office and pushed the door closed until he heard the quiet click guaranteeing the latch was secure. Shutting the blinds on the window facing the street to ensure his privacy, he tossed his gray pin-striped suit jacket with the red and white striped silk lining on the back of his chair and loosened his green silk tie. Worried sweat would stain his bespoke shirt; he ran a finger around his collar to pull the expensive Egyptian cotton fabric away from his skin.

He threw himself into his chair and opened his mouth wide in a silent scream. Waving his arms, slamming his head against the air, he pantomimed stamping his feet. No relief. He pawed through his desk drawer for the anti-anxiety pills his clever wife, the doctor, had prescribed.

Trudy had had her uses.

This was the worst time for him to be interacting with the police. Or to have a panic attack. Harmon poured himself a glass of water from the carafe on his desk and swallowed the pill. He had to appear normal. The botched robbery focused attention on him at a time when he most wanted to blend in. Those moron wannabe robbers had made him seem like a fool instead of refined and competent, a man above reproach who managed his affairs with precise equanimity.

The whole town was probably buzzing with how he'd failed to keep the bank safe, and how the world's most inept robbers had threatened his customers. Of the long list of things he loathed, Harmon most hated being viewed as ineffectual.

Footsteps approached his office door, stopped, and someone knocked. "Mr. Rutledge?"

"Not now," Harmon called out in what he hoped was a controlled voice.

Whoever the intruder was went away, but the brief exchange grounded him. Ethel Goodman—he'd learned the intrepid bank patron's name by eavesdropping on her police interview—had been quite remarkable. Who knew what would've happened if she hadn't shown him even a senior citizen could thwart a bank robber? Those two thugs might have escaped with cash.

He would restore the bank's solid reputation and by extension boost his own by hosting a public event at which the bank honored Ethel for her quick thinking. The board could award her a check for fifty dollars, even one hundred. They could afford to be magnanimous.

Harmon pulled up Ethel's account on his computer and was surprised to discover she was worth more than half a million in his bank alone. Her customer profile had been updated recently to widow, which the bank needed to know for tax reporting purposes. Why didn't he remember her? The bank should have been helping her to invest her money. The whole meme about women becoming invisible when they turned sixty must be true.

Since rewarding Ethel with money wasn't necessary, a plaque commemorating her bravery was the thing to do. They would have a ceremony covered by the media and hang the plaque on the wall. That would be the normal thing, and everyone in town would expect it. The best way to be invisible was to behave the way everyone expected.

To give himself more time to calm down before he dealt with higher-ups, Harmon opened Google on his phone in dark mode. Ethel's photograph came up on the screen opposite her name—curly white hair fluffing around her face as if blown by a sudden breeze, saucer-sized ice-blue eyes, the pink rosebud mouth. She was a real estate agent.

This was serendipity. As part of behaving normally, he would put his house up for sale. This was a tad bit sooner than he'd planned, but Harmon guessed it would take at least three months for a sale, maybe six, and in that time the complicated business about his wife would have concluded. Plus, strangers tromping through his house leaving trails of DNA might prove useful in case he came under official scrutiny.

Arrayed in her new fame, Ethel was just the person to help him blend in, and everyone would believe he was rewarding her quick actions by giving her the listing. His bosses would see him as a good man by association and memories of the whole robbery fiasco would disappear like smoke.

The desk phone rang. Harmon, expecting a call from his boss, automatically punched the speaker button. "Yes."

"Mr. Rutledge, there's a reporter on the line who wants to interview you about the robbery for the newspaper. They need an official statement for the article."

Here was his opportunity to jump out ahead of the story. After all, the best defense was a swift and decisive offense. Harmon grimaced, glad his executive assistant couldn't see him, and said, "Put him through."

"Her, sir; it's her. Millie Overbee from the *Daily*. She was here a little bit ago, but you didn't answer my knock, so I sent her away."

"Oh, really? Okay. Whatever."

While the reporter waded through her introduction, Harmon waited for her to take a breath instead of listening to her first question. He wasn't going to answer questions anyway; he wanted to make a statement and be done with it.

"Yes, well, we of course were startled by this outrageous assault in our quiet community," he said. "Nothing like this has ever happened before in the three years I've been with this bank. But I assure you . . ."

An image of the inside of Trudy's arm lying on the bed, her fingers dangling over the side, diverted him. His train of thought derailed, and he couldn't remember where he was in the sentence.

"Mr. Rutledge?" the reporter prodded.

"Oh, yes, I guess I'm far more distraught . . . about the robbery than I expected." He should try for sympathy but convey the idea that the bank was impregnable and everything was in hand. "Of course, you know we're FDIC insured and if the worst had happened and the robbers had gotten away with any money, all our customers' accounts would still be protected from loss."

The reporter said something Harmon didn't listen to.

"But, of course, they didn't steal anything, and I do want to thank Ethel Goodman for her quick thinking. Quite a remarkable stunt she executed, tackling the robber. I've never seen anything like it before. Quite surprising for an older woman. Heroism such as hers is rare."

The reporter babbled something.

The weight of his wife's body in his arms flew through Harmon's mind. He gasped, then rallied. "Well, I must go back to my work. Reports to file, people to call. Thank you for the interview. I look forward to reading your article."

The reporter was still talking when Harmon hung up, reminding him of a similar exchange he'd had with a different journalist who'd pestered him yesterday, calling his home landline.

That woman had sounded a little taken aback to be speaking to an actual person at nine on a Sunday morning. "Mr. Rutledge?"

"Yes." Still groggy from his nighttime exertions, Harmon had had to shake himself awake. He sat and swung his legs over the side of the bed.

"Are you Harmon Rutledge?" she asked.

"Yes, I said so already."

"Okay, sorry. Sophie Chandler, lifestyle editor from the *Daily*, the paper you sent the wedding announcement to."

"The what?"

"Your wedding announcement?"

"What about it?"

"We have your announcement, but it's six months old—it sort of got lost behind a cabinet—and we're wondering if you still want it to appear in the paper." She sighed and he pictured a mouth-breather with horn-rimmed glasses and dandruff.

"What is it you expect me to do?" Harmon still felt muddle-headed from being awakened.

He had discussed the announcement with his wife months ago. In his opinion, it was absurd to announce their personal business to the world, but it had been important to Trudy and her mother. All those trappings had been important to them—the whole white wedding church thing—and he'd acquiesced to make them happy.

Six months later, he had forgotten all about the announcement and didn't give a fig if it never appeared in the paper, but it annoyed him that even though Trudy had followed all the newspaper's rules for submitting it, there were still problems.

This is how you know society is falling apart, Harmon thought. *No one does anything correctly, even the smallest, most insignificant thing.*

"Do you want us to run it? The announcement." The editor's tone made it crystal clear she didn't want to go through the whole spiel again.

"Keep a level head," his father had always said. The weight of his father's hand on his shoulder, his kind gaze, used to calm Harmon. He couldn't let anything slip now, even in his tone, yet annoyance crept into his voice. "Oh, yes, no, well, I don't know. Wait a minute."

Harmon put the phone on mute while he mulled the problem. This might be one of those moments his mother had always talked about when the universe unexpectedly handed him what he needed. He unmuted the phone and said, "Go ahead, go ahead. She wants you to put the notice in the paper, so do it. It's your screw-up."

Harmon was proud of the way he'd handled this interaction when he hadn't yet figured out what to say about Trudy. If necessary, the conversation with this Sophie person would provide third-party proof that on Sunday, October 12, he was at home and had communicated with his wife.

The editor was a witness, of sorts. It didn't matter that he hadn't actually talked to Trudy. Sophie Chandler could testify she had waited on hold while he consulted his wife, even if that were hearsay and not actually true. But that wouldn't be necessary. Harmon was sure his plan would work.

Recalling his own ingenuity fortified Harmon. Before another flick of fate's tail sent him sailing in the wrong direction again, he dialed the number on Ethel's account. When she answered, he stood as if she had entered the room and introduced himself, surprised by how breathless he sounded. *It's performance anxiety. Keep a level head.*

Ethel cleared her throat, but Harmon didn't wait for her to introduce any complicating factors into his plan. "Mrs. Goodman, I understand you're a real estate agent. I have a house to sell, and I want you to sell it for me."

"Oh my, I haven't, I never, I wouldn't have guessed you'd call about this kind of thing at all," Ethel said. "I did want to talk to you, though. Is there a chance you could drop the charges against Charlie, the short robber? I mean, he's my stepson and his father just died, and he didn't do anything today but stand in the bank fluttering like a burned-out lightbulb. He must have been coerced in some way."

Oh, Christ. She babbles. Harmon drew himself up to his full height, feeling each vertebra inch higher in his spine. "What Charles Goodman is charged with is up to the county prosecutor. But he did try to rob my bank. There are a half-dozen witnesses, including you. I expect there will be jail time."

"But you could put in a good word for him, couldn't you? You must have seen how baffled he was when you intercepted him. He was probably drunk or stoned. Wouldn't that be diminished capacity, and therefore he's not responsible?"

Ethel slurped something, the *swup, swup* sound coming through the receiver loud and clear. She cleared her throat again. The woman was extremely noisy. Harmon began to regret his decision. If she agreed to sell his house, all her noise would invade the quiet sanctuary of his home.

"I couldn't put in a word, no, but are you able to sell my house anyway?" He sounded too desperate. "Selling my house would be as beneficial to you as to me."

"Sorry. I'm so thirsty after my exertions at the bank. My head hasn't cleared yet. You're saying you want me to sell your house? Of course, I can. Let's set up an appointment for me to see it, and we can talk about what's involved."

That was businesslike enough. He gave her his address, and they made an appointment to meet on Wednesday afternoon. Two days was enough time to make sure the house was in order with no telltale signs of Trudy's mess.

After they hung up, Harmon realized he was exhausted also. Still, he had work to do, and he would do it. He could manage anything. Well, except for bears. He'd always been terrified of bears since his mother had stopped the car to let one lumber across the road when he was four, and it had nosed his window, leaving a gauzy circle of breath on the glass.

For an instant, he pictured a large grizzly bear turning her head to stare at him. He shuddered. But there weren't any bears around here. He flipped over a page in the report on his desk, and as the lines blurred, he closed his eyes for a minute, remembering what it felt like to sleep alone on sheets Trudy's body had never touched.

CHAPTER 2

ETHEL Goodman plopped into the cushy green chenille chair in her great room and put her feet on the ottoman, glad she lived five miles outside the town where she was born. All the buzz today would be about how she'd tackled a bank robber. Mouths would flap, but she didn't need to hear them.

The police had taken so long to complete their interviews, she felt like she'd been away from home for a year. Legs weak, mind spinning, Ethel stared out the bay window of her mid-century clapboard and brick split-foyer and saluted the old oak trees hugging her cul-de-sac.

On this block, no house was closer than two hundred feet, which, in Ethel's opinion, was what kept everyone cordial. She was not a share-a-cup-of-sugar kind of person, although unlike her late husband, Ethel liked people. George couldn't stand them. When they'd moved into this exurban subdivision ten years before, he'd tilted his head toward the nearest house and growled, "You're not going to make friends with them, are you?"

She'd laughed and assured him that she had no such intention. By then, she hadn't even wanted him to be there.

Picking up the blue teapot from the table next to her chair, Ethel poured the aromatic chai into her favorite cherry-blossom mug. A surge of deep satisfaction moved through her. Everything was better without George.

The morning's events replayed in her memory without her permission. Seconds after men wearing ski masks had burst into the building, she had warned anyone within earshot, "They're going to rob the bank!"

Employees, trained not to draw inferences from customers' clothing choices and behavior, had ignored her, as if she had Tourette syndrome.

Bank patrons stared at their phone screens. For a minute, Ethel thought she might be wrong.

Your imagination is running away with you, as always, her dead husband said.

Fierce whispering between the robbers developed into a tussle which concluded with a shove. The short robber wobbled to the center of the lobby, his red sneakers squeaking on the polished floor. He thrust out both arms, his fingers arranged in the gesture kids used when they played cops and robbers—pointer fingers straight out, thumbs raised—and turned in a circle. When his face swiveled in her direction, his body jerked and he turned away, shaking.

Something familiar in his gait triggered goosebumps across Ethel's arms, but she couldn't put her finger on the cause.

The tall robber had shouted, "This is a robbery!"

"See, George, I was right," Ethel said as she tossed her head and scanned the lobby for a place to hide.

One time. Don't make a big deal out of it. George always had to have the last word.

When the hoopla was over, that nasty deputy had asked so many questions about the attempted bank robbery, he'd almost convinced her she was embroiled in the whole sordid affair.

The fact that she turned out to be the short robber's stepmother and was in the bank at the same time as the attempted robbery was a coincidence, pure and simple. How could the police not understand this fact? The officer would've been happier if she'd been an accomplice.

"After all, you entered the bank before your stepson, and you signaled to him."

Ethel studied the officer, who surely was no older than the twelve-year-old who skateboarded around her cul-de-sac for hours every day. "I did not signal to him. I had no idea he would enter the bank. I didn't even know he was in the state." Adrenaline from her jiujitsu moves half an hour before had still been flowing through her veins, jangling her nerves. She'd fidgeted in the chair, anxious to go home.

"You motioned to him that there was no guard on duty," the deputy insisted, his fleshy cheeks inflating like a pufferfish. "The teller who pressed the silent emergency alarm said you smiled at the robbers when they entered the bank and then glanced down, like some kind of pre-arranged sign."

Ethel used her most deflating snicker. "There's never a guard in this bank. Of course, I looked at the robbers. They were wearing ski masks, for heaven's sake. Besides, why would I assist them and then try to stop them?"

"You're related to one of them." The officer seemed to think he had her, and if he kept at it, Ethel would admit her complicity.

"I'm also related to George Washington. Does that mean I'm responsible for whatever happens in this country? I hope not."

The officer made a note on his pad. Was he going to check the veracity of her ancestral lineage? He could consult her family tree, of which she was justifiably proud. Her mother, a certified Daughter of the American Revolution, had had one drawn up and framed to prove she was directly descended from the founding president's younger brother, even if her line started with his illicit tryst with an innkeeper's daughter.

The family tree hung above the mantel in Ethel's great room now that George was dead, and she'd been able to remove the portrait of his first wife. History was malleable, and she could be descended from whomever she wanted, even if her husband had always scoffed at what he called her "highfalutin phony-baloney princess shit." She wasn't pretending. She was living her one life, although at times she felt like the last bit of toothpaste squeezed out of the tube.

The phone rang and the screen declared, "Unknown caller."

Ethel considered letting the call go to voice mail and then worried she might miss an opportunity for another real estate listing. Sitting up in her chair, she swiped "accept" on the phone screen. A voice identified itself as Millie Overbee, a reporter from the *Daily*. Ethel immediately regretted her decision to take the call.

"Is this Ethel Goodman?"

"That's right."

"The Ethel Goodman who thwarted a bank robbery at First Charles Town Bank today?"

"Correct." Maybe one-word answers would bore the reporter, and she'd give up.

"Mrs. Goodman, could you tell me what made you so heroic at the bank today?"

"I was a teacher in the public school system for thirty years—which was pretty damn heroic even if no one ever acknowledges it." The last thing Ethel had expected in her retirement was becoming famous for stopping her stepson from robbing a bank. "Truth is, I have no idea why I was so daring."

"Could you expand on that?" the Millie person prompted.

"I don't know what came over me today." Ethel sighed. "It seemed like the thing to do, you know, what needed to be done. I'm no superhero. But someone needed to do something."

"May I ask how old you are?"

"Why does my age matter?"

"Readers like to know that sort of thing."

This was the reason old women were desperate to appear young; age was seen as a communicable disease like leprosy. Ethel remembered herself in her forties, still full of juice and dreaming of possibilities. Vague memories of a younger George played through her mind. The heat she'd felt when his hand brushed hers. Those eyes.

Ethel collected herself. "*Humph*. I'm sixty-seven years old and proud of it." Maybe her actions today would change people's ideas about being old. She lifted her chin even though Millie couldn't see her.

"How did you come to be so agile that you could tackle a man less than half your age?"

There it was again, a question implying age was a disability. "Well, I play pickle ball."

Millie snorted.

"I'm on a team. And I've taken yoga and self-defense classes for years. Did you know yoga is so powerful that Alabama banned teaching it in public schools?"

"What? Why?"

"They didn't want children learning the dangerous words *namaste* and *om*."

"Oh, my God. For real? I didn't know that."

"Well, now you do." Delighted she'd knocked the reporter off course, Ethel said, "I should have just yelled 'Namaste' at the robbers."

Millie chuckled. "That would've stopped them in their tracks. And you are currently a real estate agent at Steptoe and Fritter?"

Ethel stiffened. "Being a real estate agent has nothing to do with what happened today. I don't think you should include that in your story. The company might object."

"Okay. I'll check with them. So, you unmasked the robber who demanded money from the tellers?"

"The tall one. Yes."

Ethel instantly relived sprinting across the shiny marble floor and striking the tall robber in the face with her heavy handbag before he could duck. He covered his head with his arms and backed away, but she threw herself against him and he went down with a thud, banging the back of his head on the floor. His eyes fluttered and closed. Ethel pounced on his stomach and pinned his arms with her knees.

"I'll have to tell my self-defense instructor this move works," she'd whispered.

"Did you know the man?"

"Never saw him before in my life." An image of the stranger sprang to her mind—a man in his twenties, skin the translucent blue color of skim milk, dark curly hair, gray eyes, and gaunt looking as if his mother had never fed him enough. A whiff of week-old garbage had seeped from him.

"His name is Don Whitley. You never met him before?"

"Nope. Like I said, he's a stranger to me."

"Have you lived in the Charles Town area long?" Millie asked.

"I've been in this county all my life. I was born here, like my mother, and grandmother, and her grandmother, I might add going back to the revolution."

Millie cleared her throat. "Um, and the other robber was your stepson?"

Ethel pushed herself out of the chair and paced the great room to think about how to respond to this intrusive question. When Harmon Rutledge had unmasked Charlie, all the blood in her body had risen to her face accompanied by a buzzing in her ears. Her nose got cold, and the room spun. Perched on the tall robber, she worried she would faint. She did not want to go down this road with a reporter.

"His name is Charles Goodman. Is that correct?" Millie prodded.

"That's his name."

"Were you surprised to see him in your bank this morning?"

Ethel tried to tamp down her anger. She had always hated the thoughtless way Charlie behaved, expecting his father to clean up after him as if he'd never been properly toilet-trained. She'd also hated George for being a crap father, a failing she'd hoped her presence would improve but instead exacerbated. *Charlie acts out to get even with George for marrying me.* It was a little late for that bit of enlightenment.

But just as she had gotten free of George and begun to anticipate riding a camel in Egypt or kayaking with whales in Alaska, the boy involved himself in this stupid robbery. Now she'd be saddled with taking care of him until she died.

"Ethel? Hello? Are you still there?" Millie asked.

"I'm here. You can't call Charlie a robber since he didn't steal anything, and he didn't demand any money. He was just . . . for show. An accessory."

"How did Charlie know Don Whitley?"

"I have no idea. He hasn't lived at home for years."

"So, you're a local hero, Ethel. You must be feeling pretty good."

"Frankly, I feel tired. I need a nap." Ethel regretted snapping at the reporter. What if Millie included that statement in her story? That would make the whole aging meme seem true. Ethel could picture the headline: *Bank Antics Fatigue Retiree.*

The reporter made a humming sound in her throat. "You've had quite a few troubles recently. Didn't your husband, George Goodman, die two months ago? The paper ran his obituary."

"I don't see how George has anything to do with what happened at the bank today. I did what I did because I didn't want my bank robbed," Ethel said. "I didn't think about it."

This wasn't the whole truth, which was always too complicated, had too many overlapping layers, and took too long to explain. She would never tell anyone that George had tormented her. Not in the normal way married people harass each other, but with a sustained cruelty no one detected.

George's weapon of choice had been the silent treatment, which was ironic because now he was dead, he wouldn't shut up. He had alternated silence with random barrages of criticism generously sprinkled with variations of the words "psychotic," "useless," and "stupid."

Now that she thought about it, she'd lived with a psychological terrorist for two decades, never knowing when or where his bombs would explode. No wonder she was tired. The more he attacked her, the more she craved his death. The day she decided to solve the problem, everything had changed. Ethel could still smell the burning sage at the Herbs & Remedies shop and feel the healer's hands on hers.

Focus, Ethel, George said, *you've got too many tabs open.*

What do you know? Ethel thought.

"You also had a serious accident in Maryland, wasn't it?" Millie asked, bringing Ethel back into the present. "Your car was totaled. Didn't that happen the same day your husband died? You were in the hospital for a week?"

The collision, her terror, beeping machines, nurses and doctors, the endless pain in her head, the smell of bleach and ammonia crashed through Ethel's memory. "How do you know about my accident? Who told you? What about privacy laws?"

"Your accident was reported in the Montgomery County paper where the crash happened. I did my research before I called you. A little background information helps me create a picture of you for our readers." Millie took an audible breath. "Your husband's death must have been quite a blow. You were married for almost a quarter of a century. That's something."

"I know people who've been married for fifty years," Ethel said. If those marriages were anything like hers, though, she had no idea how the wives endured it so long.

"What would your husband have said about your heroics today?" Millie asked.

"George was a utilitarian," Ethel said. "He would tell you when the car got totaled, my brain got rattled."

But he would have reacted with shock and dismay, Ethel thought, when Harmon Rutledge unmasked Charlie. *It's a good thing you're already dead. That would've killed you.*

Millie chuckled. "You certainly have spunk. Could we have a photographer take a picture of you for a follow-up story in the weekend edition? You could meet us at the bank."

"A photograph?" Maybe having her picture in the paper would result in more real estate clients like Harmon Rutledge. "Okay, sure, why not?"

They set a day and time for the photography session and ended the call. Ethel sank back into the chair and closed her eyes. Staying alert for the whole conversation had drained her. At any minute, she might have slipped and told the reporter what she was really thinking.

CHAPTER 3

AFRAID to sit anywhere in a cell that smelled like mildew, piss, and something worse, Charlie Goodman paced, six strides back and forth across the floor like a goldfish in a small bowl. No one could blame him for being frustrated. To make everything more confusing, hoping that Ethel would extricate him from his troubles messed with his fixed ideas about life, people, himself, and Ethel in particular.

Everything always went sideways in Charlie's life. First that stupid wannabe bank robbery, and now he had to wait to see if his stepmother—an honorific he had never accorded Ethel—would bail him out of jail. It was humiliating. But worse than that, the day's events validated what his father had always said about him. He was a loser. Going along to get along was always a bad idea. He should've known that by now, but he hated confrontations.

Bottom line, though, this wasn't his fault. He'd done nothing except help a guy who'd asked him to come along on a ride. No one could expect him to know what Don was up to. Maybe he could've asked, but Don was offended by questions.

Charlie had long ago acknowledged he was doomed to failure. He drank on days he dreaded going into the office and on the days he didn't have to work, as a celebration. A vodka at breakfast minus the tomato or orange juice, a few beers at lunch, and he was good to go. He was also known to down a Dewar's on the rocks at dinner if someone else was buying. He liked that about himself, that he wasn't a one-drink kind of guy and thought of himself as in charge of the problem.

The main problem caused by his drinking, as Charlie saw it, was that sometimes when he typed *inconvenient* it came out *incontinent*, *excremental* for *expeditious*, *ludicrous* for *lovely*. The verbs were worse, as if someone else were typing, someone who loved to screw with him. A tendency for error wasn't helpful in public relations, and he never caught his mistakes until after he hit Send, and then it was too late to recall the email or edit the release.

There was nothing he could do about it. His fingers had their own fill-in-the-gap app, autocompleting his sentences the wrong way. Even though he proofed his work, he never caught those sneaky word substitutions as if his dark side had taken control when he wasn't paying attention, which his father would have said was all the time.

He couldn't be the only one this happened to, or they wouldn't have built Ctrl z into keyboard functions. Or had confessional booths in churches. Nevertheless, when he accidentally included a television news director in an all-employees email telling them to expect imminent personnel changes arising from a forty-million-dollar hole in the company's books, his boss had fired him. Charlie took that insult hard.

A masked guard rapped on the bars of the cell with his baton. Charlie guessed the mask was to protect him from germs. Or the smell. From the vacancy in the man's eyes, Charlie knew prisoners were invisible. No point in trying to make small talk or be charming.

"Your lawyer's here. Let's go."

"Go where?"

"To the room where your lawyer's waiting for you." The guard tapped his baton against his palm.

Charlie waited for the next instruction, working hard at not asking pesky questions.

"I don't need to cuff you, do I?"

"No. No, you don't." His wrists still hurt from being cuffed at the bank.

The guard led Charlie to a small, windowless room that must have been painted last in the previous century. A young woman with wild, curly brown hair sat at the steel table. She wore a tweed suit, white blouse, and black-rimmed glasses. Freckles dotted her tawny face, and she was stunning. Smart women terrified Charlie; beautiful women made his tongue go numb. Palms sweating and tongue-tied, he stood at attention waiting for the next instruction.

"Take a seat, Mr. Goodman. I'm Angela Markey from the public defender's office. We're going to talk about your case and how I can help you. Your stepmother's got clout at the courthouse. Apparently, her uncle is Judge Monroe? Anyway, she pulled a few strings, and I was assigned to assist you, perhaps to get you a pre-trial diversion. She indicated you had certain disabilities?"

Charlie's lips smiled without his permission. Ethel had played both the family and the disability cards. His father had always sneered at him for having an attention disorder, as he called it, but in this case, Charlie was willing to go with whatever worked. He folded his hands on the table to show he intended to behave the way he was taught in kindergarten.

But what if I am disabled and that explains everything?

"Focus, Charlie," he remembered his father saying.

Charlie gathered some words together he hoped would come out the right way. "You're going to be my lawyer?"

"Yes, if that's what you want, I'm your lawyer."

"Okay. Great. Yeah." Charlie stared at his knees so she wouldn't see him grinning.

"You're charged with attempted bank robbery. This is a serious charge. I need to know what happened so I can develop a strategy to defend you."

"From the beginning?" Charlie asked. "Like when I was born?"

She smiled. "Not that far back. Just begin with how you agreed to rob a bank."

"But I didn't agree. Honest."

She frowned.

Charlie held up his hand. "Okay. I get it. This whole mess with the bank robbery started when I was fired from my job. I was doing okay for about four years until then."

"Okay. Let's start with when you were fired."

"So, it took me six years to get my bachelor's degree in communications, and then I got this job right out of college at a big communications company in the DC area, first as an intern and then full-time." Charlie glanced at her face and thought he read disapproval. "Ridiculous, I know, but I did it, and my dad was proud of me."

She coughed into her fist. "You don't have to tell me about every year of your life, just what happened leading up to the robbery."

"Yeah, right, that's what I'm doing," Charlie said. "So, the president of my division wanted to prepare the rank and file for layoffs, to let them down easy. Internal communication was part of my job. But I didn't realize when I sent the memo that I'd also informed the media until my boss called me into his office. He found out from the CEO, who had gotten a call from a TV reporter about the pending layoffs. My boss was really pissed."

"Wait," the lawyer said. "When was this?"

"Well, maybe six months ago, about."

"Does this have anything to do with the bank robbery?"

"It's all connected."

Angela twiddled her pen. "Go ahead." She made a note on her pad.

"Anyway, what could have been a messy public relations fiasco became a downright disaster 'cause the new corporate partner they needed for a big money infusion didn't like the bad publicity about the layoffs and threatened to pull out of the deal."

Defending himself felt good. Plus, if Angela understood him, she would like him. "But the shit hit the fan, excuse my French, when a major national newspaper ran a story about the company going bust. Then three hundred people were laid off in one fell swoop to balance the books so they could look profitable on paper, and they all blamed me."

Charlie wiped his forehead. He was surprised by how easily the story spilled out. He'd been holding it in until the right person came along to hear it.

"I wasn't the bad guy, you know. I'm not the one who embezzled forty million bucks to buy a yacht and tried to claim it was an accounting error. But it was useless trying to explain this to anyone. In the world of zeros and ones, there's sent or not sent, yes or no, on or off, alive, or dead. I knew which zone I'd fallen into."

Angela flipped the page on her pad. "You have a colorful way of talking."

Charlie smiled at the off-hand compliment. "Well, I tried to apologize to my boss, but I'd been swigging with regularity from my pocket flask because I was nervous, so maybe I didn't. Apologize, I mean. I don't remember what I said."

The lawyer gave Charlie a look he couldn't interpret. "Do you drink a lot?"

"Well, yeah. I'm what you might call a maintenance drinker," Charlie said. "I binge on weekends and holidays, but if I get anxious, I take a swig or two to calm down. When I'm drinking, the line between what I imagine and what actually happened gets blurry, so . . ." He hadn't wanted to tell the lawyer this. Stuff just slipped out of his mouth.

He drew a breath, and the lawyer held up her hand. "Wait, let me catch up." She scribbled on her legal pad.

While he waited, Charlie remembered how panicked he'd been when he was fired. When his unemployment insurance ran out, he couldn't pay the rent on his studio apartment or his electric bill, and the cupboard was bare. But his father wouldn't give him any more money.

STOP GOING TO BARS IN THE MIDDLE OF THE DAY. STOP BUYING ROUNDS FOR EVERYONE, his father had texted in response to Charlie's request for maybe a thousand or two to tide him over. Along with bullshit about tough love and bootstraps, his father had typed, THIS IS THE WAY YOU'RE GONNA LEARN.

In that moment, he began to understand what hitting bottom might be like.

Then he contemplated telling his father how to undo all caps but refrained. The old man was at the end of his tether. Nevertheless, to coax him into one more loan, Charlie claimed he'd applied for a job and was waiting for the manager's decision. Which wasn't true in the sense of being real, although he wanted it to be true, so it half-counted. In fact, he'd spent the previous four months on the couch playing Royal Match in his underwear.

"By the way, are you on any medication?" Angela asked.

Charlie squirmed. The sweats had started. Pretty soon he'd be dripping on the table. Hoping Angela wouldn't notice, he wiped his forehead with his hand. His hands were shaking. *I need a drink.* "Supposed to be but I stopped refilling my prescription about two years ago."

"Is that because you couldn't afford it?"

"Well, mostly 'cause I didn't need it anymore."

Angela made a note. "Okay. Go on with your story."

"Well, two months after being evicted from my apartment, I was living in my car. But then my car was repossessed while I was in the restroom at the gas station. So, I hitched to my father's house and begged Dad to let me come home. He just stared at me like I was a red-lipped batfish."

"A what?"

"It's kind of like the aquatic equivalent of the blue-footed booby. You know, the bird? Never mind. I watch a lot of nature TV. Point is, he acted like he'd never seen anything as weird as me in his life."

The lawyer's hand scooted across the lines on the pad. "And what did your father say?"

"He said, 'For Christ's sake, grow up. When you're here, you steal from us, you get so drunk you pass out on the kitchen floor, you bring your drunken friends home to steal from us, you make a mess of everyone's life and never clean up afterward or apologize.' My dad always exaggerated. Anyway, he batted his hand in the air and walked away from me."

"Okay. Then what?"

"My father said he didn't trust me anymore. 'You gotta plan better,' he said. 'Think things through before you pull the trigger. Stay in a shelter, get sober, find a job, any job, and save money for an apartment. Make a plan for your future. I'm done.'

"I'm like on my knees, saying, 'Please, Dad, I don't know what I'm supposed to do.' And he's like, 'You're thirty fucking years old. Figure it out.' Of course, I wasn't thirty yet, but he never knew how old I was. Anyway, he slips the address of the local shelter and two twenties into my shirt pocket, says, 'Don't drink it away in one day,' and closes the door in my face."

"When was this?"

"About six weeks ago?" Charlie shrugged. "But don't hold me to that. I'm not great with dates and timelines."

"So how did you get to Charles Town, West Virginia?"

"I'm getting to that."

Angela flipped to a new page on her pad.

"I couched it for a few weeks at a friend's apartment in Frederick, Maryland. On the morning I was ready to tackle my father again, I'm talking to my friend's bird, and I spot a photo of my dad in the newspaper that's lining the bottom of the birdcage. I yank out the paper and the article is an obituary. While I was lying around scratching my balls and eating popcorn, my father died. And no one, in particular my step-witch, Ethel, called to tell me. I was levitating with fury. Then I remembered no one knew where I was, and my phone service had been terminated because I didn't pay the bill."

"Stop for a minute," Angela said, shifting on the chair and crossing her legs. "Let me recap. After you lost your job, apartment, car, and phone, your father died."

"Right." Charlie stretched. "Is it okay if I stand up and walk around?"

"No. It's not okay. Where's your mother?"

"She died a long time ago in a car accident. My father was driving. I was little."

"Got it. Tell me the rest of the story."

"Okay. So, I borrowed fifty bucks from my friend's wallet and Ubered to Dad's house and everything looked normal, which is weird, right? Because now my dad's dead, everything should be different. Anyway, the doors and windows are locked and no one's home. Believe me, I tried all the doors. No cars in the driveway, no sign of life inside the house. Even the back porch screen door was secured by an inside latch.

"I rang the bell, pounded on the windows, yelling, 'Ethel, Ethel,' at the top of my lungs. Nothing. The bitch didn't open the door. Sitting on the front steps, I considered what to do between nips besides banging on the front door and yelling, 'Ethel, open the damn door.'

"After a few hours, I fell asleep on the porch, still hoping to shame her into giving me some of the old man's money to tide me over until I got a job. Around midnight, the cops woke me. They have their hands on their tasers, which is scary, you know, and the flashlight is blinding me. One of them says, all formal like, 'Sir, we've had a complaint about the noise you're making. Do you live here?'

"So, I stagger to my feet, trying to be dignified, and say, 'Yes. No. I should, I did, but I don't.' Blowing it, in other words. Anyway, they ask for ID, and I hand them my wallet. The cop reads my license and says, 'The address on your driver's license says you live in Maryland. Is that where you live?'

"So, I say, 'I did, but I lost my apartment, and I just found out my father died, and nobody told me about it, and I missed the funeral, and I'm an orphan, and now no one's home.' I mean, I'm in tears at this point. But the cops are like meh.

"They haul me away in their patrol car. To add insult to injury, they don't even put me in jail where I could have gotten three meals a day and a cot to sleep on. Which, by the way, might have saved me from this particular mess. Instead, they drive me seven miles west of my dad's house and drop me off in this small town the size of a dot with a warning not to venture back within *county* limits or I'll be arrested for vagrancy."

"So that's how you got to Charles Town," Angela said. "County deputies dropped you in town."

"Yes. I was stranded here. With nothing."

The lawyer raised her pen off the pad. "And?"

"Can we continue this tomorrow?" Confessing was tiring.

"No. I hope to have you bailed by tomorrow. How did you get involved in a robbery?"

"I'm getting to that. I just wanted to give you the context."

Angela smiled and then composed her face.

"Well, so now I'm homeless, penniless, and orphaned. Charles Town looks like it must have in 1786 when the original plan was drawn up. I walk the five-block-by-one-block-deep town center, and check where the parks, alleys, and public benches are, and what services are available to people like me who my father calls bums."

"Could you speed up this part?" the lawyer asked.

Charlie pressed his lips together. "It's all of a piece. You have to hear the whole thing."

She rotated her hand in a circle twice, which he took to mean he should go on.

"So anyway, I spent a couple weeks in the shelter, which is kind of like rehab 'cause no drugs or alcohol, and I picked up some free clean clothes." Charlie waved at his body to indicate his togs. "During the day, I went to the library where there's computers, bathrooms, and soft chairs. By the fourth week I was feeling a little anxious that this was going to be my life forever. I could feel like a normal person in the library, which was always near empty and so quiet sometimes I wanted to shout something, but I restrained myself. If the librarian threw me out, all the homeless might be barred, and that wouldn't be fair to them."

Angela glanced up and made a note on her pad.

"I'm an accidental vagrant. I haven't chosen the drifter life. It just sort of happened. I'm still expecting to be rescued." Charlie smiled his most charming smile and then remembered he hadn't brushed his teeth in days.

"So, where did you meet Don Whitley?"

"At the library about a week ago. I had scrolled on my socials for a while, and I was wiped out. I should have searched the job listings and applied for at least one position the way Dad always nagged me to, but I couldn't bring myself to do it. Every time I try to talk myself into planning my next move so I can survive on my own, my inevitable failure bubbles up. I get depressed, the darkness crushes the air out of my lungs, and my head gets so heavy, I have to lay it down."

Angela reached across the table and put her hand on his arm. Charlie stared at her, amazed at her reaction. "Go on," she said.

"Anyway, I fell asleep and dreamed I was Charlize Theron, stunning in a gold lamé dress and a necklace dripping with diamonds and pearls like in her perfume commercial. I'm so rich in this dream I don't have to wear socks. Everyone applauds; people love me. Then someone squeezes my shoulder, interrupting my moment, and when I glance up this skinny guy's blue lips are moving.

"He says, 'Hey man. Need a place to stay? There's room at my place.' That was Don Whitley."

"At last," Angela said. "What was Don doing there?"

"He said he came in to use the facilities. He seemed harmless. I figured there was no problem in going along for the bed until I got hold of Ethel. More privacy than sleeping at the shelter. I had nothing to lose, and I was grateful he was willing to help me. So, when a couple days later he said we were going for a ride, I went along."

"Is that it, then?" Angela asked. "Don took you in when you were homeless, and you had no idea he was planning to rob a bank?"

"Nada. Zip. I'm not sure he's the kind of guy who plans anything. He talked about robbing a bank like a super-jock fantasy he was having, not a real job he wanted to pull. We watched movies where guys got away with robbing banks and stuff but nothing dangerous. I had no idea he was serious. Not till he pulled me out of his truck, yanked a mask over my head, and pushed me into the center of the bank lobby."

"Have you ever been convicted of a felony before in this state or any other?"

"No. Not that I remember, anyway. Like, I got a moving violation and a DUI when I was a teenager, but nothing serious. No dealing or stealing if that's what you're asking."

"Okay, I might be able to do something with this," Angela said, packing up her briefcase. "Hang tight. Your initial appearance before the Magistrate is tomorrow. You'll be taken to the courthouse. Try not to look too wrinkled. Just say 'Not guilty' when the judge asks you how you plead. Your stepmother, whatever you think of her, is going to bail you out. I'll try to get it reduced to an amount she can manage."

Charlie was escorted back to the small cell feeling sorry for himself. He was the same as everyone else, trying to go along, live his life, have a few good friends, and nothing ever worked out right.

Hands shaking, he walked the four steps from the cell door to the bunk, sat down, and put his face in his hands to consider his grim future. He did still have something to lose—his freedom—which of course he'd never valued until right now when the two people who could save him were a slip of a lawyer and a stepmother who hated him.

CHAPTER 4

TWO hours after their arrest, a deputy dragged Don Whitley from the county sheriff's holding cell to a tiny, windowless room with walls the color of puke, shoved him into a chair, and linked his handcuffs to a metal ring on the table in front of him.

Don had been waiting for transportation to the regional jail following his arrest for bank robbery and didn't expect an interview. He kept telling himself to chill, but he found it hard to be relaxed about his situation. Charlie was a wild card. Don didn't know the guy and had no idea how he'd react under pressure. Charlie might get caught by a trick question or tell the police the truth because he couldn't think of anything else to say.

He could hear Charlie saying, "We were copying a movie, the one where they nab fifty thousand dollars, and no one gets hurt during the hold-up. Don said we'd be set for life. We were going to go to Las Vegas. We worked it out on paper."

The county sheriff entered the room and stared at Don for two minutes before she said anything. Worms squirmed around in his pants. *This ain't gonna be good for me.*

Pacing the small interrogation room, Sheriff Jo Hammersmith read Don his rights and then said, "Caught you in the act, dimwit. Best if you plead guilty and save the county a bundle in court costs, but for my peace of mind I gotta know what you think you were doing in the bank."

"I wasn't out to hurt anyone," Don said. "Anyway, you didn't catch me. Old Mrs. Busybody did." He sucked air through his teeth as it hit him that he'd just admitted he tried to rob the bank. He reminded himself that the sheriff was tricky.

She must have gained twenty pounds since the last time he was arrested five years ago. She was the deputy who'd nabbed him for the liquor store heist when he was eighteen. The buttons on her regulation brown shirt were barely holding on to the buttonholes for dear life.

For a second, this observation made him feel superior to her because thin people were supposed to be better than fat ones according to the commercials on TV. He raised his chin and scowled at her.

"You are dumber than a box of rocks," Sheriff Hammersmith said. "Didn't you learn from the last time you tried it that you're no good at robbery?"

"I don't know what you're talking about." Don tried not to feel insulted, but the sheriff calling him dumb reminded him of every time his mother had done it. And teachers, the principal at his high school, his employers—they all got around to saying the D word. And when they did, they always made the same face, like he smelled like month-old cheese covered in green fungus that they'd dug out of the back of the refrigerator.

The sheriff glared at him. "Look, kid, this is serious stuff. The county's going to prosecute you to the fullest extent of the law. You're gonna wind up in prison. For God's sake, we've got you on video trying to rob the bank."

Don shrugged. "Photographs can be faked."

"You parked right in front of the bank where the camera had a fine view of you exiting your truck. You didn't put on your masks until you got out of the vehicle. We got you storming into the building and more footage of you inside the bank trying to rob it."

"Wait a minute now," Don said, trying to sound like he knew what he was doing.

"We've got half a dozen eyewitnesses. Aside from the obvious question of why you imagined you'd succeed in robbing a bank, why would you announce you had a gun when you didn't?"

Sweat dribbled down Don's forehead. *I'm screwed.* The sheriff wouldn't believe him no matter what he said, but he'd been sure if he thought he could rob a bank, then he could. "I want a lawyer."

"C'mon, kid," Hammersmith said, her voice sounding like gravel unloading from the back of a dump truck. "This kind of attitude isn't gonna earn you any respect. Everybody saw you robbing the bank. You were unmasked by an old lady who's the new local hero. It'll be all over the papers. What do you think is going to happen here?"

"I want to talk to a lawyer. After that, I'll talk to you with my lawyer present." Don closed his eyes so he couldn't see her face.

"Okay. If that's the way you want to play it, but this is your second offense, it's a felony, and you're going to prison for a while, lawyer, or no lawyer."

Don couldn't tell if he'd won or lost this round, but they let him call his mother, who was not kind on the phone. "Your idiot face is all over my social," she screamed at him. "All my friends know you robbed the bank."

"I didn't rob it, Mom. I didn't end up with any money. I attempted it."

"Cheese and crackers, Don. What am I gonna do with you?"

"Get me outta here, Mom, please."

CHAPTER 5

THE cleaner had come on her usual Tuesday, but in Harmon's estimate, she never did the job the way he would have and wasn't thorough enough for Ethel Goodman's market assessment walk-through. He also needed to check the entire house to ensure that no telltale signs of the scuffle with his wife remained.

Harmon hated that the botched bank robbery on Monday had put him under police scrutiny, and now he had to scurry around to amend his original scheme. Plans needed to age before they were deployed. Consequences needed to be weighed. Otherwise, one might be surprised by how things turned out. He liked to take his time and do things in the right order. On the other hand, certain provocations demanded an immediate response and sometimes improvisation was necessary. Winging it, in his experience, was tricky.

Of all his mother's teachings, what had stuck with Harmon the longest was protecting his boundaries. She'd insisted he was worth fighting for, and anyone who stepped over the line was in for a battle. His wife should have known that, not that he'd told her anything about his late unlamented mother. But Trudy should have picked up on this fact by the way he comported himself. For a smart woman, she could be slow to grasp fundamentals.

Harmon's brittle imitation of someone who cared about his wife had snapped the moment she questioned his fashion sense. But anything could have set him off. Truth be told, he had just needed an excuse; it had been such a long time since he'd scratched that itch.

On that fateful morning five days ago when the blinkers had fallen from his eyes, Trudy's mouth had stretched thin and then pouted, and the little lines that would incise her cheeks in another ten years became visible. He'd had to act. His autonomy had hung in the balance. Harmon had no regrets now, but he had to be careful, and this stupid bank robbery had put him in jeopardy.

Plumping up the pillows on the sofa in the living room, Harmon scrutinized the window wall for smudges, spraying a small spot and wiping it with the special cloth he'd purchased for this purpose.

When he'd realized Trudy had to go, it had taken him a day to formulate a plan. He took no notes, made no diagrams or lists, left no fingerprints for anyone to reverse engineer his design. In his estimation, this ability to keep a complicated plan in his mind was a sign of his genius.

Harmon swabbed the interior of the wall oven's glass door until every sign of the last roast he'd ever cooked disappeared. When the task was done, he removed his mask and admired his image in the gleaming glass. He loved a clean kitchen. After all, the house reflected him, and he wanted to show it off in the best light.

Like buildings seen at night through the rain-streaked window of a moving train, a new plan began to form, indistinct but pressing toward his consciousness. He just had to wait. The phone rang, startling him.

"Just calling to remind you of our appointment," Ethel Goodman's voice chirped from the phone. "I'll be there in an hour."

"Yes, yes. I'm at home," Harmon confirmed. But now he'd lost sight of his plan. This woman was as infuriating as his mother and wife.

As with everything else, he blamed his mother for his receding hairline, the curly red hairs on his big toes, and the Dudley Do-Right good looks that demanded heroic acts he had no intention of committing—well, except for saving his bank. His mother, whose philosophy had twisted him for life, was also on the hook for the fact that he'd married someone who was wrong for him. Trudy was like his mother—sure that she was right about everything.

There was something anti-biological about marriage, Harmon decided, even if it was a social necessity. Cells divided and doubled their nuclei; they didn't cut themselves in half and join up at the navel. The degree of closeness required by marriage was psychologically claustrophobic. Harmon was sure society's demand for couple-hood was the mark of an immature civilization.

Yet at black-tie functions and casual company picnics, the bank president and chairman of the board had always asked him when he was getting married, as if being married were part of the job description. They would clap him on the shoulder and boom, "Where are you hiding your lady, young man?"

It didn't help matters that he had hinted he was engaged even before he'd met Trudy on an online dating service. He'd felt pushed into an arrangement for which he was unsuited, and then he'd had to produce her like a magician pulling a bouquet from his sleeve.

Harmon dusted the blades of the overhead fan in the master bedroom and tried to focus on his new plan but kept being swept up in a tide of old recriminations. Had he known in advance marriage would be disgusting, for instance, the sharing of body fluids part, he would never have said yes when she asked.

Not that he didn't enjoy a satisfying purge once in a while, but the squishy embracing afterward, her wet thighs, and the swampy smell of sex made him squeamish. Even remembering how his wife rarely closed the bathroom door made him nauseous. How could his doctor wife think it was acceptable for her husband to witness her biological functions? He'd wanted to suggest she close the door but refrained out of fear of the consequences. Her tongue left marks.

He moved on to polishing the brass knobs on every door, stepping back to examine each one to ensure he could see his reflection.

A sudden memory of mounting his sleeping wife three nights ago—straddling her hips, holding a pillow down over her face, her body thrashing, her muffled screams—made his groin throb. Harmon held his breath. A thrill of freedom pulsed through him, and, for a second, he felt as if he could fly.

The hard part had been driving the speed limit afterward so as not to be stopped by police with Trudy's body in the trunk. His normal highway driving speed hovered around eighty miles an hour; the effort of going sixty-five made him sweat. His brilliant plan had involved leaving her in the trunk of her own car in the long-term parking lot of the Baltimore Washington International airport in Maryland. Harmon had presumed airport personnel would discover it a month or so later when the reek from the trunk would have indicated something was wrong.

Before he arrived at the remote parking lot, Harmon had slipped on his gloves and baseball cap and pulled up his hoodie. Randomly selecting a parking space on the acres of asphalt, he parked and took a photo of the space number with his phone. Then he opened the trunk and squeezed her still-limp fingers against the parking ticket dispensed by machine at the entrance to the lot. He slipped the ticket behind the garage door opener on the driver's side sunscreen.

Taking Trudy's debit card, he left her wallet with the license and credit cards in the large tote bag on the floor of the car. He hadn't found her cell phone anywhere in the house, so he assumed that it was in her bag as well. Checking in the rearview mirror to make sure the hoodie and baseball cap obscured his face, he locked the car using his own key fob and strolled to the bus stop to wait for the airport shuttle.

There'd been no need to wipe his prints off the car. Of course, his prints would be there; he was her husband. He would have been in the car hundreds of times. He'd left her wallet so she could be identified, reasoning police had to confirm she was dead so he could get his hands on her trust fund money and the life insurance.

The thought of fingerprints reminded Harmon to dust the doors inside the house, picking up the smallest particles of dirt from the decorative detailing. This was tedious work but necessary if the house were to sparkle and sparkle it would.

Keeping his head down to ensure the camera on the ATM machine did not capture an image of his face, he'd used Trudy's debit card to get cash at the airport at 1:30 A.M., mentally thanking her for insisting they know each other's PINs. His gloves ensured he'd left no prints on the machine's keys. The bank activity would make it look like she was still alive, or that someone had stolen her bank card and forced her to give them her PIN number before they killed her, if anyone checked. Then, he took a cab to Baltimore's inner harbor, threw the ATM card and cap into the murky water, tossed the hoodie in a public trashcan, walked to the Sheraton hotel and from there hailed another cab back home. He had started at 12 A.M. and was home by dawn. Quite efficient if he said so himself.

As he polished the last brass knob, the lavender smell of Trudy's nightgown wafted around him. He waved off the memory. The benefits of his actions outweighed the negatives. He would never have to court another woman again, he'd get sympathy for having been abandoned, and soon, he'd be a rich man without ever having to defer to a wife or pretend to be carried away by lust.

Buoyed by this compensation, he applied the special granite cleaner to the kitchen counters and rubbed them until they shone while he assessed all the times in the past six months he'd had to hang from the chandelier, as he referred to their extended love-making bouts. Trudy took a long time to climax. The memory reminded him to dust the Venetian glass chandelier in the dining room.

The things he had done to please that woman. Did she know his heart wasn't in it? *What if her heart wasn't in it?* Harmon stopped dusting. It was one thing to acknowledge he hadn't loved Trudy; it was quite another to stumble on the idea that she might not have loved him either.

He rubbed his forehead to rid his mind of such absurdities and plugged in the vacuum, cleaning the steps leading to the family room and three more bedrooms downstairs. He had done his bedroom on Sunday morning; it wasn't necessary to do it again. As the vacuum blared, he couldn't help thinking he'd been nothing more than a boy toy for his wife, sitting in the corner until *she* wanted to play.

No. That's absurd. She loved me. The beginning of his relationship with Dr. Trudy Davis, who'd kept her name when they married because her name was her brand, had been promising. His stock went up at the bank, and in her navy pants suit and buttoned-up white silk blouse, the lady doctor was perfect.

Their honeymoon had given him another version of bliss—for one week, he was the center of her universe. He had all her attention, and every day she told him how brilliant he was, how handsome, how happy being seen with him made her. Her face lit when she spotted him across the room. And, best of all, she listened to him. In his thirty-eight years on the planet, the one other woman who had listened to him was his mother.

But the second they returned home to Shepherdstown, the problems started. All courtship behavior ceased. She'd expected him to do the cooking, the dishes and vacuuming, to put up with her late rounds at the hospital and tolerate her early morning patient phonathon in complete silence. Even the rattle of a cup on its saucer induced a scowl as she waved him away.

Nevertheless, he'd applauded Trudy's work ethic and her dedication to her career and enjoyed introducing her as "my wife, the doctor" to other bank executives. Even the way they ogled her made him proud. But Trudy's ability to ignore him as if he weren't standing right in front of her waving his arms and shaking his hips irritated the hell out of him.

She never smiled at his antics anymore. Smiles had been part of the courtship phase and now that she'd snagged him, the corners of her mouth had settled into a downward dog position, never to turn upward and salute the sun again. Using his pent-up exasperation, he attacked the floors in the bedrooms and hallway with the vacuum. No dirt would escape his vengeance.

The final straw for Harmon came the morning she questioned the selection of his favorite periwinkle silk tie to go with a pink bespoke shirt and dark charcoal suit. In the mirror, he'd been gorgeous, if he said so himself.

"Purple? You're going to wear purple?" She'd put her phone on mute while her patient continued her lament. "Honey, isn't purple with pink a little over the top, even for successful bankers?"

"It's blue." He put his hands on his hips and huffed.

"Really?"

Her supercilious tone implied she knew what successful bankers wore by dint of heredity and her upper-class childhood, and he didn't. If she had *suggested* he wear the green paisley, he would've complied. But with that ring on her finger, she was now his monitor, his boss, his tastemaker, and could tell him the way his mother had what clothes to put on in the morning. Years of hard-won independence dissolved in a second.

"What do you think I did every day before I met you?" Harmon had retorted, feeling seven years old again. "I'm good at this."

In an instant, he was transported to the moment of his earliest humiliation when he'd first understood his mother was to blame for everything that would ever go wrong in his life. After homeschooling him through first grade, with no warning she had sent him off to the second half of second grade on a yellow bus that belched like a sick dragon at each railroad crossing stop.

His mother explained that she had to follow her bliss, and he had to go to school for her to do that. "How come I'm not your bliss, Mommy?" he'd asked as he climbed that first steep step into the belly of the dragon.

"You are, sweetie, but other things make me blissful also." Her answer had made him feel empty.

As he handed his new teacher the note the kind lady in the school office had given him, he knew being in that classroom was a terrible mistake. The teacher read aloud, "Sweet Harmony Rutledge is joining your class."

The class tittered and whispered. The teacher smiled at them, and Harmon hated her. Trembling, unable to understand why everyone was talking about him, his face heated as if he'd sat next to the kitchen wood-stove for too long. Within seconds of a girl's whispered jeer about his clothes, Harmon made decisions that affected the rest of his life.

Shaking his head to let go of the memory, Harmon stowed the vacuum in the assigned space, gathered his cleaning supplies, and went through the downstairs door to the flagstone patio. The steady motion of his arm as he sprayed and wiped the wall-to-wall window put him into a kind of trance. As if he were watching a movie, he could see himself stunned into immobility at the front of that wretched classroom. His mother had failed to tell him about the ferocity of children.

In her youthful exuberance, his mother had renamed herself Everlasting Beauty. When Harmon called her Beauty, she would scoop him up and twirl him around until he was transported to the spot in Van Gogh's *Starry Night* painting where the stars rolled out across the night sky and made his throat ache.

But standing in that horrific classroom with the torn, brown paper shades on the soot-streaked windows, Harmon knew his mother had betrayed him by giving him a goofy name. He would always be the butt of a joke, and that was intolerable. He had decided then and there to shorten his name as soon as he could.

That night when he'd told his mother about his first day at school, she'd said, "Fight back." Her lips had trembled as she gripped Harmon's shoulders. "There are boundaries. You don't have to take abuse. Some things are worth fighting for, and you are one of them."

She was right about protecting himself, Harmon had concluded, but she'd sent him out into a world she hadn't prepared him for, and that was her fatal mistake.

Now as he stood in the foyer of his beautiful house and surveyed it from a stranger's point of view, he understood everything had happened for a reason. He was the man he was because of his experiences and the decisions he'd made when pushed to extremes.

The house was perfect, and he would regret leaving it, but he had been in West Virginia long enough. It was time for him to move on. Being the president of a nice mid-western college would suit him. His background in banking should make any recruitment committee salivate as they imagined a burgeoning endowment under his stewardship. He could always pay the geek who'd created his brilliant Harvard and Yale transcripts to do another for a doctorate from Brown, maybe also gin up a few well-placed papers in the appropriate journals.

Picturing himself greeting prospective donors and handing out honorary degrees at graduation ceremonies, Harmon stood straighter. He imagined how, wearing a red gown and velvet cap, he would shine in the sun at commencement ceremonies. The speeches he would give. Harmon stroked his chin and decided to grow a beard.

CHAPTER 6

ETHEL winced at Charlie's odd clothes—tweed jacket, green corduroy pants, and orange t-shirt—as he'd stood in front of the Magistrate on Wednesday morning. Next to him stood his bright-faced public defender. Until she piped up, "Not guilty, Your Honor," when Charlie's tongue stuck to the top of his mouth, Ethel had mistaken her for a high school cheerleader doing an internship at the court.

Humiliation mounting by the second, Ethel drove to her bank, cashed one of her certificates of deposit, and then rushed back to the court building. She waited in line to pass a cashier's check from her bank through the metal grill to the clerk of the court to pay his bail. Every moment of the process was like being locked in the public stocks herself, minus neighbors pelting her with rotten tomatoes and eggs. Good thing her mother couldn't see her.

Charlie said nothing as they'd trudged the three blocks to the follow-up meeting at the lawyer's office in a century-old building with cracked plaster and creaky floors. Ethel stared at her stepson's red sneakers while the cheerleader told them she was going to try to work out a deal for leniency with the county prosecutor. Everything would be fine, she said, if Charlie stayed out of trouble. Then the lawyer asked her to wait in reception while she talked to her client in private.

Pfft, Ethel thought. *What does she know? She's young enough to be my granddaughter.*

Ethel doubted Charlie knew the difference between trouble and a chocolate-covered donut. She still didn't understand what on earth could have persuaded him he could be a successful bank robber. He probably didn't know either. He'd been sideways with every authority since he was eight, which didn't bode well for his future decisions.

But, recalling George's routine after Charlie's rehab stints, Ethel took her stepson to Walmart for new clothes, a burner phone so she could get hold of him if she needed to, and the thickest Stephen King novel on the shelf.

"I'm not rewarding you for bad behavior," she said. "I'm just resetting you to zero. What happens next in your life is up to you."

Charlie hung his head and said nothing.

She rented Charlie a room on a month-to-month lease in the Lazy Eight, the cheapest motel around. At least he wouldn't freeze to death sleeping on the street before the trial, which could be months away. The motel room had a television with HBO, easing her concern that Charlie would be so bored that he'd do something dangerous or stupid.

Using her best old-lady-in-distress persona, Ethel also wrangled a pre-paid food plan for him at Uncle John's diner next to the motel. Mortification had swamped Ethel ever since she learned he'd been standing in line at the soup kitchen in town. *What if someone I know saw him, and everyone in town is talking about how horrible I am?*

Securing room and board for Charlie satisfied her sense of duty without having his actual body reside in the same house with her. Her conscience pinched for a second; she might be failing her stepson. Fate could have dealt the cards another way.

At random times every day since her car accident, she experienced the freak crash as if it were happening again. *The truck came right at me as if it meant to hit me.* The roaring sound. Screeching metal, splintering glass. She gasped and Charlie side-eyed her.

"You never told me how Dad died," he said.

"Oh, sorry about that. He had a heart attack on the day my car was totaled by a truck. They couldn't revive him."

She could've died instead of George, whose massive coronary appeared to have been triggered by learning that she'd survived the crash. That was some kind of karma. Or was it intention? But if she had died, her husband might have taken his boy home to live with him and prevented the whole bank robbery disaster.

Charlie's eyebrows rode up. "You were in an accident?"

Ethel nodded.

"Were you hurt?"

"Concussion, broken collar bone. Stuff like that."

"Like in the hospital broken?"

"Yup."

"I didn't know. Sorry."

It's not like the kid went searching for trouble, Ethel thought, but disaster had a way of zeroing in on him with unerring accuracy, and he'd always welcomed it like he'd been standing there waiting for the arrows.

She pulled the car into the parking space right outside his motel room door. Charlie glanced at her. "Here's your room key," she said and held out the key for him to take.

"Thanks."

"You can eat two meals a day at Uncle John's next door." Ethel tilted her head in the direction of the diner on the other side of the parking lot. "They're open six 6 A.M. until nine P.M." She handed him the cardboard card he was supposed to get punched for each meal he bought.

"Okay."

Ethel took that to mean he understood. "Don't go anywhere or talk to anyone, including on that online social thing you like, and don't let anyone in your room. I'll be back to pick you up on the day of your trial, assuming your lawyer hasn't got you a deal, and I'll call on the new phone to remind you. If you have an emergency, call your lawyer before you do anything."

To her ear, she sounded like GPS giving clear directions. Not that Charlie, a boy who could get lost on the way to the bathroom in his own house, would follow them. A feeling she'd done something wrong needled her. *Well, I'm not a perfect person.*

You said it, George sneered as if he were sitting in the back seat.

Ethel sniffed. "Wait, Charlie. I have to ask what you were saying to the other robber, Don. In the bank on Monday?"

"Honest, Ethel, I'm not a robber."

Ethel ignored his attempt to circumvent the truth. "But what were you whispering about?"

Charlie rocked his head from side to side. "Don wanted me to act tough. I didn't want to." Clutching the plastic shopping bags she handed him, he got out of the car and marched to his motel room. He unlocked the door and turned to wave goodbye.

The gesture cracked her heart a bit.

WENTY minutes later, Ethel pulled up on the semi-circular driveway in front of Harmon's house. Still early for their scheduled 4 P.M. appointment, she sat in her car watching the autumn wind thrash trees still in full leaf until branches swept the grass. The weather, sunny in starts and stops all day, was sending her a message.

"But what is it saying?" she muttered.

Her nerves were on edge, her stomach churning like a blender set on whip. At least being early gave her enough breathing room to prepare for the meeting. *I'm discombobulated from spending the morning with Charlie, that's all.* She had to pull herself together. The last thing she wanted was to display the wrong emotion during her first professional meeting with a potential client.

Ethel gazed around Harmon's neighborhood, and patted her heart, which was still a little undone. Checking the rearview mirror for lipstick on her teeth, she shuffled through her briefcase to make sure she had the necessary equipment and papers to secure Harmon's listing. *I'm just a little bit afraid of him, but I do have a backup.* She patted her purse, said a brief prayer that something would go her way for a change, and emerged from the safety of her new Subaru.

Opening the Notes app on her phone, she typed *Rutledge House* as the title and made a note that the driveway was paved with stone. The address put Harmon just outside Shepherdstown, a posh village seven miles north of the county seat. Professional landscaping set off each property in this subdivision with rich, dark mulch and variegated leafy shrubs. Taking a photo with her phone from the front of the house, she zoomed in on the carved wood front door and, using the dictate function, added *unique design touches* to her notes.

Harmon opened the door to her knock, and after shaking his hand, she excused herself to make a note about the white marble-tiled floor in the foyer. "Notes help me remember special features so I can complete a market comparison and set the right price for the house," she explained.

"Don't forget to make a note about the view," Harmon said, pointing through the living room wall-to-wall windows to the wide expanse of the adjoining well-landscaped golf course. "The house sits on a third of an acre bounded by that creek."

Ethel could picture the words in the listing typing themselves onto a photo of the house. She imagined the animated slide show she would post on Facebook. A quiver of delight flashed between her shoulders.

"Your house is lovely." Ethel added to her notes: *Well-kept contemporary stone and clapboard lodge, high ceilings, presents well.* "First impressions are always important."

Harmon led her through the formal living room where a baby grand piano took center stage.

"Oh, what a beautiful piano. Do you play?"

"No, my wife, Trudy, Dr. Trudy Davis, she plays."

Ethel noted the odd quaver in his voice as he said his wife's name and typed the name into her notes so she wouldn't forget it. From there, they walked into a large dining room big enough to seat twelve guests.

"You can see there's lots of light from the bay windows, and wood floors throughout where there isn't tile," he said as he opened a door to a book-lined study.

Ethel took room measurements with her laser tape measure and jotted them down, added *built-ins, bright, cozy breakfast nook*, and followed him into the huge kitchen designed with every possible modern amenity, including a glass-front, sliding-door refrigerator, built-in wine cooler, and grill.

The great room adjoining the kitchen had a cathedral ceiling with huge, exposed timbers which Harmon said matched the ceiling in the master bedroom at the other end of the house. Few agents in her office had ever had a listing like this, easily in the nine hundred thousand range, maybe a million. She hadn't had a listing at all in her entire first year of being an agent, although she'd made two sales on other agent's listings. The idea of her first listing being worth a million dollars made her feel as if she were sailing single-handed across a lake, the jib pregnant with wind.

"How long have you lived here?"

"Not quite a year," Harmon said. "The house is too big for us," he added, answering the question she hadn't asked. "It's time to move on."

His voice is so cold. Doesn't he care about his home? Harmon's plan for a large family must have been derailed. She couldn't ask him personal questions, but something must have happened for him to have changed his mind about living here.

"Did you buy this house as an investment?"

He shrugged. "My wife, fiancé then, liked it. I wanted a threshold to carry her over." His face mottled.

"Has she changed her mind?"

Harmon strode down the hall to show her the bedrooms. "She went on a trip for work. She said she was going to a medical conference. But she hasn't come back."

Ethel trotted after him, confused by his answer. "What do you mean, 'she hasn't come back'? Have you talked to her about selling the house? Is her name on the deed?" She should have known there'd be a glitch. None of her plans ever worked the way she anticipated.

Harmon paused at the bedroom door and swiveled to face her. The slight twitch on the left side of his mouth warned her this might be a ticklish subject. Ethel stepped back. *I hope he doesn't flip out.* He was far too tall for her to clobber with her bag.

"She's been gone for four days. I expected her back on Monday at the latest. But, as you can see . . ." He spread his arms out and then let them drop to his sides. "I think she's left me. I tried calling her, but I get that 'this phone is not in service' recording. I'm worried she's missing."

"Missing?" Ethel's spirits sank; her misgivings rose. *He's not being honest with me.* The listing was no longer the golden opportunity it had been the moment before.

The last thing she wanted was to be caught in the middle of one of those messy divorces where she had to chase down the other party to secure a signature on the listing contract and then again at settlement. She'd heard horror stories in the office about such a scenario.

"Does she know you're selling the house?" It was important to be clear about this point.

"No. She's not here for me to tell her, is she?" Harmon's tone sharpened. "If she left me, it serves her right."

Ethel pulled her shoulders up to her ears, as if that would protect her if he smacked her with one of his huge hands. "Have you reported her missing to the police?"

He lumbered into the luxurious master suite and sank into the leather wingback chair in front of the black marble-faced fireplace. "Her mother might have, or someone at her office. I prefer to think she'll come back." Touching the remote, he turned on the gas fireplace.

Well, that's an odd response, Ethel thought as she stayed ten feet from him and typed a note about the fireplace. Harmon's whole attitude was odd, but she was no social worker. She wasn't going to try to iron out his relationship problems.

Her husband wouldn't have reported her missing either. George would have just been glad she was gone. But if Harmon's wife wasn't officially dead, and her name was on the deed, her written permission was required to sell the house before anything else happened. Unless he'd bought the house in his name.

"Do you own the house by yourself, then, without your wife?" Ethel held her breath. Whatever he said, she'd have to check the records because instinct told her this man didn't always tell the truth and might be lying this very minute.

Harmon's face was as self-assured as any of the hundreds of men who'd ever explained anything to her. "I bought it before we were married if that's what you mean."

Ethel smiled with relief. *He didn't say, "We bought it."*

"Well, let's see the rest of the house. Then you'll answer some questions for me, I'll explain how I work, and I'll draw up an exclusive contract and arrange the listing for you." Giddiness restored, Ethel's thumbs missed a few keys as she took notes on the rest of the property details.

But even as she oohed and ahed over the marble-tiled bathrooms, enormous rec room, and flagstone patio, the sense that Harmon was lying about something important wedged its way into her mind like a fist. This sense of unease might have been exacerbated by the one gray linen pillowcase on a king-sized bed covered in snowy white pillows.

CHAPTER 7

DRUMMING his fingers on the white granite counter in his kitchen while he stared out the window at the serene landscape, Harmon waited for Sheriff Hammersmith to come on the line. It was Thursday morning. He'd recruited Ethel to liberate him from the house Trudy had wanted, and now he needed to tackle the next task, the one he would have completed Monday afternoon if the bank robbery had never happened.

Feelings of imminent doom had dissipated at work. The tellers had stopped cringing every time someone dropped a pencil, and the state police had figured out he was the victim in the bank robbery and not the inside man. Now, he had to set in motion the discovery of his wife's body and establish that he was the bereaved husband instead of the most likely suspect.

I can do this. I am calm and capable. I am the one who gets things right.

A female voice on the phone said, "Sheriff Hammersmith."

Harmon was caught off guard. *Why is she so perfunctory?* The clerk must have told her who was calling. He had expected a warmer reception given how cooperative he had been following the attempted bank robbery. Anxiety vaporized his prepared presentation.

"Oh, good morning, Sheriff, I was calling, ah, to report, huh, well, my wife, you know, Dr. Trudy Davis . . ."

"Yes, Mr. Rutledge?"

The sheriff's brusqueness threw him off. "Well, my wife is missing, and I don't know where she is."

He hadn't wanted to rush the announcement this way, but the sheriff tricked him. He'd wanted to lead up to it, tease it like a good TV commercial announcing a new car, but here he was, and now it was a matter of record. Did the sheriff's department record its calls? A tremor swept through him. *Keep a level head.*

"I'm sorry, sir. I didn't quite catch that. Say again. Your wife is missing?"

"Yes, yes, that's what I'm trying to tell you."

Harmon considered telling the sheriff the same story he'd told Ethel—his wife had gone to a conference and hadn't come home at the expected time—but that could get complicated. The sheriff might check to see if Trudy was expected at some physician conference somewhere. Of course, he could always say she lied to him. People always lied; he might as well make use of that human trait.

"Okay. Tell me what happened." Hammersmith's tone was soothing.

"Thank you. My wife left the house in a huff on Sunday, the day before the robbery at the bank, and she hasn't come back. But, well, I was traumatized by the robbery, and I thought she'd gone to a medical conference, and I'd just forgotten. But then I couldn't get hold of her, and I started to worry. I thought I had to wait three days to report that she might be missing because she's an adult, but now I see your website says I wasn't supposed to wait at all. Anyway, I didn't report her missing when I should have, and then I waited longer, thinking for sure she'd come back, but she hasn't gone to work all week. She would never miss work, and her mother hasn't heard from her." He breathed in, hoping it sounded like a ragged sob.

"Okay, let's back up a little," the sheriff said. "What day was the last time you saw her?"

"Sunday. In the morning." That would match the timeframe he'd set up with the newspaper editor who called about the wedding notice, and it was true. He could say it with a straight face. He hadn't seen Trudy since he dumped her limp body in the back of her car at 12 A.M. on Sunday and closed the trunk.

"So, she's been gone four full days, and she hasn't called or texted or communicated with you in any way since then?"

"Correct."

"And you're just now reporting her missing."

"Yes. That's what I'm saying. We argued. She left here in a huff. We've been married for six months and, well, you know how newlyweds are. I expected she'd be back by now."

The sheriff asked Harmon to spell out Trudy's name, which he did while congratulating himself for doing so without rancor at the absurd request.

"How old is she?"

"She's thirty-seven. What does her age have to do with anything?"

"Height and weight?"

"Not sure. Maybe five-foot-six and a hundred-twenty pounds?"

"So thin, then."

"If you say so."

"Do you remember what she was wearing?"

Harmon wasn't prepared for this question. He pictured the lace across Trudy's bare arm and at her throat, how her head lolled when he lifted her. His neck warmed, then his cheeks. His breath came faster. "How on earth does it matter what she was wearing?"

"Her clothes might help us spot her when we search for her."

"Oh, got it. Let me try to remember."

Trudy had been wearing her nightgown when he saw her last, but he couldn't say that. He felt the silk cloth brush his cheek, her hip bone press against his ribs and shuddered. She couldn't be wearing the nightgown when the police found her, because no respectable woman would go driving off in her bedclothes. The nightgown placed her at home at the time of her death. He drew a breath across his gritted teeth, making a slight hissing sound. *I should have anticipated this problem before I called the police. I should have planned better. I'm an idiot.*

His mind took another leap—whatever he told the sheriff she was wearing when she left the house is what she had to be wearing when they found her, which complicated matters even more. Inventing something on the spot was how plans got bungled.

Harmon managed to repress an involuntary groan. He had time before authorities found her to rectify his error. Holding the phone between his cheek and shoulder, he dashed into Trudy's closet and reviewed the clothes in her dresser, selecting the first items his hand touched.

"So, she was wearing jeans . . . and a white T-shirt . . . and she threw on a green sweater. She might have had a baseball cap on. Orioles. She's an Orioles fan. And her flip-flops." As he talked, he piled the clothes on the top of her dresser so he wouldn't forget what he'd said.

The sheriff was silent for a few seconds, and Harmon assumed she was taking notes.

"Also, she drove her car, a white Volvo, and took the shoulder bag with her laptop. She wasn't going for a drive around the block. I don't think you'll find her in town." Was he pushing it, going too far? Had he given himself away with those details? He picked up Trudy's laptop from the bed and walked with it into the kitchen.

"What's the license plate number on the vehicle?"

"One, W-V, underscore, D-O-C. It's a vanity plate she got when she passed her medical boards."

"Was she on any medication, have any illnesses we should know about?"

"No, no, she's healthy."

"What was the argument about?"

Harmon wasn't fooled by the innocent-sounding question. Whatever he said could come back to haunt him. He couldn't tell the sheriff they'd argued because Trudy had criticized the color of the tie he wanted to wear. He would sound unbalanced.

"Oh, you know, stupid newlywed stuff—the toothpaste cap and the toilet seat." He raised his eyebrows to signal recognition of his own foibles even though Hammersmith couldn't see him. "We're both pretty opinionated. And stubborn."

"What did you tell her mother when she called you?"

What an odd question. How did the sheriff know Trudy's mother had called? Harmon couldn't stand talking to Mrs. Davis under the best of conditions. Her super cheery voice always made him want to reach across the ether and strangle her. He'd let her three calls roll to voice mail, but he had to tell the sheriff something.

"I told her we had an argument and not to worry." This *was* what he would have said if he had returned her call. He made a mental note to call her before the sheriff did.

"What about Trudy's work? Did her supervisor call?"

"Trudy's the supervising physician at the practice." Harmon couldn't help smiling from the pride her status inspired in him.

"What practice is that?"

"Jefferson County Health Clinic. I told Mrs. Romero, she's the practice administrator, the same thing I told Trudy's mother." He had, in fact, talked to Romero yesterday in case the sheriff checked with her.

"But now you're worried something happened to your wife?"

"Well, yes, of course, I'm worried something happened to her, or she would have been in touch with someone at work by now, even if she was still angry at me. She would never abandon her patients." He huffed for effect and was gratified that his voice trembled when he said, "I'm so sorry we argued. I don't know where she's gone, but I think something terrible has happened to her."

"Have you tried calling her?"

"Yes, of course." Harmon hoped he sounded indignant.

"And?"

"I just get the out of service recording." The sheriff's question made Harmon worry. Could the police do some techno thing to locate her using the phone?

"Was she having an affair?"

Harmon fell into a chair. He had never considered the possibility that Trudy might be cheating on him. He bellowed, "What? Of course not. How could you even ask such a thing?" He had to admire the sincerity in his voice.

"Okay, Mr. Rutledge. My deputy will come to your house to search for anything that might tell us where she's gone. Please give him a recent photo of Dr. Davis. We'll share the information about her on a missing person alert with neighboring counties. We'll do our best to find her."

He'd have to discard Trudy's laptop before the officer got to the house. Since he couldn't transfer her funds online without getting the bank's two-factor verification code from her phone, he didn't need the laptop. But first he had to get rid of anything on it that would make him look bad. The best option was to F-disk the hard drive, a method he'd heard about for removing any trace of existing files. But, of course, he needed her password to open the operating system before he could delete everything, and nothing he'd tried had worked.

For the time being, he put the laptop out with the trash. Worst case, he could just run over the damn thing with his car. That would solve the problem. Unless she put files in the cloud, like photos of him wearing that glitter ribbon she'd dressed him in on their honeymoon. The thought made his face flame. He couldn't deal with that; he had to focus on the positives.

"Thank you. Is there anything else I need to do?"

"No. There's nothing else you need to do right now," Sheriff Hammersmith said. "I'll take it from here. I'm sure we'll need to talk again, so let us know if you're going out of town."

"Do you think it will take a long time to find her?"

"Depends. There are a lot of factors at play. We'll keep you informed about our progress."

Harmon stood in the middle of his bedroom, wondering if Trudy had been having an affair. He gagged thinking about it. *Why would she have an affair when she's married to me?* On the other hand, if she had been having an affair, she was a more interesting person and not the all-work-and-no-play individual he believed he'd married.

Also on the plus side, the notion of a lover might lead the police in the wrong direction, although he didn't want to string the investigation out. Even if the methodology had to change, his goals were the same: the police had to declare her dead so as the established successor in her trust fund, he'd get her money.

Harmon needed a week before the police found Trudy. He needed to re-organize a few things, like where her body was located in addition to what she was wearing. His initial plan had been perfect, but now she had to be wearing the clothes he'd identified for the sheriff. He couldn't be the one to dress her, and she couldn't be dressed in a public space where someone could spot him handling a dead body. And now, those clothes couldn't be in his house when the deputy arrived.

That meant Trudy had to be redressed by someone else, somewhere other than in that very public parking lot. That person couldn't be clever enough to blackmail him with the fact that he was disposing of his wife but still capable of following instructions. *Who do I know who's dumb enough to do this without asking any questions? And strong enough to lift a body.* At least, rigor mortis would have worn off by now so the body would be flexible.

He'd made a mistake. Harmon gasped as if he were in a runaway elevator plummeting from the penthouse to the basement. He could've told the sheriff Trudy was so angry she ran out of the house in her nightgown. Too late now. He had to see his new plan through.

Like sunshine breaking through after a storm, Harmon realized he knew two perfect dupes. With a little finesse, he could make the wannabe bank robbers into Hammersmith's prime suspects in the Trudy Davis kidnap and murder. Harmon patted himself on the back for being flexible and able to plan with such clarity.

CHAPTER 8

A T chow in the regional jail on Thursday night, Don heard the rumor that Charlie had been bailed right after the Magistrate's hearing, right when *he* was being transported to Martinsburg in the Corrections Department van. Here Don was eating slop and the doofus he'd tried to help was out in the wild scarfing down Mickey D's. Life was not fair.

Not that his mother had ever promised him a rose garden, as she reminded him whenever he complained he didn't have what the other kids had—skateboards, bikes, Gameboys, money for the movies. Don hadn't the wildest idea what gardens had to do with life being unfair, but no flowers grew around their house.

Worry had eaten away at him the whole time he was being finger-printed, photographed, and swabbed for DNA at intake. The guards had taken his stuff and handed him gray sweatpants and a sweatshirt. Through the entire process, he kept wondering how Charlie would mess him up. He'd tried to coach Charlie when he'd seen him before the hearing.

"Don't tell 'em nothing," Don had whispered to Charlie as they'd waited in line to be escorted by guards into the courtroom. "Keep your mouth shut." Charlie had stared at the chains around his ankles.

Flanked by his way-too-cute lawyer, Charlie had gaped blank-faced at the judge while the prosecutor went on and on about their heinous behavior, harming the community, terrorizing good citizens, yada, yada. Although he'd pleaded not guilty, Charlie appeared dumbfounded, which is what worried Don.

Dumbfounded would put them in the most danger. The guy would cop to anything, he was that gullible. During interrogation, the police could've brought up every unsolved robbery from the last year, and Charlie would've sat there saying, "But, but, but . . ." They would have bullied and ragged on him until he confessed to anything to make them shut up.

Or maybe Charlie had ratted him out for a lighter sentence. An icicle stabbed Don in the chest at the thought.

Don knew about jail time. He had served nine months in the regional jail and two years' probation for the nothing liquor store robbery that netted him a whole thirty bucks because the judge had considered his juvenile record before sentencing. He should never have copped to the charge when the officers showed up at his house an hour after he held up the liquor store pretending the hand in his pocket was a gun. He knew now that was stupid, even in his own estimation.

But that story was water over the bridge, as Don's mother liked to say. Whenever she said it, Don pictured a flood with trees, cars, and houses being swept over a bridge by a huge wave of water like the tsunami in Japan he'd seen on TV.

Although his teacher had said, "The water goes *under* the bridge, Don" when he used the phrase at school, there was no correcting his mother. If he had dared to say, "It's under, Ma, the water is under the bridge," she would have smacked his head. Whichever way he said it, he was drowning.

After he'd gotten out of jail and finished his probation, he'd found a job and kept it for six months. As hearse driver, body hauler, chair arranger, doorman, and custodian, he'd done the grubbiest chores at the Eternal Destinies Funeral Home. But he had been necessary; that's what was important. So what if his weekly wage wasn't enough to pay his bar bill for the one night a week he bought a round for everyone? It was a job, he showed up every day, and he was good at it. Successful. He had a future in the funeral business. Don told himself he could climb the ladder and be someone.

The job had even made him realize clothes were important. When Don had asked the funeral home owner, Sigmund Frohler, why he and the missus dressed up every day, Sigmund had said, "You never know when someone is going to die, Don. Our clothes convey our profession-alism. We're the service we provide, and that service is impeccable."

Don had been astounded by Sigmund's words. This was the wisdom of the ages, as important as how the earth was suspended in space, a phenomenon that had worried him since second grade when the string holding the carboard galaxy to the ceiling of his classroom had snapped, and the planets had plummeted to the floor with a clatter.

"What if that happens for real?" he'd asked his mother. "What if the world falls down and the people on it are killed?" He'd held his breath waiting for her answer.

She'd poured two splashes of whiskey into her glass, lifted the glass to her lips, taken a swallow of her drink, and closed her eyes. "Not the worst thing that could happen."

He'd felt so lonely at that moment that the end of the world couldn't have happened soon enough.

Even with the funeral parlor job, though, his mother had still been short with him. She hadn't forgiven him for going to jail. "Go away from me, Don," she said, pushing him away when he came into the kitchen to hug her after work. "You smell."

A crack had opened in his chest each time she did that, and a chill crept in. Maybe he smelled a little like formaldehyde and other chemicals they used for embalming at the funeral home, and like the dead, who smelled like mice disintegrating inside a wall.

To solve this problem, Don had hung ten Christmas tree deodorizers from the rearview mirror in his truck, hoping the dead smell would wear off him before he got home every day. He worried that the odor had seeped inside his body and wouldn't go away even if he sprayed himself with Lysol. He had tried dousing himself with the deodorizer once, but his mother went nuclear.

"Cheese and crackers, Don, what the hell did you do?" his mother had shouted at him. "You smell like the inside of an old refrigerator left at the dump."

Since then, he'd taken a shower the minute he got home whether he smelled bad to himself or not. He should've asked his mother what she expected of him, anyway. He was just a guy who'd grown up in one of the five occupied houses in Bridleburg, someone doomed to failure. But Don kept the idea to himself in case saying the words out loud guaranteed that fate would get him sooner rather than later.

Bridleburg, according to the description of his hometown he'd read in the county paper last month, had been left to collapse in on itself. "A half-hearted artifact of the industrial age," the article said. In honor of the twentieth anniversary of the town's ruin, the paper had run a huge story on the old factory with old and new photographs.

Everyone who'd worked in the factory had been laid off in one day when the business closed. "The End of Made in America," the big type above the story spelled out. All the stores had closed, the windows boarded up, the town unincorporated, and the mayor had disappeared with the employees' pension fund. If a whole town could be wiped out like that, what hope did he have for a life?

His father wasn't going to rescue him. He had disappeared with a spray of gravel and dust in the driveway one afternoon right as Don got home from kindergarten. Didn't even wave goodbye. Don might have blamed his father for how their lives had skittered out of control afterward, but the guy was too much of a ghost to matter.

His mom had tried to keep it together, Don wanted to give her that. At least, they weren't living in a car. His latest mess was her last straw. Now he was locked up, waiting God knows how long for his mother to get bail money together, and Charlie was out there blabbing his mouth off. Don knew in his gut that Charlie would screw him.

By Friday afternoon, Don had stored up enough hatred to burn down the entire world. Standing in the hall, gripping the wall phone receiver, the heat in his belly made him shake. "It's four days I've been in jail, Mom. Two days since the hearing that I'm in regional. There's crazy people in here. You gotta get me out." He had told her this on each of the daily five-minute phone calls he was allowed. "They're gonna kill me for my cigarettes."

"I'm going as fast as I can, Don," Marge said. "This whole damn disaster is my worst nightmare. Do you know they charge fifty bucks for these collect calls? Your uncle warned me twenty years ago, when you weren't even potty trained, that you would 'walk on my head' someday. I shoulda listened."

"Mom, please, I'm dyin' here." Don fingered his split lip. "I don't even know what uncle you're talking about."

"That dumb foreigner couldn't even speak English," Marge shouted, "but he was telling me how to be a mother. I had no idea what the hell he meant, but now I get it. Cheese and crackers, Don. You're old enough now to wipe your own ass."

Don remembered overhearing bits of his mother's phone calls to her sister when he was a teenager. "I'm at my wit's end," she said almost every day. "I got no kind of life. Who's gonna set up housekeeping with me and a kid who bushwhacks me every day? I can't get ahead for going backwards."

He'd had no idea what a wit was, but he'd pictured their dead end street with a big wooden barrier and a sign on it saying, "Wit's End." Standing with his forehead against the jail's yellow and gray cinderblock wall marked with scratched images of dicks and balls accompanied by suggestions of what he should do with them, Don tried hard not to cry.

"Mom, you gotta help me. I got no one else."

"I'm doing my best. It's like crawling over broken glass to get your deserter father's brothers and sisters to help me. They're handing me twenties and fifties, like that's gonna help. I even asked my boss and everyone at work for money. You know I can't ask my sisters. They're so poor they add extra water to the Jell-O to make it go farther."

He got it. His mother didn't want him in jail with the riffraff, but she didn't have five thousand dollars, the ten percent in cash she had to put up against the fifty-thousand-dollar bail the judge had set. It might as well be a million.

No one was more surprised than Don when his mother found a way to put up his bond and spring him later on Friday afternoon. By the time he walked out of the detention center, she was shaking, and her face was bright red.

"I had to put up my house to get you out," Marge shouted the second he slid into the car. "The bail bondsman made me sign a document. You better not make me lose my house."

Don got it. She'd been steaming for the twenty miles she'd driven from the bail bondsman's office in Charles Town to the regional jail in Martinsburg to pick him up. Her lips chewing on words she didn't say, she drove eighteen miles in the other direction to the lawyer's office for a consultation. He stayed as far away from his mother as he could in her small tin-can car. They were like two lit sticks of dynamite just waiting to explode.

The building housing the public defenders' offices didn't give Don much hope. Older than his house and divided into tiny offices the size of shoeboxes, the place made him feel more of a failure than he had before. *Bet Charlie didn't have to come to this crap hole to see his lawyer.*

His mother flipped through a magazine while they waited in the reception area. A Black woman in a gray pants suit stopped to talk to the receptionist. Marge secured her purse under her arm as she snuck glances at the woman. "None of my business who comes here for help," she muttered.

The woman walked toward them and said, "Don. Mrs. Whitley, I'm Jada Greene, the lawyer assigned to Don's case." She held out her hand.

Marge froze. "This can't be right," she whispered. "She's not even a real lawyer. They did this on purpose 'cause we're poor."

Don stared at Ms. Greene, momentarily paralyzed. "Damn, Mom," he whispered. "I met her in jail." The lawyer reminded him of his high school principal and the hours he'd sat outside her office waiting to be scolded. He shot out of his seat like he'd been ordered to attention and shook the woman's hand. Marge glared at him but rose from the chair.

Ms. Greene led the way up creaking stairs to an even smaller office than the ones on the first floor. When they were seated, the lawyer opened a file on her desk and scanned the first page. Don stared at the two fancy, framed university diplomas hanging on the wall behind the lawyer.

"Guess she's for real," he whispered to his mother.

His mother cleared her throat and smacked his arm.

When the lawyer looked up at him, Don pictured a doctor in a soap opera about to deliver a death sentence. Then she turned to Marge. "I wanted to ask you, Mrs. Whitley, if you thought we should use a diminished capacity defense?"

"A what?" Marge's face looked like she'd walked in on a cat peeing on the rug.

"That's when a defendant is unable to assist in his own defense," Ms. Greene explained, her voice calm and her demeanor respectful.

Marge tossed her head. Her ponytail swayed. "There ain't nothin' wrong with my boy. They tested him at school, and he's got a solid eighty-four."

"An eighty-four?" Ms. Greene drew her eyebrows together over her nose.

"IQ. They tested his brains. He just don't use them."

Ms. Greene nodded. "Okay, I see. I'm going to give it to you both straight. The prosecutor told me he isn't taking any chances. He's going to ask the grand jury to indict Don on multiple counts—bank robbery, conspiracy, assault, committing violence to a person, whatever else he can find the slimmest basis for. One of those charges will stick at trial and they'll put you in prison for at least ten years. It's your second felony. If you're convicted, which you likely will be, you'll go to the state prison in Huttonsville."

"I told you, I didn't assault no one." Don folded his arms over his chest and glared at Ms. Greene. "That old lady assaulted me. She should be going to jail."

Marge writhed in her chair. "I don't understand. I know people who got eighteen months for killing a kid with their car while they were drunk. Don didn't kill no one. He didn't even steal any money."

The lawyer smoothed a stray hair back into her bun and leaned forward in her chair. She clasped her hands together on the desk and furrowed her brow. Don assumed this was Ms. Greene's serious face, so what she was about to say was important. His mother smoothed back her own hair, tightened her ponytail, and leaned forward also.

Don shrugged. What did it matter what the lawyer said from here on? She'd pretty much already said he was going to jail anyway. But the lawyer kept going.

"The lowest sentence for bank robbery in this state is ten years, even if the robber just passed the teller a note demanding money," the lawyer explained. "A judge gave a bank robber in Salem fifteen years for leaving 'a lifetime emotional scar' on the tellers when he robbed a small bank like the one here in Charles Town."

"What's that got to do with us? I don't even know where Salem is," Marge said.

Ms. Greene waited a beat. "The prosecutor wants to indict Don for first-degree robbery because he threatened deadly force even though he didn't have a gun. He says Don placed the victims in fear of bodily injury. Premeditation counts, whether or not Don succeeded."

"This don't make no sense," Marge said, her voice rising. "Don told me he didn't do anything to hurt anyone. Anyway, I don't think he even premeditates going to the john."

"Yeah," Don said, "I *said* I had a weapon, but I didn't hurt nobody."

"Shut up, Don," Marge snapped.

"Mrs. Whitley, I appreciate your coming to this meeting with Don. It helps me get a picture of my client. But would you wait downstairs, please, while I consult with him?"

Marge huffed for a few seconds and stood. "My son may be stupid, but he's not evil." When Ms. Greene didn't respond, Marge left the room, closing the door behind her.

Don studied his shoes. His neck heated. He hated his mother for saying that. He'd rather be evil and smart. Anyway, it was none of Ms. Greene's business how he was or wasn't. He wasn't stupid; stuff just happened to him, and he didn't know what to do about it. His mother was mad at him for putting her smack dab in the middle of his mess. *That's water over the bridge now.*

Ms. Greene gave him a minute to calm down and then asked him to tell her what had happened on Monday at the bank. Don repeated what he'd told her when she came to see him while he was rotting in jail, but this time he added, "I'm sorry I upset everybody. I just needed some money."

Ms. Greene pointed her shiny dark blue nail at Don. "I got it. Here's what the prosecutor thinks. You planned to rob the bank with an accomplice and terrorized people to get what you wanted. Even if you didn't think people would be scared, you threatened to shoot them, and they were scared. The law considers scaring people into handing over money or valuables to be attempted robbery and a felony. Even if I got the charge knocked down to second degree robbery, you'll serve five years or more. If you're convicted of the top count, you could serve up to fifty years in prison."

Don squirmed. *She is just like my principal.*

Ms. Greene unbuttoned her gray wool jacket and inhaled like she wished she had a cigarette. "I'm not saying I agree with the prosecutor, or I won't argue against it. I'm telling you what he thinks he can prove because of the video they have of the event. He will play the video for the grand jury and at trial. Juries are emotional. They'll convict because you intended to scare the tellers, no matter what you say. The tellers' reactions are compelling. You wore a mask, you were loud, and you meant to frighten them."

"Lots of people wear masks these days," Don said, folding his arms across his chest.

Ms. Greene ignored him. "There's also a rumor the other man, Charlie Goodman, may turn state's evidence in exchange for a better deal. He didn't say anything in the bank. According to one witness, you pushed him, and he appeared to resist. He can claim he was coerced. In addition to the video, there are seven witnesses, one who can identify you without a doubt."

"The old biddy, you mean? The one whose picture was in the paper?" Don asked. "She's probably blind as a bat."

"She saw you face to face, close up."

Don huffed. "Well, can you keep me out of jail or not?"

"Since you didn't have a weapon, I think I can get you less time if you change your plea to guilty to a lesser charge and save the court time and money. There'd be no trial and the prosecutor and judge might consider a more lenient sentence if you show remorse."

Don jumped out of the chair and paced the small office. "But I'll still be in prison with those bad men who did real bad things."

"Also," Ms. Greene glanced at Don from above her glasses, "it seems this guy you persuaded to be your accomplice had no prior convictions and might be cognitively challenged. It could be hard to find a sympathetic jury."

Don could hear his mother saying, "Cheese and crackers, Don. What's the matter with you?"

"Of course, the beauty of juries," the lawyer continued, "is they're regular Joes. I've seen the other man, Charlie Goodman, wandering around town. He's been homeless and on the verge of being charged with something. A jury might be persuaded you meant to help him."

Don stifled a yawn and raised his arms, crossing them on the top of his head, and stared out the window. "I did help him. I gave him a place to sleep. Mom was too drunk to notice he was in the house."

Ms. Greene glanced at Don. "Okay, we have about a fifty-fifty chance of a hung jury. We need one juror to vote against conviction. So you could go free because of a hung jury unless the prosecutor wants to retry you. Since you didn't walk off with any money or hurt anyone, it's unlikely the county would entertain another trial."

Don picked at the hole in the knee of his jeans. Ms. Greene tapped on the desk with her finger. She must have been a teacher before she went to law school. The tap meant, "Listen up here, I'm talking to you." He glared at her.

"If you can't stand waiting months to see what happens," Ms. Greene said, "the sure bet is for you to change your plea to guilty to attempted robbery and take a deal. I might be able to get the sentence reduced to two years in the regional jail up in Martinsburg, so your mother can visit you. You could be out in less time if you're good, with a couple years' probation." She stood and opened her office door.

Don nodded, but he was lost, and it sounded like things were going to get worse for him, not better. Ms. Greene walked him downstairs and into the reception area.

Marge rose from the chair and squared her shoulders. "Look, I don't care about justice or the law," she said, ignoring the lawyer's disapproving stare. "I don't want my son in jail again. The first time, when he went to jail for the nothing robbery in the liquor store, was enough. If we'd been rich, I coulda paid the store back, paid the court fine or whatever they call it, and everybody woulda just laughed about the caper because it was dumb shit kid stuff. But we ain't rich so he went to jail. And going to jail made him into someone I don't like at all."

Don closed his eyes. If his mother didn't like him, who would?

"My boy does not go to jail again. He's not a dangerous criminal. Can't he have one of those ankle bracelets so he can live at home and go to work?"

Ms. Greene opened the outer door. "I'll see you in circuit court on the date the judge sets for your trial. Please let me know as soon as you can if you change your mind and want to make a deal with the prosecutor."

Don's brain spun like a merry-go-round. He slinked out of the building but waited on the front step to eavesdrop on his mother and the lawyer.

"Make sure he shows up for his court date, Mrs. Whitley," Ms. Greene said in her sternest voice, "or the judge will issue a warrant for his arrest, and there'll be nothing I can do to protect him."

D ON folded himself into his mother's car.
    "How could you do this to me?" She slapped him across the head. "You're gonna make me a laughing stock." Marge screeched out of the parking space and sped toward their home seven miles south of town.

"Damn, Mom. Damn. I wanted some cash so I could buy the right clothes and look respectable."

She backhanded him, muttering, "You're an idiot," then swerved to avoid hitting a car cutting in front of her. "You don't get it by stealing it from a bank, for God's sake. Where'd you get a crazy idea like that?"

Don's head snapped against the passenger side window. He rubbed the sore spot and glanced at his mother. "You're supposed to be on my side, Mom."

"You're exactly like your father." She gripped the steering wheel with two hands and stared straight ahead. "Useless."

Don could have sworn she was crying, but maybe it was just allergies.

Two cigarettes later, Marge pulled onto the gravel driveway next to their tumbledown house in the worst part of the all but deserted village where his father had abandoned them when booze and drugs became his highest priority. Don doubted the house with its peeling paint, missing roof shingles, collapsing chimney, and tilting porch, could take another winter. Everything about his life made him feel helpless. Maybe his mother felt that way too.

"Sleep in the basement, you idiot," Marge said. "I don't want you anywhere near me. You make me crazy."

She stomped into the kitchen, dropped her purse and keys on the Formica table, and poured herself a good two fingers of whiskey in the glass already sitting next to the bottle. Plopping into the white plastic patio chair she'd picked up for nine dollars at the supermarket where she worked as a cashier, she snapped a cigarette out of the pack with a little jerk of her hand, lit it with shaking fingers, took a deep tug, and glared at Don until he left the room.

Don trudged down the stairs into the basement and threw himself on the old sofa the dog used to sleep on. The sofa had that mildew, dog fart, sour-sweat smell Don associated with his whole house, and the basement still smelled of wet dog even though Spot had run away while Don was in jail five years ago.

His mom had said, "Good riddance," and didn't even try to find the dog. The dog was smart. Don should have taken a cue from him and never come home after his first incarceration. He missed Spot, though. The dog was someone to talk to. Too bad he didn't have Charlie's phone number or know where the guy was. This whole mess was so unfair. He had tried to improve himself. Why didn't anyone see it the way he did?

If they'd pulled off the bank heist, they would have been far away from here already, on the way to Texas or someplace else where they could blend in, and his mother would never have to see him again. She wouldn't have to worry whether he was dumb or how he was doing. She'd be able to have her own life, although Don couldn't imagine his mother living anywhere else but this house in this crappy town.

Then it struck him—what had gone wrong in the bank was that they hadn't had real guns. If they had, no one would've touched them, and he'd be far away from his mother's basement. Heat started in Don's gut and wound its way out to his skin, making him restless. He jumped up from the couch and paced. Everything he did always turned to shit. His whole life he'd been treated like crap, and now his mother had banished him to the basement. *I could still run away.*

Don could see it in his head like a movie: throwing his shit in the back of the truck and taking off down the road. All that would be left of him would be his cigarette smoke floating out of the window. He'd feel mildly guilty about leaving his mother in this dump. But before he left, he had to get revenge, payback for all the wrongs done to him.

There was one small problem to deal with first. He didn't know who to take revenge against, but he would work it out and then he'd leave this small town faster than dust settled on a table.

CHAPTER 9

ETHEL had set aside Friday to develop a market comparison for Harmon's house, but flashes of her car accident intruded every fifteen minutes. *I must have PTSD.* Taking a sip of tea, she leaned her head against the high back of her comfortable chair.

That fateful September morning, she'd left George ensconced in his recliner, earbud wires hanging from his ears, and staring at his laptop screen as if it were a spaceship console, like a lost alien who would never find his way home. He hadn't even looked up when she said goodbye. She couldn't have known it would be the last time she saw him.

Ethel had tapped the address of Herbs & Remedies, the specialty shop in Maryland she'd found online, into the GPS device and backed her Subaru out of the garage. Reviewing the text to lock the general direction into her brain, she'd returned to the map view.

The first part of the drive from West Virginia into Maryland was familiar, and she hadn't listened to the GPS instructions. Determined to enjoy the beautiful fall day on what GPS said would be an hour's drive, she had tuned in to public radio's classical music station and hummed along to a Mozart *divertimento*.

By the end of the first year of her marriage, Ethel knew she had entered into a duel to the death. George was enacting *The Taming of the Shrew*, and she refused to play Kate. The obvious solution, divorce, wouldn't work—not if she wanted to win. In their no-fault state, he would get half her money and property which included her teacher's pension, her IRA, and her social security pension, at least that was how she understood it.

Besides, divorcing him would have been embarrassing. Everyone in the county, people she'd known since birth, would know she'd failed, again. One divorce from a youthful marriage everyone agreed had been a mistake could be forgiven. Two, on the other hand, meant something was wrong with her.

Once Ethel had identified her dilemma, she'd been determined to find another solution to save her sanity. After twenty years of using every psychological method to modify his behavior from carrots to sticks and back again, she'd had her breakthrough moment.

Undetectable poisons.

She'd seen it work in hundreds of episodes of her favorite television series. Diligently researching her options at the public library so George couldn't track her online history, Ethel hit on the perfect toxin disguised as a homeopathic remedy. *Wolfsbane, such a lovely name.*

Even as she drove away from her house, Ethel hadn't known if she dared to follow her plan to reach its logical conclusion. *It's not like I owe George anything. But do I have the nerve?* That remained to be seen. At least she had a nice drive.

"Stay in the right lane. Turn right onto Route Thirty in one-hundred-fifty feet," the GPS device's female voice said out of the blue. "Then continue straight for ten miles."

Ethel gazed around at the world outside her car. She had no idea where she was or what roads these were. She could've been on another planet. Thank God for the GPS. She lowered the volume on the radio to hear the next instruction.

"Turn right at Wodehouse Drive and then get in the left lane," GPS said.

Ethel panicked. She was in the wrong lane to follow the directions and hemmed in by cars on both sides.

"Turn around when possible," the GPS device said.

"Damn," Ethel muttered, again missing the opportunity to change lanes.

"Take the next left at Martinet."

Confused, she maneuvered the car into the left lane and executed a U-turn.

"Recalculating," GPS said. "Make the next right at Poppet Street and stay in the right lane to return to the highway. Then go straight on for two miles."

Ethel concentrated on following GPS instructions and exhaled when she merged onto the highway.

The notion that with enough patience George would come to love her had been naïve. Such nonsense was the result of having read too many Jane Austen novels, or misread them, because surely Mr. Darcy had loved Elizabeth from the moment he set eyes on her.

George had never loved her. He had even warned her. "You're not the one," he'd said when he proposed. "But I have to marry you." God had ordained their union, he declared, and he couldn't escape it any more than Jonah could escape God's will. He had no choice.

Head over heels, Ethel had believed he meant their love was greater than any obstacle. She hadn't heard what he left unsaid: marrying her was like being swallowed whole by a whale.

She got it now. Delusion was a powerful drug capable of changing the meaning of words, the way people appeared, and even one's sense of reality. Hate, she'd discovered, was equally potent. George had been right about one thing; their destinies were entwined. She'd had to learn that one-sided love wore out like the silk fibers in a rug walked on for decades, and George was the one to teach her. And as a corollary, she'd found she was happier alone. Maybe some pots didn't need a lid.

"Take the next right to exit the highway, then use the left lane to turn left onto Wooddale," GPS said.

Ethel appreciated that GPS never stopped talking to her simply because she'd made a mistake. George should have been more like GPS.

In one last ditch attempt to save their marriage just the week before her trip to Herbs & Remedies, she'd perched in the chair opposite his recliner, cleared her throat, and said, "We can't live like this."

He'd glanced up over his glasses. "You can leave. I can buy every service you provide. I've already checked the prices." These were the first words he'd said to her in three months.

"Why don't *you* leave, then?"

"I pay the mortgage." He gave her a little smirk as if he'd played his trump card and won the game.

Ethel had kept her body still but blurted, "Why are you like this?"

He'd inhaled, looked away from her, and said through clenched teeth, "You violated my circle of truth."

Her bones vibrated as if she'd been transported outside in her pajamas into subzero weather. He wasn't angry at her for an infraction of his secret rules, he was certifiably crazy.

Circle of truth? He's never said anything about this before. Has he read it on some online guru's blog? Are there different truths for different people? His circle, like some invisible planetary orbit around an alien sun, was what was important to him.

"Am I part of your circle of truth?" After twenty-two years, he might consider her to be a satellite, like a moon to his earth.

His face twisted into a grimace. "No, you have your own circle of truth," he said as if she should have known this because the law on circles of truth was written on the first page of a primer titled *Instructions for Living for Dummies.*

As far as Ethel could grasp, this lunatic idea was another way of erasing her. Still, from a long habit of forgiving him, she tried once more to understand. "Is there an overlap of the two circles, like a Venn diagram, a place where we share some truth?" To demonstrate, she made two circles with her thumbs and forefingers and overlapped them in what looked to her like a love knot with a diamond in the center.

He'd shaken his head and gone back to reading whatever was on his screen. That conversation ended any lingering illusions that he had ever cared for her. They didn't share a scrap of truth between them, and she wasn't part of his universe. No wonder they didn't get along.

She hadn't thrown away her life, she'd sold it for the fantasy that she was like other women who married and had a family. He'd wasted his life also, selling himself to get his hands on the hefty annual income from her mother's trust fund. Ethel was as much to blame for the ache in her heart as he was, agreeing to live without being loved and convincing herself she loved him.

"Take the next right onto Somerset Lane," GPS said.

Ethel flipped on her blinker and followed the instructions.

She jammed on the brakes in the middle of the street. *Oh, my God, that's it. I don't love him.*

"Go one block and turn right on Snookers Lane."

"I don't love him," she said, trying the words aloud.

After two decades of exhausting mental gymnastics, she was free. *I must have already known this. I just didn't know I knew it.*

"I don't love him," she shouted. She felt such jubilation she could've sung Beethoven's entire *Ode to Joy* in German.

At this moment, GPS had said, "In one-hundred-fifty feet, you will reach your destination." There was a brief pause as if GPS had to take a breath, during which Ethel drove the car into a small gravel parking lot.

"Your destination is on the right."

Ethel checked the address she'd written down on a piece of paper against the hand-painted sign, Herbs & Remedies, hanging from the porch roof of the gray clapboard cottage right in front of her. Sitting in the car for a minute, her heart pounding hard, she'd waited to change her mind.

She would remember forever that she hadn't.

Stumbling up the three stairs, she'd knocked on the red door, pressed the old brass latch, and stepped over the threshold. A bell tinkled. The shop was lit by dozens of candles, which struck Ethel as quite dangerous, but the smell of burning sage enveloped her.

Potted aloe and snake plants thrived in the window. The woman behind the counter, white hair held back from her face by a green ribbon, looked up and smiled. Ethel wouldn't have been surprised if huge white wings had unfurled behind her.

Lurching to the counter, Ethel had stammered, "I'm hoping you have aconite. I read it sometimes helps with anxiety. I've tried the usual over-the-counter remedies. They don't work. A friend gave me the name of your shop. I came here because I thought you might be able to help me."

These were the most lies she had uttered at one time in weeks. Breathless and embarrassed, she'd forgotten to begin the conversation with the social amenities, like saying hello and smiling. She dipped her head and mumbled, "Oh, sorry, I should have asked your name . . . but . . ."

"My name is Hannah. I'm glad you found me. Could I see your hand, please, dear?"

"My hand?"

"I can tell from your hand what kind of illness you have and whether aconite is the cure you need."

Ethel offered her hand. The woman took it in both of hers and pressed her thumbs in the center of Ethel's palm, cradling her hand for two minutes while gazing straight into Ethel's eyes. Time expanded. The warmth of the woman's fingers seeped through Ethel's skin. No one had touched her in months. Her arm warmed, then the rest of her body, and she floated in a sea of blooming multi-colored lights. The feeling of weightlessness went on and on. She relaxed, hoping the sensation would never end.

Hannah said, "I see," and placed Ethel's hand on the counter as if it were a rare artifact.

Ethel's lips twisted with the effort to hold back tears. "The aconite, can I buy it?" she whispered.

"Yes, my dear. I am going to give you twenty milliliters in a single ampoule. You administer it in one dose. Put it in something to mask the taste, like coffee. Its action will be quick. Be careful not to spill a single drop on your skin. It's best to wear gloves, and throw the ampoule, the cup, spoon, and gloves into a plastic bag and discard them right after administration."

"Will it have the effect I need?" Ethel wanted to be clear she understood what the woman was saying.

"Yes, indeed. He will have a heart attack. He will likely vomit first, then his face will seize up. There will be excruciating pain. He'll know he's dying, and he'll know you caused it. This is what you want, right?"

Ethel gasped. Hannah knew what she wanted and didn't judge her.

"The aconite will be undetectable in a normal autopsy if no one is testing for it." Hannah handed Ethel a small paper bag with the shop's logo stamped on it.

It was hard to believe this tiny, lightweight bag held something powerful enough to end a life. Ethel's hand trembled a little. She put the bag down on the counter and opened her wallet to pay cash for her twenty-five dollar purchase.

In the car, Ethel placed the bag on the passenger seat next to her purse, cleared the route on the GPS device, and set a new course for home. She felt so light she might float away.

"It must be from breathing in the sage." Her voice sounded like the woman she used to be before she married George.

She clicked her seat belt, started the car, and rolled down the windows to allow air to circulate through the vehicle. Thinking the bag holding the aconite was unprotected, she placed it inside her purse and put the purse on the floor in front of the passenger seat for safekeeping. *Just in case someone tries to steal it.* She'd heard of thieves sticking their hands through open car windows and swiping a necklace right off a woman's neck while she waited at a stoplight.

Ethel, her mind full of white noise, exited the parking lot, made a right, and drove for a while, oblivious to the GPS instructions. The device said, "Turn around when possible," and "Recalculating," offering her alternate routes. Disobedience gave Ethel an odd feeling of satisfaction she hadn't had in a long while. This was her first taste of freedom. She could hear a testiness in the device's voice, but GPS was still talking to her.

Ahead, a long line of cars waited to cross the intersection, but she wasn't in a hurry. Her shoulders uncrimped; her twenty-year headache had dissipated. Time, once a luxury commodity, was now abundant. She didn't have to do anything right away. She could solve her problem whenever she was ready. The idea made her giddy. For the first time in two decades, her fate was in her hands.

The traffic light changed three times before her car reached the intersection. GPS repeated, "Turn around when possible," because she was going the wrong way, but she was in the wrong lane to do anything about it.

With the same joy she'd always felt when the first pink buds unclenched on her favorite cherry tree every spring, Ethel understood that being lost didn't matter. Being in the wrong place didn't matter. Eventually, she would follow GPS' directions to go home.

Her car had arrived at the head of the lane just as the car ahead of her ran the yellow light. She stopped, proud of herself for obeying the signal. When the light changed to green again, the long line of cars behind her surged forward, horns honking like a gaggle of anxious geese awaiting takeoff.

Jolted out of her reverie, she slammed her foot on the gas pedal. Her car vaulted into the intersection. In her peripheral vision, she glimpsed a Dodge Ram truck racing toward her. It slammed into the driver's side of Ethel's car before she had time to think. Her vehicle spun 180 degrees, skidded across three lanes, and smashed into the cars on either side of her.

Windows shattered, glass flew everywhere, stinging her face and hands. The car was tossed from side to side like a sheet flapping on a clothesline in a windstorm. Airbags slammed against her, pinning her in the seat, suffocating her. Ethel might have screamed, but later she couldn't remember. Her purse holding the tiny ampoule of poison lodged under the front seat of her car.

"Recalculating," GPS said. "Turn around when possible."

When she awakened to a nurse leaning over her, stroking her arm, and saying her name, Ethel thought she'd died and gone to heaven.

Ethel wrenched herself back into the present and refocused her attention. "Well, if I survived all that, I can sell Harmon Rutledge's house."

CHAPTER 10

CHARLIE leaned on the counter in Uncle John's diner, waiting for his takeout of fried chicken, cornbread, fried apples, and mac 'n' cheese—his father's favorite meal. Inhaling the mixed aromas of sweet fruit pie, pickles, burned coffee, and chicken frying, he sent his father a mental hat tip. *To the best days, Dad.*

This restaurant, where he and his dad used to eat after a day of fishing since they never came away from the river with any actual fish, hadn't changed in twenty years—red vinyl benches in the booths, shiny chrome stools, and Formica counter. Even the waitresses looked the same to Charlie.

"Hey, hot stuff," he said to the waitress, whose name was embroidered on her white polo shirt, as she handed him his drink in a takeaway cup.

Barb flipped her ponytail, batted her lashes, and said, "Thanks," in what Charlie took as an invitation to continue flirting. He smiled his best smile. This was his sixth meal at the diner under Ethel's arrangement with the management, and he was liking the whole set up. It wouldn't hurt to ingratiate himself with the staff.

Admiring his new flattop haircut in the mirrored tiles behind the milkshake machine, Charlie spotted Don pushing open the door and creeping into the restaurant as if he meant to surprise him. Charlie's stomach lurched. *He's the last thing I need.* Even before Don reached him, Charlie caught a whiff of the man's mothball odor.

Don came up behind him and squeezed Charlie's shoulder. "Whatcha doin', kid?"

"Hey, man." Charlie rubbed his thumb along the stainless-steel edge of the Formica counter, trying hard not to look at Don.

Don's claim on him made him uneasy. Just because Don had given him a place to sleep and junk to eat didn't mean the man owned him forever. As sure as male dogs lifted their legs to pee, Don would suck him into another crazy scheme destined to land them in jail again. Jail was the last place Charlie wanted to be; the thirty-six hours he'd spent in a cell were enough.

But if there was one thing he knew about himself, it was that he had zero willpower. As his father would say, he could be convinced to do things he didn't want to do faster than a ping pong ball sucked through a vacuum tube. All of which meant that Don equaled danger to his current comfortable status quo.

Concentrating on writing his name with his fingertip on the counter, Charlie asked, "When did you get out?"

"My mom bailed me this morning. I'm back living at home in the basement. My lawyer's workin' on a deal to get me off."

Charlie doubted this was true, but he knew nothing about the law. His attorney, Angela Markey, had explained that unless he told the prosecutor everything, he was going to jail. Meaning, if he snitched on Don, the prosecutor would cut him a break. Angela said she thought she could get Charlie probation before judgment on a misdemeanor mischief charge. He'd do no jail time unless he screwed up again. The choice was snitch and go free or be a good friend and go to jail.

"You should take this deal," Ethel urged. "It means you won't have a record. Misdemeanors can be expunged after five years. Ms. Markey said so. You'll still be able to get a decent job, have a real life."

He'd wanted to tell Ethel this life was real enough, thank you very much, he didn't want another. But he'd held his tongue and patted himself on the back for keeping his mouth shut.

Charlie had promised Angela he would think about taking the deal, but the minute she'd told him about it, he knew he would. Free or in jail; it was an easy decision, even for him. His delay was to make it appear that he had scruples. Charlie planned to call Angela in the morning and say he'd do whatever she thought was best.

All of which made him reluctant to spend any time with Don. He wasn't supposed to talk to the guy, and he didn't want anyone to see them together, so of course Don turned up in a public place where he couldn't just tell him to go away.

Don plopped down on the stool next to Charlie and ordered a Coke. "How'd you know I was at this restaurant?" Charlie asked.

Don's lips curled. "I saw your post. You know, the pics."

His scowl made Charlie's stomach lurch again. *He knows. He knows I'm going to give him up. He wants to blast me into a bubbling mass of goo.*

It wasn't like he owed Don anything. This dude had gotten him into the kind of trouble he would never have stumbled into on his own. Who could imagine trying to rob a bank—much less pretending your finger was a gun—was on anyone's list of things to do before you die? On the other hand, Don had also given him a place to stay when no one else had. So he was obligated. Although maybe being forced to be an accomplice in a bank robbery evened the score.

Barb slid the frosty glass toward Don, and he sucked on the straw like he hadn't had anything to drink in four days.

"You could come back and stay at my place instead of the motel," Don said when he came up for air. "Be like old times."

The sound of Don swallowing his soda made Charlie want to cover his ears. "Nah. Better stay where I am. At least until this court thing is sorted out." Don knowing he was staying at the motel gave Charlie the willies.

Don was his kryptonite. Before the robbery, Charlie had driven while intoxicated and failed to pay his bills on time. Well, maybe nicking money out of Ethel's purse and petty cash at work was illegal, but he didn't count as stealing the times he had taken money from his father or friends when they weren't paying attention. Not that he'd ever repaid anyone who covered his debts, but he might someday.

Actual theft, as Charlie understood from watching movies, required entering a stranger's house and taking something of value like cash, jewelry, or electronics. Therefore, in his mind, he had never committed a crime. Borrowing stuff wasn't stealing as long as he planned to return whatever he'd taken.

These complicated questions occupied a fair amount of his headroom. Since he had nothing to do all day but ponder his life, he allowed such reflections to peck around in his mind like crows on roadkill. He would have spent several hours a day on social media to take his mind off his predicament, but Ethel had cautioned him in no uncertain terms he'd better not make public statements about his legal situation "on that online social thing." His account, she warned him, could be subpoenaed as evidence in a trial.

Charlie reasoned that instead of posting about his experience in jail, he could write about the book he was reading, his new duds and digs. He had posted a selfie in his motel room, in front of the library, at the galleries, and pics of his meals. After all, she hadn't said he couldn't do that.

"So, what d'ya think?" Don put his hand on Charlie's shoulder.

Charlie shrugged off Don's hand. "About what?"

"Like, about staying at my place?"

Ethel had warned him that he shouldn't open the door of his motel room to anyone but her. She said he shouldn't talk to anyone except her and the lawyer. Charlie hated the fact that saving him from prison meant Ethel could tell him what to do. He was a grown up; he had his own life. He could make his own choices.

Charlie closed his eyes and inhaled, like taking back a birthday wish, before he said to Don, "I guess you could hang with me in my room for a couple of hours if you want. They clean it every day, and I got HBO." The minute the words were out of his mouth, he regretted them. The last thing he wanted to do was spend time with Don.

"But nobody can see you come in my room. I don't want to mess up my deal with Ethel. She's taking care of everything, and if she found out we hung out, it would be over, and I'd be in jail. And I can't . . ."

Don glared at Charlie. "Okay, man. I'm checking in with you. Remember, don't say nothin' to nobody about you know." He dismounted from his stool the way a cowboy would from a horse and punched Charlie on the shoulder.

"Okay. See ya." Charlie rubbed his shoulder, hoping Don's laser beam eyes wouldn't melt the skin off his face.

"Yeah."

Charlie felt a brief twinge of guilt as Don left the diner. He liked his new comfortable routine more than he liked Don. After waking at ten in the morning and eating a hearty breakfast at Uncle John's, he'd amble down to the library and hang out online for a few hours.

In the afternoon, Charlie would chat with his fellow displaced Americans arrayed on public benches in town, or check out the exhibits in Main Street galleries, and then walk back up to Uncle John's for a takeout dinner he ate in his room while watching whatever was on HBO. He read until he fell asleep, the novel having the same effect on his brain as alcohol—he zoomed away from his life into someone else's and wasn't responsible for anything that happened.

This was the good life and messing around with Don would ruin it. Charlie did have a yen for a few beers now and then, but he also had no work stress, no car troubles, no bills to pay, no worries about dating and relationships. He could do this. Add some cash to buy a six-pack every day and living this way would be bliss.

All the American hustle, the demand to be productive, to make money and have stuff, to build monuments and solve world problems ran counter to his mental health. He considered himself a different kind of animal, a go along to get along kind of guy. Who needed achievements memorialized in framed pieces of paper some stranger would throw in the dumpster when he died?

Of course, Ethel was paying for him to live this way and she'd be fed up pretty soon. Like his father had always said, Charlie needed a better plan for his future. He should be applying for jobs, but he was still having those downward spiral dreams he'd had when he was fired.

He'd read enough Stephen King now to know the dreams meant something bad was going to happen, and he was sure Don would be involved. There was no point in spending the effort to reverse course. Anyway, spiraling upwards would take a superhuman amount of energy.

Bottom line, his father said in his head, *you're a lazy fuck*.

Charlie gathered up the plastic bag with his food in it, but he waited by the glass door until Don's pickup left the parking lot. Walking across the cracked asphalt parking lot from the diner to his motel room, he realized Don had scoured the town looking for him.

He followed me on my socials. He recognized the diner from the photo I posted. He's stalking me. He's going to suck me into some other crazy scheme that's doomed to failure, and I'm stupid enough to fall for it.

Charlie scampered the last ten feet to his door. Don was like a contagious virus corkscrewing into his brain. Staying away from him would make Ethel happy, and, after all, Ethel was the one parent he had left. He owed her. It should be simple enough to avoid getting into another scrape. *Saying a thing could make it true, couldn't it?*

CHAPTER 11

"HOW'S it going?" Debbie asked, walking into the real estate agency's computer room early Friday evening.

Ethel glanced up from the screen at the broker's perfect cheeks, the kind that plastic surgeons were crafting on movie stars' faces. Debbie was young, though, and her cheeks complete with adorable dimples were natural.

"Oh, fine," Ethel said. "I'm just trying to figure something out."

"Can I help you?"

"Maybe. I want to make sure Harmon Rutledge has clear title to his property and is able to sell the house before I talk to you about the listing."

"You mean the Harmon Rutledge who's vice president of the bank that was just robbed?"

"Well, it wasn't robbed. The robbers didn't succeed."

Debbie's face brightened. "You're the one who stopped the robbery there, right? The story was in the paper."

Ethel blushed. "Yes."

Debbie's indigo eyes sparkled. "You were so brave. We're proud to have you as part of our team. And Mr. Rutledge asked you to sell his property?"

"Yes, he called me right after the police rigamarole was over and asked me to list it. I was going to tell you about it after I did some research." In Debbie's presence, Ethel felt faded, like a photograph exposed to the sun for too long.

"Wow. Wonderful. This is your first listing, isn't it?"

"Yes." Ethel held her breath. If Debbie assigned a seasoned real estate agent to help with the listing, all the work Ethel had already done would be for nothing. The senior agent would get the credit for the sale and the lion's share of the commission. Ethel had to get Harmon's signature on an exclusive listing agreement with her before that happened.

"Well, I'll give you any help you need." Debbie leaned over Ethel's shoulder to stare at the computer screen. "You're examining his title?"

"Yes. Records show the house isn't old. It was built ten years ago, although it has an air of permanence about it, as if it's been on the site for half a century. Mr. Rutledge is the second person to own the house."

"Where's the house located?"

"It's off Shepherd Grade Road, in a neighborhood on the riverside, half a mile from the country club. The development is part of a parcel subdivided thirty years ago from the remains of a plantation dating back to pre-Civil War days."

Ethel could see the dollar signs rolling up in Debbie's eyes. This was a premiere neighborhood, which meant big real estate price tags.

Debbie ran her hand through her blonde hair. "I know where you're talking about."

"Each house has its own design and is built individually," Ethel said. "There are stringent covenants, like 'no artificial materials,' meaning aluminum siding, I guess, and no cloven hooved animals."

Debbie snorted. "I think they mean farm animals like pigs and goats."

"Right." Ethel grinned as she imagined a drove of pigs wobbling across the golf course behind the fancy houses. "Some of the larger lots are still vacant. You must know the original plantation house, the limestone mansion on a bluff overlooking the river."

"I've been there for weddings," Debbie said. "It's an upscale neighborhood." She patted Ethel's shoulder. "Sounds like you've got a handle on this but come find me if you run into any trouble. Remember, I have to sign the contract before you put the sale in the multiple listing system." She gave Ethel a friendly wave and bounced out of the room.

Ethel checked again to make sure the current deed was registered in Harmon's name. Her relief at discovering she wouldn't have to deal with an angry, discarded wife was offset by an increasing discomfort she couldn't put her finger on. There was something she didn't know, and if she didn't learn about it in time, it would guarantee her downfall.

Don't be so melodramatic, Ethel.

"I hate it when you're right, George."

To make sure she had scrutinized every item that might trip her up, Ethel searched for Harmon's birth record in the county's vital statistics database and found nothing. After a second's panic that he was lying about his name, she collected herself. *He could have been born anywhere.*

"But where?" Ethel trawled through Google looking for Harmon Rutledge's biography and spotted the announcement of his appointment at the bank. He hailed from a small town called Manitou Springs in Colorado. His father had been the local doctor. *How interesting.* Digging a little deeper, she found an old news report that said both his parents had been murdered while he was away at college. The killer had never been found.

"So sad for Harmon. No wonder he's a little off." She was about to click on the next story and stopped herself. *Can't go down this rabbit hole now.*

But the thought that she was missing something important stuck in her craw. Ethel examined her notes again. *Wife Trudy Davis is missing.* A jolt of electricity flared through her. She scrolled through the photos she had taken on her phone in case she'd captured a framed photograph of the couple on an end table or bookcase shelf. Nothing.

No family pictures were displayed in any of the rooms, not even their wedding photo. So odd. Didn't people display at least one photo from their wedding? Harmon must have read somewhere he should remove personal photographs before showing a house for sale and had followed the advice.

Come to think of it, the house's interior had made her think of a model home, a blank canvas onto which anyone could project themselves, good for selling the place but strange for living in. It would be like living in a hotel. Maybe Harmon and Trudy were both with the CIA, their jobs were a cover, and the house was a façade they kept clean of personal references in case their false identities were penetrated.

Ethel took a breath. It was times like this that she'd needed George to drag her back from the brink of her wildest speculations. How odd to discover he was good for something.

But what if Harmon had lied about ever having a wife and had just made up the name Trudy Davis? *Ethel, cut it out.* Her wild speculations were making her anxiety worse. Fact was, if the woman didn't share ownership of the property, then she didn't matter as far as selling the house was concerned. Cold perhaps, but this was business. Time to be pragmatic.

Ethel scanned the Rs in the county's marriage license database. There was a record. *Halleluiah*! Six months ago Harmon had married Trudy Davis, just as he'd said. The woman existed and the marriage was recorded. Ethel had everything she needed to proceed with drawing up the contract. *Stop dithering. Debbie will think you're too old to do the job.*

"Hey." Betsy, the real estate agency's top seller, tapped Ethel on the shoulder. "Did you see the paper today?"

Ethel jumped and swiveled in the chair to face her. "The paper?"

"Yeah, today's *Daily*. Your client is in it." Betsy tugged down her gold shirt, the way Picard, Ethel's favorite *Star Trek* captain, always did right before he commanded Star Fleet officers to go to their inevitable deaths.

Ethel's heart froze. Had something happened to Harmon? She grabbed the paper from Betsy and brought it rustling in her hand down to the desk where she could see what her colleague was talking about.

"Oh, the wedding announcement. Yes, I saw it," she lied. Noting the wedding photo, Ethel was reassured that Harmon and his wife might be normal people who did normal things.

"Yeah, well, see the date of the wedding?" Betsy put her finger on the paper. "Six months ago. It's a little odd, isn't it, having the notice in the paper so long after? I mean, why bother? Did you meet his wife?"

"No, ah, she's, she wasn't there for our appointment."

"Well, that makes sense because on page six there's a news item saying she's missing." Betsy patted her perfect auburn French twist. "Isn't it strange both the wedding announcement and the police report saying she's missing are in the paper on the same day? You'd think the newspaper people would read their own stuff and ask a question or two."

"I knew she was missing." Ethel's voice squeaked.

"You knew? And you took the listing anyway?" Betsy's coral-colored lips frowned, reminding Ethel of the emojis on social media apps.

All Ethel's insecurities now circled her head like angry dragons. Betsy was a top seller. If Betsy was questioning the listing, something must be wrong with it.

"I checked county records," Ethel said. "Harmon owns the house on his own, in his name, I mean. The wife's not on the deed."

"Oh, well. I guess it's okay then. Maybe he can't manage the property on his own. But still, it's weird, right when his wife goes missing, to sell his house. Don't you think?" She stared at Ethel for a beat and walked away. "Good luck with it," Betsy said over her shoulder.

It didn't sound like Betsy was wishing her luck. More like a prediction of abject failure. Anxiety wrapped its arms around Ethel and squeezed. *I should find out more about Harmon before I list his house.* She reminded herself she wanted another tour of the house to snap more photos. *Maybe I'll stumble on something to help me make sense of his situation.*

Ethel pulled up the residential multiple listing system to check if Harmon had tried to sell the property before. Just as he'd said, he'd bought the property a year before from the original owner. Ethel schooled herself to stop worrying. As far as the world was concerned, he was legally qualified to sell the house.

Opening the market comparison app, she plugged in the house's attributes and examined similar houses the system found that had sold in the last six months. Her hunch had been right; she could price the property at $995,000 and leave room for bargaining or a bidding war.

Glee bubbled in her chest. This would be a big sale, even for Betsy. Ethel grinned at the computer screen. "We did good," she whispered to her reflection grinning back at her from the screen.

While the market comparison was printing, Ethel began filling in the blanks on the real estate company's contract form. Harmon would have to sign and date it before she could put the house on the market. She called him to set an appointment to get his signature and got his voice mail. In the background of his recorded voice mail message, Ethel heard a woman whispering as if she were telling him what to say.

Harmon hadn't struck Ethel as the kind of man who needed that level of instruction. His wife must be a nag. A spurt of empathy for him made her remember how stifled she'd felt living with George, how he had questioned her every action down to whether to buy brand name or brand X canned beans.

Living in a straitjacket could drive one to extreme measures. After George died, she'd cleaned out his stuff, and it was almost as if he'd never existed. Harmon must have cleared away his wife's things when she left him and claimed she was missing because he couldn't face the embarrassment of having been abandoned. He was such a meticulous person, he would have waited until the last possible moment to assume the worst, just as Ethel would.

Ethel skimmed the daily newspaper online and found the police blotter post reporting Trudy missing. It was accompanied by a different photograph from the one in the wedding announcement. Based on the lightweight dress Trudy wore in the photo, Ethel presumed the picture was taken on their honeymoon.

So he does have photos of her. Maybe they're on his phone. I just jumped to the wrong conclusions.

His wife was attractive; perhaps he loved her. For no reason, a memory of Othello smothering his beloved Desdemona flashed through Ethel's head. *Love is no guarantee against murder.* Ethel waved her hand in front of her face to push away the association. She thought of the lengths *she* had been willing to go to secure her sanity. Perhaps Trudy had tried a similar solution and failed. Then, desperate to save herself, she ran away.

A memory of the odd gray pillow on the snowy white bed floated by. Maybe Harmon was the one who'd been desperate. Ethel dismissed the image and loaded her photos into the listing application for Harmon's house, sure there'd be immediate offers even without a walk-through. The house was beautiful. Harmon had taken impeccable care of it, and the market was hot. The first people to call her would be other agents with lists of clients looking for this exact house, but she wanted to find her own buyer.

Her share of the six percent commission if she were both the listing and selling agent was almost thirty-thousand dollars, with the rest of it going to her bosses at Steptoe and Fritter. She didn't need the money; it would just throw her into a higher tax bracket. It was winning she craved. She wasn't ready to settle down to noontime television and Mahjong like her friends.

It was the idea of success, even at what some snotty-nosed youngsters considered her advanced age, that drove her. Selling one expensive house would lead to selling another. She pictured herself striding into house after house, shaking hands, signing contracts, smiling as the settlement lawyer handed her a check. *I could be this year's million-dollar real estate agent. The top seller.* Ethel smiled at her fantasy. *I could beat Betsy.* She glanced around hoping no one had heard her thoughts.

All she needed was a buyer. In her mind, she had already designed the postcard featuring a picture of Harmon's house with the word SOLD in a bright red banner. She would send the postcard printed with her name and telephone number to every household in Harmon's neighborhood.

Ethel got up to pour herself another cup of tea. Her knees wobbled as if her body had run out of power. After she secured Harmon's signature, she still had to put the For Sale sign on the front lawn and drop off the open house flyer for his review. She needed to get his key and put a lockbox on the door, advertise the open house, and make pamphlets that listed the data home buyers needed to know—property taxes, electricity costs, size of the rooms. There were so many details to keep track of she felt breathless. Oh, and she should make a walk-through video of the house for the website.

When she left her message on Harmon's voice mail, Ethel tried to be cheery so her voice would convey confidence, but she worried her "See you soon," hadn't quite hit the right note. It wouldn't be helpful if he picked up on her uncertainty. He was a big man who could snap her in two with one hand.

CHAPTER 12

MILLIE Overbee stuck first her head and then her entire body into the office of the *Daily's* executive editor. "There's something odd about this," she said. She took a deep breath and shook the newspaper clutched in her hand.

"Yes?" Erik said in the pained voice of someone coping with a migraine.

Millie set aside Erik's unhappiness. She had to talk to him, and invading his office was better than cornering him in the hall. She'd waited to make her move until her immediate supervisor, the news editor, left for dinner. Martin didn't like junior reporters going over his head. He would find a way to get back at her, even if that took a long time. But for this story, Millie was willing to take that risk.

Blinking, Erik glanced away from his screen and groaned. "What's odd? Is there a misprint?" Although he appeared to be talking to his desk, Millie knew from office lore that he was addressing her.

"The Rutledge-Davis wedding announcement and the police blotter report about Trudy Davis being missing for five days is what's odd," she said. "They're both in today's paper."

Bewilderment spread across the executive editor's face until his features appeared sand washed.

"Did you see today's paper?" Millie asked.

Erik winced and smoothed his sparse mustache. "Of course, I read the paper every day, although I must admit I expect the wedding notices and police blotter to take care of themselves. All the information comes from primary sources."

He smiled, which Millie read as an attempt to mollify her instead of dealing with what was an obvious mystery. His office smelled like wet newspaper. The bank of bookcases behind him reminded Millie of the ready-made backgrounds on Zoom. They were supposed to frame the man, give him context. The backdrop wasn't working. For one thing, his desk was too neat, like the desk of someone who thought one thing at a time. That was boring. For another, the blinds on the window-wall through which he was meant to observe the newsroom were almost always drawn.

Millie almost explained to Erik that she couldn't help herself; she had succumbed to her terminal curiosity. It was in her nature, after all, to tease the lid off secrets. Someday her inquisitiveness might kill her, but regardless, she considered nosiness to be genetic like her red hair and freckles, and that couldn't be overcome by willpower.

Besides, she had been at this small-town daily, the required rung up to a big-city newspaper, for two years and was still assigned stories not covered by beat reporters—general assignment, they called it. To move on, she needed a humdinger of a story, one good enough to be picked up by the Associated Press wire and spotted by a national editor. Which meant a story with a lot of conflict and a great hook, which was what everyone else under thirty in this newsroom wanted.

She had to hustle, even though Erik preferred consulting with the editors about potential stories at the prescribed morning budget meeting and afternoon roundup. To get his attention, Millie had to knock him off his routine. While he avoided looking at her by examining his finger-nails, she studied his growing bald spot. This external indication of his biological humanity gave her courage. He would be convincible.

"Well, I talked to Soph, and she says she talked to Rutledge on Sunday morning about running the wedding announcement six months late, and he consulted with his wife, and they said to go ahead."

Erik jiggled his tie. "So, what's the problem?"

"The police blotter item says Trudy Davis has been missing since Sunday morning. How could Rutledge consult with his wife if she were already missing?"

"Maybe she went missing after Soph talked to him."

Millie stared at Erik.

"You're saying we printed the wrong date she went missing? And we need to issue a correction?"

"No." Millie plopped herself into the visitor's chair opposite him. "I'm saying Rutledge lied, either to Sophie or to the police. Either his wife hadn't gone missing on Sunday, or he pretended to consult her."

"I'm not following you. Did he say he consulted his wife?"

"He told the sheriff his wife was gone at the same time he implied to Sophie that she was there. What good reason is there to do that?"

"Implied? Did he say he consulted his wife? And why does what he told Sophie matter?"

Millie rocked her head from side to side to unkink her neck. "Soph drew the inference when he put her on hold." *How is it the minute a good reporter becomes management he loses his capacity for knowing a news story when he sees one?* "Okay. I interviewed him right after the bank robbery attempt on Monday. Rutledge is . . . weird. I'm sure he had something to do with his wife's disappearance and is covering it up."

Erik rocked back in his chair, put his hands up behind his head, and laughed. "Wow. What a leap. You know we report the news, right? We don't make it up."

Millie ground her teeth. "You have to search for the news. Murderers aren't going to call you up and confess on the phone, well except for the one guy who confessed to the night desk editor last year, which was a complete fluke."

Erik's eyebrows shot up. "So, you're asserting Trudy Davis was murdered by her husband?"

"I'm not claiming she was murdered. I'm wondering if a murder occurred and if he did it."

Erik huffed. "What do you want me to do about this . . . this coincidence you've spotted?"

"I want your backing. I want you to tell me I can dig into it, sniff around, talk to some people, keep my eyes open—whatever an editor is supposed to say to a reporter. Direction, leads, contacts."

"Did you talk to Martin about this? He's the news editor."

"I did."

"And?"

"And he said it was a non-starter. I don't agree, so I'm coming to you."

Erik glowered. His look said all the words he didn't.

Millie's face flamed. *Dial it back, Mil. Your tone might be the teeniest bit insubordinate.* She pictured waves rolling in on the beach, light blinking off the ocean, a seagull flying overhead, and felt the tingle of cold water washing over her toes. Her shoulders relaxed but her determination stayed.

"I want to check out my hunch, and I'd rather you give me the okay, but I'm probably going to do it anyway so you might as well . . ."

"Okay, whatever," Erik said. "But nothing goes to print without my approval. If you find anything, you bring it to me. Before you write it. Got it?"

Millie grinned. "Got it." She had her phone to her ear before she left his office.

CHAPTER 13

HARMON paced his office. These late Friday bank hours took a toll on his patience. *His father's sleeping face. Blood splattered everywhere. A hand tossed the ax into fire.* Why was he thinking of that now? He'd hated killing the old man. His father had been a good guy, but it was a bad idea to leave a witness.

"Just have to let go of things that weigh you down, son," his father had always said. Harmon had taken the man at his word.

Time was wasting, and impatience made Harmon uneasy, which increased his exasperation with the people around him. He'd been curt with his administrative assistant. Backing her up against the wall and telling her to just do her job and stop trying to manage him had been the wrong approach. She'd scrunched her shoulders, and her lip trembled.

Since then, she'd shot him hurt looks all day instead of her customary adoration. To regain her esteem, he'd called the florist and ordered a bouquet of lilies, roses, and carnations to be delivered to her desk at the bank. *Thank you for keeping your head when all around you are losing theirs*, the card said. The chorus of oohs and ahs when the flowers arrived just before the bank lobby closed was satisfactory proof that he'd done the right thing.

But Harmon felt rushed, and he worried he would miss something important. Worry made him hesitate, and hesitation made him feel weak. This was not the time for weakness. A memory of his mother whirling him around the living room unrolled in his mind like a carpet, dizzying him. *Why am I even thinking of her now? I dealt with her.*

He had to figure out what to do next, and whatever that was, his clues couldn't be obvious. The police needed to believe that they had pieced together the story that Trudy had been abducted, killed, and her car had been stolen and then ditched. How to feed the authorities this sequence of events in a plausible way without seeming to do it was the problem.

His first plan—to park Trudy's dead body in her car trunk at the airport's long-term parking lot—had seemed perfect until he realized he'd left her there in her nightgown. *Who storms out of the house in a nightgown?* Harmon railed at himself. *How could you be so stupid?* The minute the police found her, they would know he'd been lying. But he resented having to change his plan on the fly, and his resentment got in the way of thinking clearly.

Getting the wannabe bank robbers to change her clothes would solve his problem of being seen near her body or her car. But people, in particular stupid ones, couldn't be trusted, not because they were malevolent but because they would introduce another layer of uncertainty by virtue of their own mistakes.

The list of things he couldn't control grew larger with every additional person involved. There was no way to tell in advance if the dopey duo would execute his plan as instructed. To be flexible, he had to let go of certainty. He'd have to be able to switch his story on the fly as unexpected consequences developed. But he'd proved years ago that he was nimble. He could adjust.

It also worried him that his experience executing a complex plan and evading police detection afterward was so many years ago, it almost didn't count. The police had better forensics now and cameras were everywhere. To make matters worse, this situation brought up his old issues with his mother. The sheriff, after all, was a woman. These factors had to be taken into consideration in his new strategy.

Use the uncertainty. That's it. By using the dumbest guys possible to do his bidding, their mistakes would cover his own, like fingerprints. The police wouldn't see his hand for all their messes. There was no time to waste. Trusting his gut, Harmon picked up his cellphone and searched the internet for Don Whitley's phone number.

CHAPTER 14

THE last person Don expected to hear from was the vice president of the bank he'd tried to rob five days before, but here was the guy on the phone, introducing himself in the cup-rattling voice he'd used the day of the attempted robbery. Harmon Rutledge sounded like he was giving orders even when he wasn't.

He was probably calling to make Don feel small and stupid, although Marge had already done that job for the day. For twenty seconds, thinking about how he hated being bossed around and told he was dumb, Don didn't listen to anything Harmon said. The man represented every person who'd ever insinuated he was smarter than him. But as the buzz of Don's animosity subsided, he heard the words "job" and "Charlie" and "pay you."

Don sat up on the couch. "Wait. Are you saying you're going to give me a job in the bank even though I tried to rob it?"

The minute the words were out of his mouth, Don wanted to suck them back in. He had now confessed his crime to the prime witness expected to testify against him in court. *What if this call is a trick and the police are recording it?* The sheriff was right, his mother was right, he could never escape how dumb he was. He ran his hand through his hair and switched from hating other people to hating himself. *Rocks are smarter than me.*

"Not in the bank," Harmon was saying. "A job for *me*, something I need done right away, within the next day or two. Are you and Charlie available?"

"Available." No one had ever asked Don if he was "available." His shoulders squared on their own. He stood up at attention. Maybe robbing the bank hadn't been a bad idea. People who would never have known he existed were calling him. He had potential customers; he could start a new business, a kind of Uber for odd jobs. People would go to a website to schedule their job, and he and Charlie would show up and do it. They'd be paid online.

What's the word he'd heard app coders at his local bar use to brag about their work? Seamless. It would be seamless. He could call the business Odd Jobs R Us. Like Sigmund Frohler and his funeral business, Don would provide a service the community needed. He would dress well and snub Mrs. Frohler if he ever spotted her in the supermarket because he would be richer than she was . . .

"Don? Did you hear me? I'm offering you a job. I'll pay . . . fifty dollars."

"Fifty dollars?"

"Each, I'll pay each of you fifty dollars."

"Is this a job at your house?"

"No, no. Not here. You'll need transportation. You have a truck, right?"

"Yeah."

"Well, you'll need your truck."

A vibration went off in the back of Don's head, the way tonsils jiggled in cartoons when a character screamed. The man sounded too intense, which meant something bad although Don wasn't sure what. "I don't think fifty is enough, then, if we have to drive somewhere."

"Okay, a hundred then, each."

Now he was talking. "How about a hundred upfront and a hundred when the job's done? Each." Don could barely stop himself from jumping up and down. He was negotiating, for God's sake. He had skills.

Harmon was quiet for a long time and Don paced, worried he had pushed him too far. He still didn't know what the job was, how far he'd have to drive, or if it required any other equipment. How could he be expected to know what the job was worth? *I'll have to remember these questions for my website.*

"Okay," Harmon said. "I'll meet you in the parking lot behind the county recreation center and I'll tell you what you need to do. I'll text you when it's time to meet. You get a hundred now and when you're done with the job, you'll text me, and we'll meet up again for the rest of your money."

"Deal," Don said. Saying the word "deal," with his tongue pressed hard against his top teeth to form the D and then rolling back on the L, made him feel in charge of his destiny.

Now, he had to convince Charlie to help him out. Two hundred bucks, although far short of the twenty-five thousand Don had promised Charlie as his share of the bank job take, should go some way toward persuading the guy to be his sidekick again. Even thinking he had a sidekick made Don feel important.

Don found Charlie in Uncle John's diner at 6 P.M., and saying, "Hey, I got us a job. You willing?" was enough to convince his friend to come along. The guy seemed almost grateful to be asked.

"I'm dying of boredom," Charlie explained.

"Huh?"

"Who knew I liked going to work," Charlie said. "Even if I didn't like the work, even if I was terrible at it, it was something to do each day, a place to go, people to talk to. Work gave my day a shape. I don't know how the rich do it. Having a whole day with nothing to do is dead-boring. How many video games a guy can play?"

"I think they play tennis a lot," Don said. "And golf." He would have liked to have such a problem, but he wasn't going to argue with Charlie about it now. After they did this job, Don planned to explain his idea for a Jack-of-All-Trades business, as his mother called it when he'd tried to explain it to her.

"You know what the other half of the jack-of-all-trades saying is, don't you?" his mother had sneered, the ice in her voice making his chest split open so Arctic air could whoosh through it.

Don had wanted to put his hands over his ears and say, "Nah, nah, nah, nah, nah" to stop the sound, but he didn't because she would've smacked him. He just said, "No, Mom."

"Expert at none, like what you are—expert at nothing." She'd lifted her glass and drained it as if she were toasting her cleverness.

This job, Don told himself, would be the start of something new, never mind his mother. Like the guy on the radio said, he had to be proud of himself; he didn't have to prove himself to his mother. The pile of rocks Don always carried on his shoulders vanished. Relief swept over him like magic when he said the words, "I'm proud of myself. I can do this." He was ready for anything.

CHAPTER 15

JUST as the sun set on Friday, Don and Charlie met Harmon in the parking lot behind the prefab community recreation building. The place was deserted. A narrow ring of trees encircled the park, separating it from a residential street. Lights from nearby houses flickered like lightning bugs between leaves ruffled by a cool breeze.

While they talked, Charlie pulled his jacket collar up against the autumn chill and looked away. Don worried that Charlie wasn't paying attention. He needed Charlie to remember what Rutledge was saying. Following Charlie's gaze, Don took in the gigantic playground awash in stadium illumination. Three sizes of red, blue, and orange slides, two sets of swings, three climbing racks, a plastic fort on stilts, and five large, yellow plastic ducks on springs were set up across a half-acre of cedar chips. *Charlie would rather play on the equipment than listen to Harmon's instructions.* He bumped Charlie's elbow to get him to pay attention.

"Look, it's simple," Harmon said. "You drive to the BWI airport long-term parking lot and locate my wife's car in section B, spot one-oh-five. She drives a white Volvo. I've written down the license plate number for you so you can be sure it's hers. From there, Charlie takes her car using the key I'm going to give you, and you drive in your truck to the Alpha Ridge Landfill on Marriottsville Road in Howard County, Maryland."

The more Harmon talked, the more Don was sure he'd made a mistake negotiating the price for this complicated job. He hadn't asked for enough money, and the mission, as Harmon called what he was asking them to do, was definitely out of his comfort zone. But that was water over the bridge now, the whole structure washed away with him paddling as fast as he could to keep his head above floodwaters.

"That landfill's not even in this state," Don said.

"Right. It's in Maryland, the same state as the airport. I'll give you the address. It's not too far, about an hour from here. After you locate the car, Charlie drives it. Get that, Charlie drives Trudy's car? And Don, you follow Charlie in the truck. Got it? You," Harmon touched Don's arm, "follow Charlie to the landfill."

"Got it," Don said, miffed because Harmon was treating him like an idiot. "We're picking up your wife's car from the airport and taking it to the dump."

"Right. When you arrive at the dump, you open the trunk and put these clothes on her." Harmon held out a lumpy plastic bag.

Don hesitated before he took the bag. There was something not quite right about this plan. "Who's in the trunk of the car?"

"My wife," Harmon said as if this fact were so obvious even a rock would understand. "Dr. Trudy Davis."

Don took the bag and jiggled it as if something inside it might be alive. "What's your wife doing in the trunk of the car?"

Harmon stared at him.

Charlie, who as far as Don was concerned had been lost in space, turned to face him. "She's dead. Don't you get it, Don? The woman is dead."

"Dead? What'd she die of? Is it something catchy? Why did she die in the trunk of her car?"

Harmon stared at his shoes and then off into the distance. "This is the way it is, Don." He bit his lip. "This is the job I'm paying you to do."

"You want us to dress your dead wife in these clothes?" Don's cheeks flushed at the prospect of handling a dead woman's body. He would have to undress her first. She would be naked. His palms itched; his lungs got heavy.

Harmon stuffed his hands in his pockets. "Yes. Because of your experience at the funeral home, you know how to do it."

"How do you know I worked in a funeral home? Anyway, those clothes are slit open in the back to make it easier to dress a corpse. Dead people are heavy. They don't sit up on their own and hold out their arms, you know."

Harmon wiped his mouth with his palm. "Well, there's two of you. And I know where you worked because it was in the news story about the bank robbery."

"Oh. I don't read the paper. I guess it's all right then. Why do we have to drive to the dump to change her clothes? Why can't we change her right there in the airport parking lot?"

Charlie and Harmon both gawked at him.

"Someone might see you," Harmon said.

Charlie held up his hand like he was asking a question in class. "Do we put her back in the trunk after we change her clothes, and what do we do with the clothes we took off her?"

Don regarded Charlie with a new appreciation. He wasn't spooked about moving a dead body. He was all business.

"You drive the Volvo with the body in it to the landfill in Howard County," Harmon said. "Don follows you in his truck. When you get to the landfill, you change her clothes and dispose of her nightgown in the dump. You put the body in Don's truck. Extract her license from her wallet and throw her bag in the landfill too. Then you drive over to the big golf club near there, Turf Valley, in Don's truck. You drop the body anywhere in the woods around the golf course. Then text me when it's done and drive home. When you hand me her license, I'll know you did the job, and I'll give you the rest of the money. Simple."

"It'd be better if you write the instructions down for us, so we don't have to remember so much," Don said.

Harmon scowled. "I'm getting to that."

Don took a step back. Something about this job gave him the hee-bie-jeebies, as his mother would say.

Charlie ran his palm across the top of his head. "What are we doing about her car?"

"The car. You leave the car at the landfill. That's why you're going there."

"With the keys in it?" Charlie asked. "Somebody might take it."

"So, you don't want the car?" Don asked.

Harmon appeared unsure about this part of the plan. Maybe he'd forgotten the detail of the extra vehicle. He scratched his cheek and glanced over his shoulder like he'd heard someone coming.

"Could I keep it?" Charlie asked. "Like, if you don't need it or anything."

"It would be a bad idea for you to keep it," Harmon said. "The police could claim you stole it, and I couldn't tell them otherwise. If you're spotted with her car after the police find the body, they might think you carjacked it and killed her."

"I think we need more money," Don said.

Harmon glowered at him.

"I mean for gas, wear and tear on the truck, for the interstate driving we're doing."

Charlie ran a hand over his eyes. "We're illegally disposing of a dead body, risking charges of carjacking and murder, and you're worried about money for gas?"

"No problem." Harmon reached into his pocket, pulled out his wallet, and handed them each a one-hundred-dollar bill plus two twenties each for gas. "We good?"

Don pocketed his money. "When are we supposed to do this?"

"Tonight would be good, tomorrow night the latest."

Charlie shoved the cash in his jacket pocket and exchanged a glance with Don.

"Tomorrow will work for us," Don said.

Harmon handed the Volvo key to Don along with a piece of paper with the information they needed typed out in neat rows: Trudy's license plate number, the BWI long term parking address, Lot B, Green area, spot 105, and the addresses of the dump and the golf club.

"Couldn't be easier," he said. "I'll expect your text telling me you're done." He waved and walked away.

"You know," Charlie said as they drove out of the park, "we could take the driver's license out of her wallet, throw the bag of clothes in the Volvo, and leave the car and the body at the airport. It would be a lot easier for us and not as risky. Harmon would never know the difference. It's not like he's going to drive over there and check."

"That would be cheating," Don said. "We made a business deal. We gotta stick to the plan."

Charlie made a sound like air escaping from a tire and stared out of his window until Don pulled into the motel parking lot.

"Give me your number," Don said, handing Charlie his phone. "I'll text you when I'm on my way over." Everything about this job made him feel important.

Charlie typed in his new number, handed back the phone, and climbed out of the truck.

For almost twenty-four hours, Don felt confident. He had a sidekick, a job, and he was going to come into money. This was what life was all about.

CHAPTER 16

O N Saturday, Ethel and Harmon posed in the center of the bank lobby for the *Daily*'s photographer. The drive-up window and the ATM machine were open on Saturday afternoon, but the lobby was closed to the public. The photographer, after pacing out the expansive interior designed to accommodate a long cordon of waiting customers, selected the tellers' stations as the perfect backdrop.

Ethel had slept with her head bristling with curlers for today's photo shoot and as a result, her head hurt no matter which way the photographer had her turn. Distracted as she was by each twinge, she also worried she had worn the wrong clothes and her lipstick was smeared, but she couldn't help smiling. She had never gotten so much attention.

Ruby Red was the lipstick color she'd chosen this morning, and it had gone on like silk and gleamed back at her when she smiled at her bathroom mirror. A minute later, the color had seeped from her lips to the skin surrounding them as the lipstick oozed into the tiny runnels of wrinkles deepening around her mouth every day. Horrified, Ethel had blotted her lips, leaving a thin red outline on the tissue. Enough color was left that she wouldn't appear half-dead in the photos.

These discomforts were a small price to pay for her fifteen seconds of fame. She had gone all her life never expecting to be known by anyone except her family and a few close friends, and now everyone in the county would recognize her. The word that expressed her feelings about this unexpected fame was joy. *I'm like Hedda Hopper, or is that Ava Gabor, no, Hedy Lamar.*

In the deep recesses of Ethel's mind, George grumbled. *Nothing good ever came from making a fuss about yourself.* He was such a party pooper.

The photographer took a dozen photos of her alone while Harmon stood to the side huffing, and Ethel imagined herself featured on the cover of *Vanity Fair* like Margaret Atwood. The writer would have appreciated Ethel's metamorphosis from handmaid to hero.

Standing next to Harmon while they waited for the photographer to pull another lens out of one of his innumerable vest pockets and screw it onto his camera, Ethel reiterated her next tasks for the property sale. "After you sign the listing contract today, I need to put up the For Sale sign and take a few more pictures. And I'll need a front door key for the lockbox. Can I do that this afternoon?"

She worried she was talking too much. Waves of antagonism wafted off Harmon, making her uneasy. *What did I do to make him angry with me?*

Never taking his eyes off the photographer, Harmon said, "No problem. Whatever you can do to expedite the sale is welcome."

"Can I set an open house for a week from now? I'll have just enough time to promote it."

"Sooner the better." His facial expression reminded her of *Star Trek*'s Spock with his constant wooden deadpan, which of course reminded her of George's complete lack of emotion.

The camera shutter whizzed. Ethel's eyes twinkled. She loved being in the spotlight, but she stopped herself before she winked at the photographer. *This is what it feels like to be seen. And I don't feel awkward at all. This attention would have driven George mad.* Ethel's smile broadened.

"Unless, of course, someone comes in with a full-price offer before the open house," she said.

"Do people make pre-emptive offers for real property?" Harmon asked.

"Yes," Ethel said. "The transaction can happen quickly if the seller agrees to a cash sale."

"Would you make a quarter turn to the right, Ms. Goodman?" the photographer asked. "And Mr. Rutledge, if you could turn to the left so you're back-to-back?"

They turned. "Yes, good. Now if you both could make a pistol with your fingers?" He demonstrated with his forefinger up in the air, his thumb cocked toward his face. "And then blow on your forefinger?"

They followed his instructions.

"Yes. Perfect. That's the one."

Ethel glowed with pride.

"After it's sold, is it possible for me to skip the closing?" Harmon asked. "I mean, if I must be at work on the day it's scheduled. Settlements take hours, there are so many papers to sign." He gestured at the bank interior. "I can't be away from the bank so long."

Ethel stepped back so she could see his face better. Not a flicker of anything off. It was an odd request but not unheard of. "You could approve a limited power of attorney for this transaction for the day of, and I could act on your behalf at the closing. Or if you're bothered by a possible conflict of interest if the buyer is also my client, you could hire an attorney to represent you at closing. The funds can be deposited into an account you specify. It's another set of documents for you to sign in advance."

"There's certainly a lot of paperwork involved in selling a house," Harmon muttered.

Ethel mugged for the camera. "We're dotting our I's and making sure there's a paper trail of the transaction to support the title, adherence to various federal, state, and local laws, and the payment of required taxes."

Standing next to him, she wondered if Harmon would go down as easily as the scrawny bank robber she'd clobbered with her bag. Doubtful. He was a big man, at least a foot taller than she. Even if she sat on him, he could flick her off like lint. It would take something powerful to bring him down. *A tank maybe. A missile, or bomb.*

Harmon gripped her hand, the shutter whirred. Ethel ignored her misgivings. Everything in her life had contrived to bring her to this moment. The rest would be downhill.

CHAPTER 17

T HE success of Millie's story about Harmon and Ethel saving the day at the bank had whetted her appetite. Everyone in town was talking about it. Around 1 P.M. on Saturday, she went in search of her most reliable local source for two years, who hung out at the lunch counter in Needful Things. Old Dave knew everything and everyone.

The second-hand store on Main Street, chock full of antiques and junk from estate sales, had twenty-foot-high ceilings from which hung real Venetian chandeliers from time to time depending on whose estate had been liquidated. In addition to its junk-tique offerings, it also sported a 1950s-style luncheonette that served everything from eggs over easy to homemade pie and brought in a daily trade of county officials, attorneys, and shopkeepers.

Above the odors of cooking grease, burned fries, mildew, and dust that caught Millie's nose when she opened the door, rose the unclassifiable smell of Old Dave, who never washed his clothes, wore holey cowboy boots, and sported an unruly beard. He also boasted a philosophy about his personal microbiome which caused him to refrain from bathing so that he wouldn't harm the helpful bacteria that called his body home. Before Old Dave gave up working, he had been the chief technology officer for one of the nation's seventeen spy organizations, although he never said which one. He assured Millie he could still put zeros and ones together.

It didn't take much nudging on Millie's part to get him to talk about the missing local doctor. "There's something off," Old Dave confided. "Sheriff Hammersmith told me Rutledge is like a rat watching from inside his hole in the wall, waiting for his opportunity to scurry away."

"Sheriff Jo Hammersmith said those exact words?" Millie asked. "She called Rutledge a rat?"

"Well, no. I'm giving you my impression of what she meant. Jo used the word 'squirrely.' It's a different species."

Millie's interest was piqued. He might have been off-putting to other people, but Old Dave was her secret weapon.

The mayor, the president of the county commission, and even one of the state's US Senators would sit on the stools next to him at Needful Things talking to each other about topics they shouldn't because they thought he didn't matter. As if he were invisible, Old Dave picked at his beard while they gabbed on and on. He had been listening for so long he could fill in the spaces between what he overheard and what he didn't. Extrapolating, he called it. He was like the walls, but he was happy to talk if she asked nicely.

"Now, I never told you this," Old Dave said, leaning so precariously in her direction from his stool that she put her hand on his shoulder to steady him. "Jo would never forgive me if I told anyone she dropped this bit of important information."

Millie pressed her lips together. The best way to keep people talking was to be quiet.

"Anyhoo, Jo said something was odd about Rutledge's manner— that's what she called it, his manner—when he told her about his wife. It wasn't anything she could put her finger on but when she set his weird vibe against the fact that he waited almost a week to report his wife missing, it made her Spidey sense tingle."

"Did she do anything about her suspicion?" Jo Hammersmith would never tell Millie any of this in an interview, even off the record.

"She said they'd put out an all-points for the woman and her vehicle in every county in West Virginia but so far nothing. It's like she's disappeared off the face of the earth."

Millie pondered this statement for a minute while Old Dave stirred his coffee. He would sit at the counter for hours every day nursing cup after cup. She admired his bladder control. Sometimes, like today, she'd buy him pie, not as compensation for his story tips but because she could, and he was always appreciative.

"Has Jo considered widening her search?"

Old Dave gave her a little smile as if she were his prize student and had guessed the right answer. "Yes, indeed. This morning, Jo said they'd sent the BOLO to Virginia, Maryland, Pennsylvania, and Ohio."

"So she must think Dr. Davis drove out of the state."

"Or somebody drove her."

Millie stared at him. "Maybe she got on a plane or took the train somewhere five days ago. She could be anywhere by now. What do you mean, someone drove her?"

"I don't think Jo's considered Dr. Davis flying anywhere a possibility. I got the feeling she thinks the body is close by."

Millie's neck heated. "Body? As in dead body?"

Old Dave stirred his cup. "I didn't say the word dead."

He must've been a lawyer before he was a spy. Who talks about a body if it's not dead. Millie tried to read his face. "Did you ever meet Rutledge?"

"I'm not the kind of person he would deign to meet." Old Dave raised his eyebrows and rolled his eyes.

Millie made a face in response. "Thanks," she said to the waitress, leaving a generous tip as she picked up the small paper bag containing her own lunch of a tuna salad sandwich on toasted wheat, a bag of chips, and a chocolate chip cookie. "You are worth your weight in gold," she said to Old Dave as she hopped off the stool.

The old man smiled a little broader and waved as she went out the door. On the sidewalk, Millie jotted down her notes from the conversation in the first notebook she found in her bag.

Jo Hammersmith thinks Trudy Davis is already dead. She added Old Dave's name as the source and the date. The sheriff must have a theory about what happened and why. Millie needed to be the one who got that story first. It was time to tackle an interview with the sheriff. She'd just have to work up her nerve.

CHAPTER 18

CHARLIE climbed into Don's truck at 10 P.M. on Saturday night. Don's eyes were shining, and he was half jumping out of his skin. *Crap. Don thinks he's James Bond on a secret, death-defying mission.* The fact that Don was thrilled to do this disgusting job scared Charlie more than the idea of moving and dressing a dead body.

"Why are we going this late?"

"Less people on the road at this hour, so no one will see us." Don held out the paper Harmon had given him with the Volvo's license number and addresses for the airport parking lot, the landfill, and golf club.

Charlie pulled purple latex gloves from his pocket and slipped them on before he took the piece of paper from Don.

"Why are you wearing gloves?"

"We're gonna move a dead body," Charlie said. "I don't want to touch it with my bare hands."

"Oh. Good idea. What about a map? Did you bring one? I forgot to."

Charlie studied the words on the paper to clamp down on a nervous laugh and glanced at Don. "I have GPS on my phone."

"Why do you have it on your phone?"

"The app came with my phone." *Jesus, what planet's Don living on?*

"I mean, what do you use it for?"

"To get around when I'm going somewhere I've never been. We're about to go seventy-five miles, give or take, from Charles Town, West Virginia, to Baltimore, Maryland. Watch." Charlie tapped the screen of his phone and said, "Driving directions to BWI long-term parking." The phone assistant repeated what he said, and a map appeared on his cell phone. "See?"

Don stared at the screen. "Wow. Amazing. How'd they store that whole map in that tiny device, memory-wise I mean?"

Charlie lowered his chin and tilted his head, peering at Don from the corner of his eye. "I don't know. Smart chips? GPS has been around for a while now, Don."

Don cut his eyes at Charlie. "Did someone tell you this?"

"No. I asked Google."

"That's the internet. How do you know it's true?"

"If I were smart enough to know the answer to that, I'd be working at NASA."

"Well, I don't like following instructions. It makes me feel stupid."

They rode in silence for an hour and a half except for occasional instructions from the GPS about exits, lanes, and roads to turn onto. Charlie chewed the inside of his lip and wished he had a flask. By the time they reached the airport exit, Don had gotten over being spooked about some woman in the sky watching him every minute.

When GPS announced, "You have reached your destination," she sounded like they should celebrate. Grinning at his accomplishment, Don took a ticket for long-term parking at the airport's B lot, waited for the arm to lift, and drove up and down the aisles in the Green section while Charlie scanned for Trudy's white Volvo.

"Hey, there it is." Charlie pointed and confirmed the license plate against the number on the note.

Don rooted around in his pocket and handed Charlie the key. "You're driving it. You should open it." He gave Charlie a little nod of encouragement.

Geez. The guy's acting like this is a big deal. Charlie clicked the remote door opener. The Volvo's lights flashed, and they high fived each other on the perfect execution of the plan. "Should I check the trunk to see if she's in there?"

"Nah. Let's get out of here. I don't like being in another state." Don glanced in both directions. "Bad guys could be around any corner."

Charlie opened the door to slide behind the wheel and stopped. He gagged, jerked back, and jumped away from the car. "*Phew.* It stinks in there."

"What's the smell like?"

"Like shit and piss and vomit and garbage gathering steam in a locked car for a hundred centuries."

"Yeah, that's decomp. Open the windows." Don handed Charlie two of the deodorizers from his rearview mirror. "These might help a little."

Charlie started the car, rolled down the windows, and turned on the air conditioning full blast. "Wow. You should've warned me," he yelled to Don. "Let's drive so air starts flowing through here. We've got forty miles to go until the dump. I've got directions on the GPS. Do you want me to set the map up on your phone?"

"Nah. I don't like the idea of her knowing where I am."

Charlie leaned out of the window and inhaled. "Okay. I'll lead. Stay right behind me."

At the exit, Charlie found the parking stub stuck behind the garage door opener on the Volvo's sunscreen. Discovering the ticket gave him pause.

How did Dr. Davis's car get to the parking lot if she was dead in the trunk?

Dismayed he was considering this question now, Charlie couldn't think of any way to extract himself from what was going to be another catastrophic mess.

You know Harmon drove her here, don't you? His mind nagged him. *You knew back in the rec center parking lot.* Whether she was dead before they got to the airport parking or after didn't matter. *There's nothing accidental about how she died.*

He inserted the ticket into the payment machine, prayed it would work, and waited through the humming and chugging noises for the next instruction. A seventy-five-dollar fee blinked on the small screen and distracted him for a second.

The machine was telling him to insert cash or a credit card. No way was he feeding the hundred-dollar bill Harmon had given him into the machine. A hundred bucks was the equivalent of ten six-packs plus tax. He looked in the rearview mirror. Don wasn't going to be any help. He was already singing along to music on his radio.

Scanning the interior of the car, Charlie spotted a woman's bag on the floor. In the wallet, he found a credit card for Trudy Davis and inserted it into the device. He held his breath. *What if the card doesn't work? What if Harmon canceled her cards, and this one sets off alarms, and the guards come running and I'm caught with a dead body in the trunk? We should've taken her license, left the car where it was, and got the hell outta here like I said after the meet.*

The machine whirred, the system spit out a receipt, and the gate rose. Charlie retrieved the credit card and drove through, sighing with relief. Maybe Harmon couldn't cancel the cards until the authorities declared her dead. A small bit of luck. *But why didn't he warn us there'd be a hefty parking fee to pay. Must have been an oversight. Or he's a tightwad and didn't want to fork over any more money.* Charlie's head spun. *Or, he wanted us to get caught.*

GPS guided him north onto I-95 and then to 695 west around Baltimore toward the exit onto I-70. For the first twenty miles, he checked the rearview mirror periodically to make sure Don's truck with the bright yellow "Don't Tread on Me" license plate on the front bumper was behind him. Although Charlie couldn't see Don's face, the guy didn't seem to have a care in the world. *And why not? After all, he's not the one with the corpse in the car.*

But as Charlie exited onto Route 70 west toward Howard County, Don's truck raced by him and swerved around other cars on the highway like a high-speed racer until he was out of sight.

"What the hell . . ." Charlie considered chasing Don, but it was safer to stay in the right-hand lane and maintain a steady sixty than try to catch up. No point in taking a chance on being stopped for speeding by a state trooper who'd demand he open the trunk.

How would he explain to the officer when asked for his license and registration why he was driving someone else's car? Then there would be the check of his driving record, which had the DUI and a suspension. If the trooper searched further, he'd discover Charlie was awaiting trial for bank robbery. The search of the license plate number would flag that the car was stolen. If the officer had a sense of smell at all, bingo, no more trip to the dump with a dead body. No quick thinking would fix the mess he'd be in, not that he was a quick thinker anyway.

By the time Charlie exited the highway onto Marriottsville Road in Howard County an hour later, he expected Don to be waiting for him at the landfill. He needed to get the body out of the car and escape from the smell before every inch of his skin and every strand of his hair was soaked in stink for the rest of his life. But when he got to the landfill gate at 1 A.M., Don was nowhere around.

What the hell? Where has that idiot gone? Charlie got out of the car and walked a quarter of a mile down to the entrance hoping to spot Don on the main road and wave him down. Never had he pictured himself alone with a dead body at a landfill in the middle of the night. *This is what happens when you hit bottom. All your worst nightmares come true.*

He texted Don, waited five minutes, and then called him. When voice mail answered, he said, "Pick up the phone, Don. Nobody's watching you. Where the hell are you, anyway? You're supposed to be at the landfill."

Charlie waited at the landfill entrance another five minutes, jumping at every shadow, sure a crazed guy with a buzzsaw would lurch toward him at any moment. He had no idea what to do next. That was always when he got in the worst trouble. When he turned back to the car, the Volvo glowed in the buzzing lights illuminating the entrance to the dump. That's when he noticed the camera mounted below the roof of the tiny guard house at the gate.

CHAPTER 19

DON was supposed to have moved the body by Sunday but by Monday morning Harmon still hadn't heard from him. It was almost three full days since he'd given those doofuses the job. Plenty of time to get it done. Harmon chalked Don's failure up to the man's general incompetence and lack of follow-through, but he still expected that what he wanted was what would happen. Eventually, Don would want the rest of the money badly enough to make contact and tell him the job was done.

Harmon was a little unnerved by the sheriff's order to come to her office on Monday. *As if I didn't have anything else to do.* While Harmon pondered Don's inadequacies, the sheriff made him wait for her in a cramped, windowless room that smelled like someone had spilled an entire bottle of bleach in it.

Finally, Sheriff Hammersmith entered the room in a rush, closed the door, and began talking before she sat down. Harmon was forced to look up at her. *Such an obvious ploy to establish her dominance.* Slowly it dawned on him. *She doesn't think I'm the victim.* Harmon resisted squirming, remembering his father saying, "Keep a level head, son."

"So, we've been able to trace your wife's travels by tracking her credit card purchases," the sheriff said.

"Her travels? Her credit card purchases?" Harmon had the sensation of being catapulted into space without a protective suit. His lungs were about to cave in from lack of oxygen. He coughed to regulate his heart rhythm. "What are you talking about?"

Waiting at home to be notified about Trudy's death by officers holding their hats in their hands and offering condolences, he had practiced shocked and horrified faces in front of the bathroom mirror. When he found the exact right arrangement of his features to signify dignified grief, he had committed those expressions to muscle memory until he could reproduce them at will. He had not prepared for this contingency.

Trudy can't be alive. All Harmon's practiced moves abandoned him. The expression of shock on his face was sincere. "What do you mean, 'travels'?"

His plan had been so simple, he couldn't imagine it wouldn't work. Trudy's car was supposed to have been found immediately by Howard County landfill employees arriving for work in the morning. Harmon had assumed the landfill employees would steal the change Trudy kept in a cup well, drive to the nearest convenience store for lottery tickets and snacks and then notify a supervisor a vehicle had been left at the dump in the middle of the night. The supervisor would call the police. The police would check the registration and learn Trudy's name. They would try to contact her without any luck because the dopey duo would have thrown her bag, which Harmon expected contained her phone and wallet, into the landfill.

The car would be towed to the police forensics lab and technicians would examine it, finding an assortment of fingerprints including Charlie's. If they were clever, they might find hairs and perhaps other bodily fluids from Trudy in the trunk. Charlie's prints would be in the FBI system from his arrest after the bank robbery. The police would send whatever they found in the car for DNA analysis and, given Trudy had done a three-year stint in the National Guard, they might get a match. Of course, it would take weeks if not months to do that.

Harmon anticipated someone from the golf club would stumble on Trudy's body when their ball bounced into the rough. Again, the Howard County police would have been called. Without any identification on Trudy, it would take the police a few days or weeks to figure out who she was, but eventually they would put the body together with the dumped vehicle.

Her clothes would match the description the sheriff had put in the missing person's report. Her face would be identical to the photo he had provided. It stood to reason, events would transpire in the order he had planned. Unless some wild animal ravaged her face. Harmon blinked away the image.

But he had never expected to be led like a suspect to the sheriff's tiny, airless, Spartan interview room that reeked of antibacterial cleaning fluids with an undertone of vomit. Who did they think they were dealing with? He had standing in this community. He couldn't be treated this way.

"Travels means the trip she's taking." Hammersmith's voice was as cool as a chocolate mint candy. "After Dr. Davis left home, she parked her car at the Baltimore Washington International airport long-term lot at one-thirty-one A.M. on Sunday, October twelfth, where it remained for six days."

"I don't understand what you're talking about." Harmon glanced over at the darkened window to check his face and was pleased to note he did appear confused.

"Does she have a lover, by any chance, or a friend who was supposed to meet her there?"

Harmon clasped his hands on the table to bolster his spine. *The police know I lied about when I saw her last. They know she was in the parking lot just after midnight, so I couldn't have seen her Sunday morning.*

He'd expected the police to believe his statement that Trudy had taken off in a huff after their argument. They were supposed to speculate that she'd picked up someone who attacked her, ditched her body, stole her car, and eventually dumped it. Forensics would show that someone was Charlie Goodman. Harmon was speechless with resentment at the idea that the sheriff didn't behave the way he'd expected.

"There's no way Trudy had a lover." *As if I were an inadequate partner. That's not even worth responding to.* Harmon inhaled and settled his shoulders. The important thing was for the police to find her body. He had to focus, to apply his will to making the discovery of Trudy's body happen. As his mother had always said, if he put what he wanted out into the universe, the universe would respond appropriately.

In the end, Trudy would be declared dead, he'd be free, and after the required mourning period, her money would be his. If the police liked the idea of her running off with a lover instead of his kidnapper scenario, that was fine. It stood to reason they would search for such a person instead of focusing on him. A lover was a much more likely suspect than he was. After all, he was happily married.

"We can't find any airline on which she booked a flight to anywhere," Hammersmith continued. "Nor did she hire a private plane. According to our review of transit videos, she didn't take the shuttle to the airport train station or buy a ticket at the kiosk or online. Even if someone else bought the ticket for her, she'd have to show ID before she boarded."

The sheriff's eyes bored into Harmon's as if she were mining for the truth. He resisted looking away although his head trembled with effort.

"So right now," the sheriff continued, "it appears Dr. Davis wandered around the airport for a week using the cash she drew out of an airport ATM at one-fifty-five A.M. on Sunday morning. Except none of the CCTV at the airport shows her anywhere in or around the facility. It's possible a friend picked her up at the airport and took her somewhere. Perhaps she went to another location by cab and then came back. There are no charges on her credit cards during this period or calls on her cell phone."

"I don't understand." Harmon was baffled by where the sheriff's narrative was headed. He needed to steer her away from noticing his obvious lie about being with Trudy on Sunday morning. "Maybe she was kidnapped in the parking lot."

How clever he'd felt taking the shuttle from the parking lot to the airport as if he were traveling, using Trudy's bank card to withdraw cash, taking a cab to the inner harbor and then walking to the Baltimore Sheraton, sitting in the lobby for an hour, and catching a different cab home. All for nothing. He stifled the urge to bolt. His next move was to bluff his way through this interrogation.

He opened his eyes wide hoping the sheriff would infer his innocence and distress. The theory Trudy had been kidnapped wasn't too far from the truth. Charlie Goodman's fingerprints would be everywhere in Trudy's car. If the sheriff saw Charlie in the kidnapper's role, then the bank robbery took on a much darker tone. The robbers had deliberately tormented him when he didn't hand over the ransom.

"You never heard from a kidnapper about a ransom, did you?" Hammersmith asked as if she were reading his mind.

"No." The truth accidentally slipped out of Harmon's mouth. He scrambled to recoup. "But maybe that crazy bank robbery was an—"

"The other problem with the kidnap theory is after six days, Dr. Davis retrieved her car, paid the parking fee with her credit card, and drove out of state. She's been staying in a motel in Emmitsburg, Maryland, had the car detailed yesterday, bought some new clothes at the Army/Navy store, got a phone charger and two books at Walmart, and ate in local restaurants. This does not sound like the itinerary of someone who's been kidnapped. We don't know where she is today. Yet. We're still tracking her purchases."

Harmon's heart clenched; his stomach roiled. *Charlie paid the parking fee with her credit card.* Harmon's mouth dried. He tried to regulate his breathing. Or Trudy was playing with him. *She must be alive.* And, to make matters worse, she was trying to drive him crazy.

"But if she's alive, why hasn't she called her mother? Or her office? I've been getting calls from them about her disappearance."

This much was true. He'd listened to the frequent messages on voice mail although he hadn't returned their calls. Talking to her mother or anyone at her office was too much hassle. Why should he have to console frantic females? *Don't I have enough on my plate?* The sheriff had to be wrong.

"Maybe she's run away from you and doesn't know what to tell her mother."

"Wait." Harmon tapped the table. "You're saying Trudy's alive and she's deliberately not coming home?"

Hammersmith shrugged. "That's how it appears." She scrutinized his face. "She bought something from a garden stand and checked into another motel this morning."

Harmon leaned his forehead on his hand. "Apples, she likes apples. It's the season. How do you know this?"

"Like I said. From her credit card transactions. Now she's left our county, the state troopers' criminal investigation unit is involved. We've also got the Maryland state police on this because of the airport and Emmitsburg angles. This gives us more resources to find her."

An involuntary shiver shot across Harmon's shoulders. *Maybe I knocked her out temporarily, and she revived and was alive in the trunk of the car in the parking lot until Charlie liberated her.* He tried to remember if Trudy kept a survival kit in the trunk with food and water in it. *Why didn't I notice?* She'd be furious. She'd be out for blood. Charlie must be helping plot her revenge against him.

"So she's still alive?"

"As I said, it's possible."

"That's astonishing news," he managed to say. "Why hasn't she called me?"

The sheriff tilted her head. "Interesting question."

Don didn't tell me the job was done because it wasn't. Trudy is alive and they helped her run away from me. Unless she'd figured out a way of getting out of the trunk herself and had driven away before those morons even got to the parking lot. She was smart that way. Handy. In that case, Don wasn't telling him they couldn't find the Volvo so they could keep his money.

The dopey duo were supposed to have gotten caught. He'd been expecting a call from the sheriff to say they'd found the men who'd abducted Trudy, or some such version of events, but he'd never imagined this. All his work to eliminate Trudy had come to nothing. Harmon felt like screaming.

Running over in his mind the ways he could be linked to Don and Charlie, Harmon ran through his calls and texts. His face went cold and then hot. He had deleted the texts and calls from his phone, hoping it would be enough to evade a more thorough search of his communications, but he didn't know about the traceability of these things and now worried Don's phone would show the contacts. *There'll still be a record on the telecommunication company's system.* Harmon's blood pressure spiked.

Maybe the police had a way of obtaining a transcript of their calls and texts. It had been a mistake to contact Don from his own phone, but Harmon was sure no one had seen them at the recreation center. Anyway, without some kind of verifiable proof, no one in their right mind would believe he'd hired those robbers to dispose of his wife's body.

Harmon could say he'd contacted Don about making amends for the attempted robbery. In his newly established gentler, kinder mode, he could claim he'd planned to appeal to the prosecutor for a sentence other than jail to compensate bank employees for the terror the robbers had caused them.

But if she's alive . . . He coughed to relieve the pressure in his chest. This is how he'd felt the first day at Harvard when he'd had no idea what any of the teachers were talking about and the smart kids were raising their hands with the answers. Being a legacy admission wasn't always a bonus. His breath came in fast spurts. He was drowning. *Keep a level head.*

"So, Mr. Rutledge, has Trudy been in touch with you in any way?"

"No. Didn't I already tell you?" Harmon's jaw tightened under the sheriff's scrutiny.

"Did she withdraw money from a shared bank account?"

"No. I don't think so. I haven't even checked. Did you contact her practice? Have they heard from her?"

The sheriff leaned back in the chair and regarded him as if he were an animal in the zoo. "I talked to the practice manager and her mother. They haven't heard from Dr. Davis. They're very worried. So unless you—or she—report that her credit cards have been stolen, it appears she's run away from you. Any idea why she might leave you this way?"

"None. We had a perfectly normal marriage. I'm not a brute or a cheat. Ask anyone."

"We plan to."

Harmon took in the implicit threat one word at a time. The police were going to inquire about him, they were going to keep their eyes on him. They believed he'd been harming his wife, that he was an abuser, and that's why Trudy ran away.

He could hardly bear the assault on his character. But unless Trudy made such a claim and there was proof of it, there was nothing the law could do to him. And then he remembered his fingerprints would be on the hundred-dollar bills he had given to Don and Charlie. *Why didn't I wear gloves?*

He had made too many mistakes; he hadn't kept a level head. Harmon's hands quivered. He tucked them under his thighs. With a gargantuan effort, he stilled his body and regulated his breathing. *Don't give anything away. Don't let them know you're scared.*

"Well, I've told you everything we have at this time," Hammersmith said. "As long as this purchasing activity goes on, she's not missing, unless you're saying she's staying in a motel and eating in restaurants against her will. Do you think someone has stolen her credit cards? Otherwise, there's no reason to continue to search for her."

The sheriff's making fun of me. If the police actually thought Trudy wasn't missing, they would stop searching for her. Which meant they would never find her body. If she were in fact dead. So, there wouldn't be a death certificate, and he wouldn't have access to her money until she'd been missing for seven years and been officially declared dead. He was stuck here in this claustrophobic town pretending to be grief-stricken. There was no point in selling his house. He would have to call Ethel and pull it off the market. Unless . . .

"Mr. Rutledge?"

Harmon raised his chin. "Someone kidnapped her and is making her do these things. I'm sure of it. Because Trudy would never shop in an Army/Navy store. Never. Or stay in a cheesy motel of all places." He wiped his face with his palm in a practiced gesture of despair. "But," he checked the sheriff's face, "I guess you don't have any proof of her being abducted."

Sheriff Hammersmith stood. "Don't leave town without notifying us, Mr. Rutledge."

He rose from the chair, ignored the sheriff's proffered hand, and walked out of the interview room. Think of the good news, he admonished himself. *They think she's out there driving around, spending money. No one has any idea I tried to kill her, except Don and Charlie. And who would believe them?*

He had his own money. He didn't need Trudy's. He could still sell the house and move away. With his reputation, he could snag a job anywhere, the farther away the better. Maybe he'd go to California. He was still golden. Those morons he'd hired would get their comeuppance, as his mother used to say, in due time.

I N the small parking lot outside the sheriff's department, Harmon sat in his car and reran the quarrel he'd had with his mother fifteen years before. Beauty had discovered her sixty-thousand-dollar check for his college tuition had gone into Harmon's bank account instead of the Harvard bursar's. He had paid for his first sophomore semester and kept the rest, thinking that by the time she figured out what he'd done, she wouldn't care.

But instead, she'd called and threatened to report him to the Harvard authorities, to the police for fraud, to anyone who'd listen. Harmon, offended to his core by his mother's incivility, couldn't have that threat hanging over him.

He had theoretically been in Massachusetts the following weekend. People swore he was walking across campus or hunched over a book at his reserved library carrel. He had said "Hi" to anyone he passed as he strolled across the quad to the library that Friday morning, then stopped at the reference librarian's desk to ask a question and gone to his carrel. Then he'd run down the back stairs and driven two-thousand miles to Colorado, stopping for gas and pee breaks until he got to his parents' ranch at 2 A.M. on Sunday.

Driving up the winding dirt lane leading to the house, Harmon had let himself admire the dark vault of the sky lit by billions of stars as he flicked off the car lights and rolled the last forty yards to the house. He'd paused outside to breathe in the clean air and tranquility of three hundred acres inhabited by two humans, a few hundred cattle, and a small herd of horses. Mares nearest the paddock rail nickered at his approach.

Harmon found the ax leaning against the wood pile in the backyard. He let himself into the house with the key his mother kept under the kitchen doormat and crept up the stairs to his parents' bedroom. Moonlight filtering through the blinds highlighted their sleeping bodies.

Afterward, he burned his clothes, baseball cap, and shoes, washed the blood off his hands and face at the outside pump, and donned the jeans, T-shirt, and running shoes Beauty kept for him in his old room.

The plan had worked perfectly. He'd made it back to his apartment with an hour to spare before local police arrived to notify him of his parents' tragic demise. His sobs were sincere. The police determined, what with his geographical distance and obvious grief, Harmon was not involved in the grisly murders.

Harmon had to admit that Beauty hadn't been a bad mother. No one else had ever made him happy the way she had when she spun him around in a room full of color, and they had laughed and laughed. It was too bad she hadn't been able to see things his way. She would have been proud of how successful he was as a full-fledged adult. Harmon raised his chin and started his Range Rover.

CHAPTER 20

NOW Monday afternoon, eight days since Trudy Davis had gone missing, Millie coached herself as she drove from the newspaper office to the county sheriff's building two miles away. *It's time to find out if there's anything new about the doctor's disappearance.* She tuned in to the local news on her car radio in case something big had dropped that she didn't know about.

She can't have abandoned the case. Hammersmith isn't the kind of person who drops the ball on anything.

Millie had been at the *Daily* two years since graduation from journalism school, but she hadn't yet figured out how to tease facts from the sheriff's grasp. While appearing to be pleasant and open with the media, the sheriff tightly controlled any information posted on the police blotter or announced at press conferences.

Nervous about the interview, Millie ran through what she knew about the sheriff. During Hammersmith's tenure, according to the FBI stats Millie had read, crime in the county had dropped to almost half of what it had been when she took office. The seasoned law officer had also navigated two elections in a conservative county.

I'll just have to go with my gut. Millie shook off her doubts.

The right information always found its way to her when she focused on a subject. News from any source—stories in other papers, overheard conversations, photographs of documents she happened to spy lying on an official's desk, even links emailed from her mother—went into one of her four working notebooks annotated with subject, date, and source.

At the natural tipping point, the data would automatically transform into a story worth telling, and Millie would hear the lede sentence in her mind. This reportorial alchemy had always worked for her. But sometimes the best way to nail down a story was to consult a human, and in this instance that person happened to be the county sheriff.

Since calling ahead to get an interview on the Trudy Davis case hadn't worked, Millie now hoped she'd have more luck barging in. If she caught Hammersmith off guard before she could duck, the sheriff might inadvertently tell her the truth. On the other hand, ambushing the sheriff might make her unhappy, and if she was annoyed, she wouldn't talk, period.

Facts were the skeleton of a story. What had happened to Trudy Davis, how it happened, who was involved in her disappearance, and what the sheriff was doing about this case, those were the questions Millie wanted to answer. But the why—context, motive, and the process of an investigation—gave the story muscle and heart. For a great story, she needed the why, and to get at the why, she needed to establish a relationship with her source.

Making a right turn, Millie spotted the new bakery in town. She couldn't resist. When she was a child, her aunt used to bring a white bakery box tied in red-and-white striped string to Millie's home every Saturday. Her mother and aunt would sit at the table and talk for hours while the sweet smell of pastry lingered in the air. Millie was named after her aunt. She should follow her example and maybe Hammersmith would open up.

Although the sheriff might see this as a clear ploy to pacify her, pastry was less obvious than doughnuts. It was around the 3 P.M. break time the police reporter had told Millie about, anyway. With any luck, Hammersmith would think of the meeting as a pleasant interlude.

A sugar high hit Millie the second she opened the bakery door and breathed in. The glass case in front of her held chocolate croissants among its enticing treats. This shop was nirvana. Five minutes later, a bakery box containing two chocolate croissants in hand, she headed to the sheriff's headquarters.

Wearing her press badge and reinforced by the aroma of pastry, she pulled open the glass door of the two-story brick building and walked through the metal scanner. "Armed with nothing stronger than a pen, a phone, and pastry," Millie said to the clerk, who didn't smile. "Here to talk to the sheriff."

"Does she know you're coming?"

"Hmmm." Millie glanced down.

"Got it. Maybe you'll get lucky." The clerk squinted and pointed. "She's here and she's in a good mood today. Through those doors. To the right." He picked up the phone on his desk and hit a button. Millie didn't hear what he said after her name.

The entire department was thirty officers strong, a portion of whom were out on patrol at any point in time. Four desks in the open area in front of the sheriff's office were empty, the monitors on them blinking the department logo. A long hallway of closed doors went off to the right beyond the sheriff's office. A large assembly room opened on the left. The holding cells were downstairs, a fact she'd learned on her tour of the facility.

Hammersmith stood in the doorway of her office talking to a deputy. She grimaced when she spotted Millie, said something that made the deputy laugh, and then her face settled into a bland mask before she nodded in Millie's direction.

Millie put on a smile, called out, "Good afternoon," and held up the box. *Maybe sweets aren't such a good idea. Too obvious. And too late now.* She'd have to use all her wiles as well as the sugar to unlock whatever secrets the sheriff was keeping. This was supposed to be the fun part of the job, she reminded herself.

The sheriff rolled her eyes but waved Millie into a tiny office with enough room for a desk, file cabinet, two chairs, a coat rack, and a credenza on which rested a fresh pot of coffee and four black mugs sporting the sheriff's department six-pointed gold star logo. The corner window looked out on a small grove of trees and the adjacent county health department building.

"I was just going to have a cup of coffee, the first one I can tolerate in the last four months," Sheriff Hammersmith said. "Want one?"

"Desperately." Millie put the white box on the sheriff's desk and opened the top while the sheriff poured the dark brew into two mugs.

Hammersmith leaned over the box and took a long sniff. "Thanks."

Steam spiraled from the top of their cups, and for a few minutes, they devoured the croissants in companionable silence. Hammersmith wiped her fingertips on a napkin, took a sip of coffee, and leaned back in her chair. "Okay, what do you want?"

"I want to know what's going on with Harmon Rutledge and his wife."

"What do you mean?"

"I think he lied about when she went missing."

"Right. We know that."

Millie felt a little glow of validation that she'd gotten that right. "So, what's happening with the search for her?"

"Off the record?"

"Yes." Millie's stomach felt the way it always did when she stepped onto the down escalator.

"On background, no attribution."

"Sure." Millie closed her pad and turned off the record app on her phone so Hammersmith could see her do it. It was obvious the sheriff had been through this experience before with other reporters. *I'm the novice.*

Hammersmith waited for Millie to put the phone into her bag. "What do you think is happening?"

"I mean, there's something strange going on, like the doctor is missing but no one's making a big deal out of trying to find her," Millie said. "I know you did the BOLO thing, but I guess nothing came of it."

"How do you know we didn't find her?"

"Well, did you?" Millie was relieved she might have a story for her effort.

"No."

"What did you find?"

Hammersmith put her head back on her chair and stared at the ceiling for three seconds. Millie held her breath. "We think we've located her vehicle in Maryland," the sheriff said.

"Where in Maryland?"

"Emmitsburg."

"Emmitsburg's like forty miles northeast of here." Millie hoped saying the name of the town would help her remember this.

"Yes." Hammersmith seemed to be studying Millie as if she were the subject of an investigation, waiting to see if she'd give herself away.

Millie tried to imitate her, but the sheriff kept her hands on the desk, her body still, and her face didn't alter. She didn't even swallow. Millie would never attain that level of control.

"Was Dr. Davis driving the car when you found it?"

"We don't know yet."

"What do you mean? Is her car still there? In Emmitsburg, I mean. Didn't anyone look inside it?"

"We're waiting to hear."

"You mean you're sending an officer out there?"

"No. The Maryland State Police are assisting us, and we're following several leads. Dr. Davis's credit card is also being used. We're tracking her purchases."

Millie held her breath for a second. "So is Davis alive, then? I mean, if she's driving around in Emmitsburg and using her credit card, does that mean she's alive?"

"We don't know yet."

"Well, what else could it mean if her car went from here to Maryland?"

"Someone else could be driving her car."

"You mean a friend is driving or . . . are you saying she was carjacked?"

"We have no evidence of her being dead or the car being stolen."

"Is there any evidence of foul play?"

"It's complicated, but we may have found a reason she's no longer living in her house."

The hair on Millie's arms stood up. "You mean a motive for killing her?"

"Not exactly."

Hammersmith's routine was killing Millie. "You mean Rutledge was physically abusing her?"

"Let's stop the interrogation. I mean Dr. Davis may be having an affair, which is not a criminal offense and therefore none of our business or yours, and that may be the reason she left home."

Millie leaned forward, her blood fizzing. "An affair with whom?"

"Can't tell you."

"For how long?"

"None of your business."

"Did she move into her lover's house without telling Rutledge? Did he threaten her?"

"No comment."

"Does Rutledge know she's having an affair, because wouldn't that be motive . . . ?"

"I've told you everything I can without compromising our investigation." Hammersmith stood. "Thanks for the croissant. It hit the spot." She rubbed her rounded belly and smiled. "I'm always hungry these days."

Millie was not going to be pulled into a different subject, alluring as it was to break a story about a pregnant sheriff, the first in the county's two-hundred-year history. She reminded herself to tell her editor and the police beat reporter this new fact, however. "So, you think Trudy Davis disappeared voluntarily?"

The sheriff stood. "I have no further comment."

Millie gathered her stuff. "Thanks. Appreciate it. Okay if I call you about this case if I find out anything or have more questions?"

"Of course." The sheriff held the door open for her. "I'll be interested to hear what you pick up." Her face was still perfectly neutral.

Millie stepped into the corridor and turned back. "Oh, wait. One more question. Why did you tell me that the doctor's car is in Emmitsburg?"

Hammersmith tilted her head. "It's a verifiable fact that can be disclosed," the sheriff said as she closed her office door.

Millie's mind boiled with questions and speculation. She loved this part of a developing story where one bit of information led to the next discovery. The minute she was back in her car, she furiously wrote out her notes, although she wasn't likely to forget a tip like this right from the horse's mouth. Which left her with the question, *who is Trudy Davis involved with?*

CHAPTER 21

MILLIE waved as soon as she spotted Old Dave nursing a cup of coffee at the counter in Needful Things. He was wearing what appeared to be a hundred-year-old, gray, hooded sweatshirt. She slid onto the stool next to him and noticed he'd achieved a perfect dog aroma.

"Hey, Dave." If he hadn't existed, she would have had to invent him.

"How ya doin', young lady?" he said, swiveling to greet her square in the face. "Looks like you're holding down a secret so hard the top of your head is gonna burst open."

"You can see right through me. I gotta know, did you hear Trudy Davis was having an affair?" There was no point in flowery preambles with Dave.

"Whoa. Such information is way above my pay grade."

Millie called out to the waitress, "Carol, would you pour Dave a fresh cup of coffee and give him a piece of your homemade apple pie? With a scoop of vanilla ice cream."

Dave rubbed his cheek with his knuckles. "I do like a woman who knows the way to a man's heart."

"Well, do you? Know anything, I mean, about Trudy's affair."

"I know things, but whether I'm gonna tell what I know or not, I'm not certain. Till it happens, I mean."

"C'mon, Dave. It's me. You know I won't tell anyone where I heard it."

He stared at the ads on the placemat the waitress put down in front of him. "Well, to speak frankly, I seen 'em in here from time to time. They're at the stage where they keep touching each other and act like no one can see them at it. You know, the sides of their fingers brushing against each other, a hand on a back, leaning toward each other like they're being pulled together by magnetism."

"Holy cow. Why didn't you tell me this before?"

"You didn't ask."

Millie rolled her eyes. "Okay, I'm asking now. Do you know his name?"

"Not 'his.' A woman. The nurse, the nice one, from the doctor's office. Her name is Lena. Lena Cruz. They come in for coffee in the morning and sometimes again in the late afternoon."

"How do you know they're lovers?"

"You just know these things. Even *you* would be able to figure it out."

Millie pretended to be offended, rocking her shoulders, and turning her face away from him. When she glanced back, he was smiling. He wasn't fooled by her pantomime.

"Has it been going on for a long time?"

"I'd say they first started meeting up for morning coffee here about eight months ago."

"Before the doctor got married?"

"Uh-huh."

"When did it progress to the magnetism stage?"

"'Bout five months ago."

"Then why did she marry Rutledge?"

"No accounting for taste." He scooped a forkful of pie and ice cream into his mouth and closed his eyes.

Millie pondered her question while Old Dave savored his pie. She wouldn't give up her singlehood for a partner of any kind. Marriage was so far in the future she didn't even bother to imagine it. She was at the stage in her life when living alone was glorious, even though she lived in a tiny three-room walkup above a lawyer's office on Main Street. No parents, no roommates, no one else's boyfriend peeing with the bathroom door open.

She could talk to herself out loud, eat cereal right from the box for dinner, leave dishes in the sink, clean the apartment, or not, and not have to negotiate with anyone about which way the toilet paper hung. There might come a time when her needs would change, when being with someone would be more important than freedom, but she wasn't ready to trade her autonomy for companionship. If she got lonely, she could get a cat.

But here was Trudy Davis juggling the demands of two bedmates. The logistics made Millie dizzy. If Trudy were having an affair, that might provoke marital strife, unless Rutledge was unusually evolved, or clueless. *My God, that's it. Trudy's affair is Rutledge's motive for killing her.*

A crime of passion would sell a lot of newspapers. There'd be a trial with the lurid details teased out during testimony. Millie pictured herself seated in the front row in the courtroom, scribbling on her pad every day of the trial. She imagined her byline on the front page above the fold, pictured readers reaching for their devices every morning just to read her story.

"Penny for *your* thoughts," Old Dave said.

"Getting ahead of myself."

Her staid newspaper wouldn't let her report a hypothetical story unless she got it directly from the perpetrator or the police, on the record, and for attribution from two sources. Otherwise, the paper's lawyers would cover the story in red ink, and she'd be left with a headline: *Local Doctor Goes Missing.* The rest would be considered gossip, which at this point Millie had to admit was all she had.

Despite her nose for news, Millie still had principles, and invading other people's privacy for a front-page story made her uneasy. Unless the story was that Lena knew where Trudy was, they had planned to escape together, and then something went wrong. Maybe they had an argument, or Trudy met someone else, or Rutledge got wind of the plan. Her mind spun with possibilities. Of course, Millie didn't know anything had gone wrong. Perhaps Trudy's disappearance was working according to plan. The person who might know the facts would be the doctor's friend.

"You're awful quiet for a nosy woman."

"Sorry, Dave, thinking about what to do with this information."

"You might want to see if Lena is still at work or if she's also missing."

"Of course." Millie grinned. "You're better than my editor. Thanks." She checked her bill, put cash on the counter and waved goodbye.

For the sake of her story, Millie hoped Lena would still be at the office. She had a brief image of herself as a beagle following the scent through backyards and under fences to wherever it led, but she laughed it off. Beagles didn't know where they were going when they headed out, and she did. At least, she hoped she did.

CHAPTER 22

FIFTEEN minutes before the physicians' practice closed for the day, Millie pushed open the glass door of the office. The single-floor modern brick building was located on a one-way street in an otherwise residential community surrounded by woods that ended at the river.

In the large reception room, two U-shaped seating areas flanked either side of the door. Based on the magazines on one side and the toys stacked in a large toybox on the other, Millie guessed the practice included a pediatrician and obstetrician as well as a primary care doctor. Mounted on the rose-colored walls were framed paintings of local artists' depictions of the Eastern Panhandle's two rivers, mountains, and historic towns. A spicy air freshener neutralized any other smells.

Three nurses and the receptionist, all in pastel scrubs, chatted together at the intake window. They turned their faces toward Millie at the same time, reminding her of how flowers turned toward the sun. These were people who liked humans, who anticipated a warm exchange with them. Millie categorized them as helpers. How different from her own colleagues, who generally mistrusted people and often used notetaking to avoid eye contact.

"Can we help you?" the receptionist asked.

"Hi, I'm Millie Overbee, a reporter for the *Daily*. I'd like to talk to Lena if possible."

"Lena Cruz? Our R.N.?" the receptionist asked.

The striking brunette who'd been leaning against the counter said, "That's me. What can I do for you?"

Impressed at her directness, Millie wondered if Old Dave was wrong about Lena having an affair with Trudy Davis. *Or I'm the one who's wrong, thinking the woman would be embarrassed or secretive about the affair. Probably the latter.* Her first impressions were often wrong. Of course, Lena didn't yet know what Millie wanted to talk to her about.

"I was wondering if we could talk in private."

"Can you tell me your symptoms? You need an appointment to see someone here. Mary can make one for you, of course, but if there's an emergency, there's a university drop-in provider six miles away. They're open until nine. I can call ahead for you."

Millie took in Lena's rose-colored scrubs, support shoes, easy-care ponytail, the absence of makeup, and tried to determine what made her beautiful. *The eyes. Maybe her candor.* Lena fingered the thin gold chain that rode the pulse at the base of her throat.

Did Trudy Davis give her that? Whatever the secret ingredient of her attractiveness, Millie couldn't help instantly liking the woman. *She's a source, not a friend,* Millie cautioned herself. "I'm not sick. I want to ask you about Dr. Davis."

Lena's cheeks pinked. She glanced over her shoulder at her colleagues. They gazed anywhere but at her. "Let's go outside."

One of the nurses called out, "Isabel said we're not supposed to talk to anyone about Dr. Davis. Especially the media."

"Who's Isabel?" Millie asked.

"Isabel Romero, the practice manager. She manages stuff like this for the doctors," the receptionist said.

"Stuff?"

"Non-medical information." The receptionist's voice scratched as if something had caught in her throat.

Lena shrugged one shoulder. "It's no secret. The paper had a story saying she's missing. Maybe I can help find her." She walked to the entrance door and held it open for Millie.

Millie followed her and sat on the low brick wall near the door. Lena smelled like the ocean layered with the scent of exotic flowers. *What is that perfume?* Millie might have befriended this woman just to find out about the perfume, but she schooled herself to be business-like now. "I've been told you're friends with Dr. Davis."

"What business is it of yours?" If Lena's face had been an acrobat, it would have nailed the landing after a triple-double flip. Whatever her heart was doing, however much Millie's question annoyed her, she kept her expression under control.

Millie wished she had that kind of composure. It was clear she'd have to press Lena if she was going to extract any useful information. "Maybe you're closer than friends?"

"Wow. People like to talk, don't they?"

So, is this an admission of an intimate relationship? Millie wanted to be clear. "Is it common knowledge in the office that you're having an affair?"

This time Lena blushed to her hairline. "Whatever our relationship, it's certainly none of your business and not a subject for the newspaper. Even if certain people like to speculate."

Millie remembered Old Dave's description of how the women were drawn together like magnets. Did Lena understand the impression they made on others? "Was she planning to leave her husband for you?"

"You go straight for the jugular, don't you?" Lena shook her head. "We didn't have time to talk about him much. What does this have to do with Trudy's being missing?"

"It might have something to do with a motive to harm her."

Lena's shoulders jerked as if she'd been pushed. "I've been worried about that," she mumbled.

Millie kept going. "Has Trudy been in contact with you during the last week? While she's been missing, I mean. Or reported missing."

"You don't actually know what you're going after, do you?"

Mocked by the smartest girl in class. Again. There was always one at every school Millie attended—pretty, well-dressed, showing up to 8 A.M. classes in perfect makeup, shining hair in long curls, bursting with the right answers.

"This is what I know." Millie stuffed down her irritation. "Harmon Rutledge reported his wife missing, but he lied about when that happened. She hasn't been to work, the police have been trying to find her, and they think there's a chance she's hiding somewhere." Millie guessed the last part but hoped it would provoke an answer.

Lena closed her eyes as if making a wish. "She's alive? Why do they think that?"

Her reaction shifted Millie's perspective. She *was* in distress, missing Trudy, and worried something terrible had happened to her. "So she's not with you? And she hasn't contacted you?"

Lena closed her eyes. "No. Do the police think there's a chance Rutledge didn't kill her?"

Her voice was so quiet it took Millie a second to register the question. "You think she was in danger, that he might have killed her?"

"I haven't heard from her for over a week." Lena covered her face with her palms, muffling her voice. "That means something's wrong."

Millie leaned closer.

"I *told* her she was in danger," Lena said, "but for a long time she shrugged it off. She said, 'Harmon would never do anything to me that would muss his clothes.' I've been worried since she didn't meet me for our usual ten A.M. hike that Sunday." Tears streaked down her face. She wiped them away with the sides of her hands.

"Where were you going?"

"Across the bridge up to Maryland Heights."

"Did you check for her there?"

Lena nodded. "She wasn't there."

"And you don't know where she is?"

Anger flashed in Lena's eyes. "If I knew where she was, I would be there."

"If you were going to go away together, where would you have gone?"

"Someplace he couldn't find us. But we hadn't picked a place. They'd been married six months, and Trudy was already planning to leave him. She had an appointment with her lawyer next week and planned go to her bank, tell her mother, stuff like that. She thought she had time before he learned about us and flipped out."

So much for uncovering where Trudy is holed up. "Was he ever physically violent with her?"

"No. She never told me about any physical fights. She never had bruises."

"Why was she afraid of him then?" This was a longshot question.

"She'd been reading about personality types and said he suffered from malignant narcissistic personality disorder."

"A personality disorder?" Millie frowned. "Like a mental illness? What causes it?"

"Maybe not an illness so much as a character twitch. It's a diagnostic term. A combination of neurobiology, environment, and childhood fears of abandonment can cause this disorder. But it can't be treated with drugs or talk therapy. Basically, Rutledge is a sociopath and there's nothing anyone can do about it."

"Did she tell him this?"

Lena shook her head. "That would be a bad idea. Trudy said he'd been charming before they married but after, she had to walk on egg-shells around him or he flared up like a three-year-old having a tantrum. She couldn't disagree with him on anything; he always had to be right. Sure, he's smart and he can be generous, but he's also unstable, impulsive, and has no empathy for anyone."

"Hmm. Like a lot of CEOs."

"But more dangerous. If she accidentally triggered him, he might be aggressive the way a bear is—you know, stand on his hind legs, roar, and charge you—but he hadn't done anything criminal she could report."

"Is there anything in his background to suggest he'd be dangerous?"

"I don't think she checked his background. He said he went to Harvard and Yale. He showed her transcripts to prove it." Lena shrugged but she sounded miserable. "I guess degrees from two reputable universities and a fancy job made him seem stable."

"Why on earth did she marry him?"

Lena wrapped her arms around her torso. "It happened very quickly. Her mother nagged her to get married because she wanted grandchildren and Trudy was already thirty-five. You know how mothers can be. They never stop pushing. Trudy thought she could have it all, that she could manage him, have a baby or two to make her mother happy, and keep me in her life. The new way to lean in and have it all."

She sounded bitter to Millie. "But why Rutledge? Why not someone more likeable?"

"Trudy met him online. He was available, local, had the right credentials, and stunning in a tux. She said her child might get his looks and her brains. She didn't want a forever thing. She was just checking a box, and she'd divorce him when the children started kindergarten."

"That seems fairly calculated on Trudy's part."

Lena dabbed at her eyes with a tissue she pulled out of her pocket. "She changed her mind about that plan by the second month of their marriage. But who knows why people do things."

"Why didn't she leave him the minute she figured out how dangerous he could be?"

Lena shrugged. "She thought she could control him, that she could get everything worked out before she told him so she could just move once and be happy."

Millie took in Lena's obvious misery. *Her arrangement with Trudy is far more complicated than anything I could tolerate.* But maybe she could help Lena by tracking down what happened to Trudy. "So, you haven't gotten a text or email or call or postcard, no sign of any kind about where she might be?"

"No. I told you. It's driving me crazy."

Without thinking, Millie said, "The sheriff thinks she's in Emmitsburg, Maryland, if she's the one driving her vehicle and using her credit card." The minute the words were out of her mouth, Millie regretted saying them. The information the sheriff had given her was off the record, not for attribution. *I'm such a gossip. Maybe all reporters gossip.*

Lena's mouth fell open. "Then there's hope. Thanks for that," she said. "I should get back." She jumped up and opened the door before Millie could ask another question.

Slipping inside the building, Lena waved and smiled briefly as she locked the glass door. The nurses inside closed ranks around their colleague, wrapping their arms around her and whisking her out of sight.

The information about Emmitsburg couldn't have comforted Lena. How much could Trudy love the woman if she was galivanting around the country pretending to be dead without contacting her? Maybe the affair wasn't about love, and Trudy had a personality disorder also. All that ego in one marriage had to be rough.

What if we all have personality disorders? Who decides what's normal, anyway?

This lead hadn't panned out. Millie needed to strike gold soon or her editor was going to put her back on writing obits. She'd rather dish up pie at Needful Things than do obituaries.

On her phone, Millie scrolled through the *Daily*'s website. An ad announced an open house at Rutledge's address on Saturday. Typing the information into her calendar, she made a snap decision to ask Lena to come with her. They would see where Trudy lived, how she lived, and maybe stumble on what had happened to her. Lena might be able to tell if anything in the house was out of place. A lead, any lead, would be welcome right now.

CHAPTER 23

B Y Tuesday, the feeling that Harmon had taken advantage of him clung to Don like a fart. He was starting to worry maybe Charlie had put one over on him also. He'd waited patiently for his so-called friend to show up in Charles Town, for the ping of a text or call on his phone, but nothing. No call, no text, no show anywhere.

The real worry began when Don finally looked at his blank phone screen on Sunday afternoon and remembered he'd turned it off at the airport parking lot because he didn't want the GPS lady to know where he was. He opened his texts. The last one from Charlie at 1 A.M. Sunday morning said, WHERE THE HELL ARE YOU? I'M AT THE DUMP. YOU'RE SUPPOSED TO BE HERE.

Don typed, I'M HOME NOW, but Charlie didn't reply. Charlie's voice mail message sounded even angrier, which was unfair. Don couldn't help it if he'd missed the turn to the dump and before he knew it, he was at the Potomac River bridge heading into West Virginia.

Didn't Charlie remember they wouldn't get the rest of the money until they gave Harmon the driver's license? Maybe something had happened to him. Now determined to find his friend, Don drove around town, stopping at each of Charlie's hangouts.

He banged on Charlie's motel door. No one opened it. He stopped in at Uncle John's, ordered a Coke and tried to pick up the waitress. Don wandered through the library and drove past the town's public benches. For some reason, each bench was painted in different colors and patterns that made him dizzy. *Everything has to be fancy all the time. What's wrong with having plain benches to sit on that don't make people want to puke?*

Don pushed himself to remember every second of their mission from the time they'd pulled into the airport parking lot until he got home.

He'd been good until they got to the exit onto I-70. There, Trudy's car had vanished as if it had fallen into a sink hole. He'd heard about those holes on TV and they scared him. They could happen anytime, like earthquakes. Whole cars fell in them and couldn't get out.

No matter how he sped up and snaked around the other cars on the highway, he hadn't been able to find the Volvo again. Charlie must have been driving like a maniac to have gotten so far ahead. Or that tricky GPS took him another way. *I never should've trusted that eye-in-the-sky woman.*

The tightness in Don's chest reminded him of how he'd felt climbing the school bus steps every day, knowing the other kids were going to torture him. He shouldn't have given Charlie the paper with Harmon's instructions on it. The instructions put Charlie in charge of the mission, which was plain wrong. *I was the one who got us the job. I was the boss of the gig. I should have kept the instructions.*

Don's mind went around and around about who was guilty of what until he couldn't see straight. He'd been stalking Charlie's social media posts, but his last one was from Saturday, three days ago. That was a bad sign. Charlie usually posted twenty times a day. Don's stomach clutched. Charlie might have had an accident on the highway and died. A sense of loss swept over Don the way it had when he'd overheard a widow praying in a foreign language he couldn't understand. Standing next to her husband's plain casket, hands pressed together, head bowed, she sounded like death had stolen her voice. A lump had stuck in his throat for a long time that day.

The next second, Don was angry again. Charlie had screwed him like everyone else in his life. He had up and disappeared for sure, leaving Don holding the bag with Trudy's clothes in it. Desperate, Don drove back to the motel and idled his truck in the parking lot, waiting for Charlie to miraculously appear.

After two hours, the manager waddled out of the office waving his hairy arms. "Get out of here," he yelled. "This is private property. I don't want none of your drug deals here. Drive away or I'm calling the cops."

Offended the motel manager mistook him for a drug dealer, Don flipped the man the finger. "I'm a regular working guy, not a criminal," he yelled back. *If you don't count the bank job.* He threw the truck in gear and skidded onto the street headed in the direction of downtown without knowing where he was going next.

He should've known the job was dangerous the minute he learned they had to drive to Maryland. Going to another state had been a mistake, but Don hadn't been able to change his mind because he would have looked like a fool, which was worse than being one. He hated being duped because he couldn't resist an opportunity to make a few measly bucks.

Charlie's vanishing trick was payback. Waiting for the stop light to change, Don smacked his head with his hand. "I screwed up. Again." He was so tired of screwing up he wanted to scream. People passing on the sidewalk stared at him. He gave them the finger, jammed his foot on the gas, and blew through the red light.

If Charlie didn't come back with the license, Harmon wouldn't give them the rest of their pay. Don had been counting on the money. He had already imagined the spiffy new clothes he would buy at Walmart—black jeans, black button up shirt with a collar, black jacket—and a round of drinks for everyone at the bar. The guys would slap him on the back and tell him he was the man. Girls would give him the eye. He'd be one of the club. The taste of success was almost on his tongue.

But the truth was, he had failed again. And he still had that damn bag of clothes to prove it.

Five blocks later Don drove past the bank. There was one thing left to do. He had to deal with the bag of clothes on the floor of his truck. He could just toss the bag out on the highway the way everyone else did, but that didn't seem business-like. After all, he'd made a deal with Harmon. But the bag linked him to Harmon and the Volvo with the dead body inside it. He had to give the bag back even though the man would be mad because they hadn't done the job he'd paid them to do.

Mr. Big Shot might want his money back, like a couple hundred bucks meant anything to him, but Don had no intention of returning the money. He'd already driven to Maryland and back, and they did move the Volvo. They did half the job, so they got half the money. Wasn't that fair? Somehow, what had been a simple way to earn money had become a complete clusterfuck. Avoiding Harmon was the best course of action, but the feeling of being used irritated Don. He didn't like feeling like a rube.

Barely missing cars parked on Main Street, he swung the truck in a U-turn back toward the bank. Don pulled into an empty employee's spot next to a Range Rover and sat in the idling truck while he texted Harmon, telling him to come out of the building. It was 4:30. The bank was closed except for the drive-through window on the other side of the building. Mr. Big Shot would have to meet up, whether he wanted to or not.

When the big man walked out of the bank like he was king of the world, Don's hands automatically curled into fists. *I hate this guy. I hate every curly red hair on his ginormous body.* Don climbed down from his truck and, swinging the bag of clothes, sauntered over to Harmon.

"Hey."

Scowling, Harmon looked over his shoulder before he rushed Don. Grabbing him by the collar of his jean jacket, Harmon pushed Don until his back was up against the truck. "What the fuck are you doing here? You're not supposed to come here. We've got cameras, for God's sake."

Don gritted his teeth. "You still owe us the rest of the money for the job." This bastard wasn't going to scare him.

"The hell I do." Harmon's face was bright red. He slammed Don against the truck. "You idiots didn't do the job. The police don't know where Trudy is and someone's driving her car all over creation."

Don's face scrunched into a scowl. "What are you talking about?"

"You don't know this? God, you're a moron." Harmon's Adam's apple bobbed.

Don shook his finger in Harmon's face. "I'm not a moron. I'm average."

"Okay, okay. Meet me behind the recreation center in two hours and I'll explain it. I have a short meeting at home first. Just leave here now before anyone sees you."

Don rubbed his neck. "Wait a minute." His head was so heavy he worried it would snap off his neck and roll away. "You can't tell me what to do. We got the car out of the lot and Charlie took it to the dump. Then I sort of lost track of him. But that car reeked like death. For sure, there was a dead body in the trunk like you said."

"I never said any such thing."

"Yes, you did. You said to put these clothes on the body, and I got the clothes you handed me to prove it."

"Did you ever see a body?" Harmon's lips scarcely moved.

"What? No. You're trying to confuse me."

"How do you know there is one?" Harmon held out his hand. "You can give those clothes back to me now."

The bag has Harmon's fingerprints on it. Inside the bag are clothes only Harmon could've put there. That proves he gave me the clothes to put on a dead body. This plastic bag is my proof. No way am I giving the clothes back without a payoff.

"What'd you give me money for, then?"

Harmon held out his hand. "Just—"

"It'll cost you." Don stuck out his chin.

"What?"

Without a blink, Don said, "Five thousand in cash," because it was the biggest number he could think of and the exact amount of cash his mother had scrambled together for his bail.

"Not a chance."

"That's the number or no deal." Don opened his truck door, tossed in the bag of clothes, and hopped inside. "You let me know. In two hours behind the rec center."

Don spun his tires and wailed out of the parking lot without thinking about what Harmon would do next.

CHAPTER 24

HARMON spotted the flowers as he pulled onto his driveway. On the doorstep sat a three-foot-high, chrome-plated vase filled with an elaborate sympathy bouquet of daisies, lilies, white carnations, and white chrysanthemums.

I don't have time for this. Ethel's going to be here any minute.

He entered the house through the door from the garage and took off his jacket. Turning on every light on the first floor, he peeked out the front window to ensure his neighbors weren't watching. Then he opened the front door a crack wide enough for his arm to slip through and plucked the card from the plastic holder stuck in the ostentatious display.

The smell of lilies was so cloying his throat closed in allergic response. He couldn't retreat fast enough. Hives broke out instantly on his neck, just as they always did when things went wrong. Itchy welts would drive him crazy for hours, if not days. He didn't need this extra hassle. Locking the door, Harmon stumbled into the living room. His hands trembled as he pulled the card from the small envelope.

Gone but not forgotten, the unsigned card read. Someone was deliberately messing with him.

The florist was local. Harmon searched for them online and called the number on the website. Before the clerk could say hello, Harmon exclaimed, "I've received a misdirected bouquet, and I'm allergic to it. It should have gone to a funeral home. Please send someone to pick it up right away."

"Who's calling, please?" the clerk asked.

Harmon stated his name and address and described the bouquet, expecting an immediate apology. Instead, the clerk said, "No, sir, you're the intended recipient of the arrangement."

"What do you mean?"

"I mean it's your name and address we were supposed to deliver the flowers to, the one you gave us."

"Well, I didn't order it."

"Then someone else did. But we didn't make a mistake. It's our best sympathy bouquet. Mr. Fred arranged it himself."

Harmon closed his eyes and put his hand over his mouth to hold in the things he wanted to say but shouldn't. When he felt sufficiently composed, he asked, "Can you tell me who ordered it?"

The clerk was silent for a bit, perhaps scrolling online or flipping through paper receipts, and then said, "I don't know who ordered it, but it was charged to a credit card. I can see the last four digits of the number, but I can't tell you those. Maybe you know who sent it?"

"For God's sake, how would I know who sent it?" Fear and fury galloped up Harmon's spine. The arrangement had to be from Trudy. This is what the sheriff meant when she said they were tracking his wife's credit card use. Trudy was taunting him. "So no one came in the shop. You didn't see anyone?"

"No, sir. It was an online order placed this morning. We hurried because it's for a funeral."

My funeral. The cells in Harmon's body shrank one by one. Someone was threatening him with death. And they were doing it remotely, intending to drive him crazy. He had to sit to absorb the message accompanying the flowers.

"Thank you," he managed to say before he hung up, remembering at the last moment he had a position in this town to maintain. *Keep a level head.*

He fell onto the sofa and sat there without moving. It was ten days since he'd killed her, or thought he had. Don said her car had the stench of death, but how would he know? He hadn't driven it. Trudy was alive somewhere, knowing he had tried to kill her, and she was doing her best to torment him. Threatening him with death. Making it clear she wasn't gone, and that she was going to get him. Driving around in her car and buying things at an Army/Navy store, for God's sake.

It wasn't like her to abandon her patients and practice without so much as a goodbye note but maybe having someone try to murder you changes a person, makes them bolder. And very, very angry. A person in that state might do anything. After all, they've faced their worst fear. They've already been left for dead.

He'd imprisoned his wife in the trunk of her car for six days. Harmon squirmed. She'd be venomous by now. He should have dealt with her the way he had his mother. He'd wanted to be so clever, smothering Trudy with a pillow, congratulating himself on the easy clean up afterward. For a split second he pictured a blade slicing through the soft flesh of his wife's neck, and then his mind blotted out the rest.

Trudy must have teamed up with the idiot Charlie, who would have revived her and let her out of the trunk. And now they were having a good laugh at his expense, traveling the country in her car, entertaining themselves by dreaming up ways to scare the shit out of him. Siccing the police on him. He could practically hear them cackling together about the joke they were pulling.

Somehow, he had to find her and put a stop to this. But first, he had to deal with Ethel's inspection of the house and then with Don. Now that Trudy had made it clear she was still out there, Harmon had no intention of handing over any of his hard-earned money to anyone. He would need it for his escape, which he needed to start planning immediately. Harmon lowered his head like a bull about to charge. Bad things were going to happen to Don.

CHAPTER 25

ETHEL walked through Harmon's house with him marveling at how well it showed without her having to do anything. He'd already placed a wooden bowl full of shiny red apples on the white marble counter in the kitchen and added charming small bouquets of white flowers in the bathrooms and on the marble-topped table in the foyer.

The house would pass anyone's white glove test. Ethel concluded she and the banker shared a perfectionist twitch, but the idea they had any traits in common worried her. She hoped she didn't appear as forbidding and standoffish to people as Harmon did, although in her secret heart she admitted George was right—she was fundamentally a snob. Strange, but that idea didn't bother her.

Discreet black votive candles in each room emitted layered scents of a crackling fire, apple pie, and cinnamon as she walked through. *Perfect for an autumn afternoon.* All the curtains were open, and the late afternoon sun shone across the wood floors. Windows sparkled. The house exuded the seduction of a television commercial for an expensive car. It was hard to believe Trudy Davis had voluntarily walked away from a place as beautiful as this. Life with Harmon must have been unbearable.

Ethel glanced at him. Red bumps ringed his neck. *I hope he's not coming down with something contagious, and we have to call off the open house.* The rash unaccountably reminded her to call Charlie and make sure he wasn't getting himself into any new trouble. At that moment, Harmon's cell phone rang, and he stepped away to take the call.

Ethel walked into the master bathroom for a quick check of the linen closet to see if the towels were neatly folded and stacked. *Of course, they are.* She randomly opened one of the drawers in the marble vanity, knowing house shoppers would do so even if instructed not to.

It was best to lock away one's belongings before an open house because people were inherently nosy. There was nothing to be done about it. Ethel had learned this in one of her many continuing education seminars to keep up her license. The contents of drawers, like the rest of the house, had to be carefully curated to neither give away too much personal information nor to appear too impersonal.

Ethel glanced over the neat arrangement of brush, comb, extra toothpaste and toothbrush, tubes of Christian Louboutin mascara and lipstick. This was Trudy's drawer. She picked up the lipstick tube, pulled off the crown-like cap, and twirled the tube revealing a red so luscious she had to repress the urge to bite it.

This is the lipstick of a young woman with a lusty appetite. As if hypnotized, Ethel drew the color slowly over her lower lip, then recapped the lipstick quickly, feeling as guilty as if she'd been peeking through a keyhole at the woman having sex. She pressed her lips together and stared at her reflection.

Who am I?

Although it wouldn't do for Harmon to find her snooping, Ethel couldn't resist pulling the drawer open fully so she could see all the contents at one time. A slim, blue plastic case caught her eye. Before she could think about violating ethics guidelines, Ethel opened the case. Inside were half a month's supply of daily birth control pills. *No way did the person who wore this lipstick leave of her own volition without taking her pills. And she didn't set off on a jaunt without that lipstick.*

Something had happened to Trudy. Ethel might have known this since her first meeting with Harmon at the house, from the moment she shook his hand and looked into his eyes. She hadn't been willing to acknowledge it.

It's none of my business. Ethel took three deep breaths in through her nose and out through her mouth, trying to calm herself. They didn't help. She couldn't keep her mind from shrieking, *You're working for a murderer. Good thing I know how to protect myself.*

Sliding the case back in the drawer, she ran the water in the sink and flushed the toilet to give herself time to think. She wiped the water spots off the sink with a tissue and tucked it into her pocket. If Harmon asked why he heard water running, she could explain she was testing the water pressure, as potential buyers would do.

I should walk out of the house right now and never go back. I should tell my broker I can't do it. But she'd just send another agent to take the listing. I could tell the police my suspicions. But who would believe me? And if I tell someone, will he know? Will he kill me too?

The commission on nine-hundred-ninety-five-thousand dollars . . . That was a lot of money to sacrifice for a little bit of integrity. On the other hand, if she took the commission, she was no better than a Mafia consigliere. Theme music from *The Godfather* played in her mind. Ethel ran her fingers through her hair to stop the sound, watching her white curls fluff up in the mirror. *I am not a good person.* She adjusted her clothing and made herself comfortable with the observation.

Besides, the police, particularly that intimidating Amazon of a sheriff, wouldn't believe an accusation of murder based on the theory that a woman would never leave home without an expensive lipstick and half a packet of birth control pills. In the old days, women were hustled off to the loony bin for claiming less. Ethel needed stronger proof if she wanted to convince anyone.

By the time she got back to the kitchen, Ethel had come around to thinking that even if Harmon was in jail, someone had to sell his house since he wouldn't be able to keep up the mortgage payments while incarcerated. The agent who benefitted from the sale might as well be her. *Silicon Valley executives call that enlightened self-interest. Why shouldn't I?* The profit from the house would be put into a special escrow account held by the closing attorney and would go to Trudy's estate in the end. So, someone else, not Harmon, would benefit from the sale. *So, I'm not his accomplice.* It was amazing how agile her brain was, solving these small moral conundrums by itself without any help from her.

"All set," she told Harmon. "You did a marvelous job of prepping the house."

"It's always like this," Harmon said. "I don't like messes."

She smiled in a way she hoped would soothe him. "Well, I think it will sell very quickly." Ethel lifted her chin and lowered her shoulders.

"You can bring buyers through any time before five P.M. on weekdays since I'll be at work," Harmon said as though Ethel weren't thinking he was evil. "In the evenings and on the weekends, I prefer you call me to set up an appointment." He handed her a key to the front door.

Ethel resisted the impulse to clean off the key with hand sanitizer before putting it in her purse. "Oh, of course. Any agent will do that. It's standard practice to call the owner in advance." She placed the shiny portfolio stamped with the realty company's logo on the kitchen counter. "The listing has been live on the website for one day with a 'Coming Soon' banner, and already one hundred people have clicked the heart icon indicating it's their favorite. I've got calls and texts from other agents on my phone wanting to tour it. We may have offers even before the open house and a contract by Sunday."

"Perfect." Harmon clamped his gigantic hand on her shoulder. "I don't want this to drag out."

Ethel repressed a shudder. "Before I leave, I'll put the lockbox on the front door and the For Sale sign on your lawn."

"Fine." Harmon strode out of the kitchen to the foyer, the stacked heels of his black leather Armani dress shoes rhythmically striking the marble floor with finality.

To Ethel that sound meant he was done with her for today. She wondered if he always wore his work shoes indoors. She always shucked her shoes the moment she got inside her house. *What a relief. We're not alike. I'm not a secret murderer.*

If she kept thinking about it, she was sure to find other differences. For instance, she was always cordial to people whether she liked them or not. *But I would have been a murderer . . .* She shrugged off the rest of her thought.

When she'd completed her final tasks, Ethel paused in the driveway and again assessed the house from a stranger's point of view. Harmon watched her from the window as if he didn't quite trust her. She rushed to get into her car and locked the doors, feeling the slightest bit safer. The disquiet lingered long after she pulled into her own driveway.

CHAPTER 26

DRESSED in the navy-blue tracksuit and matching running shoes Trudy had bought him to at least suggest he did something that involved sweating, Harmon headed to the recreation center. Should anyone see him there, they would think he was running the outdoor course.

He resented having to deal with Don. The man was a utility and should know when to sit down and shut up. Harmon had no intention of forking over five thousand dollars for a small bag of Trudy's clothes. Devising a method to silence Don permanently shouldn't be that hard.

The simplest solution was the best one. Kill Don, dispose of Trudy's clothes, end of story. Charlie wouldn't come back to Charles Town to claim a hundred dollars for moving a body. At least, Harmon wouldn't have. If Charlie had teamed up with Trudy, he wouldn't be returning to take his punishment for the bank job. And if by some miracle Trudy was actually dead, Charlie should be heading northwest where he could get lost. Not that Charlie behaved like someone who made sensible decisions.

Killing Don was the solution, but Harmon hated working without a plan. He couldn't knock the man down with a rock or run him over and leave his body in the rec center's parking lot. Too messy, with too many opportunities to be observed, and too much evidence to conceal. Disposing of the man's truck would be a hassle. And didn't Don have a mother who would report him missing?

He might be stuck giving the idiot the money he'd demanded. *Unless Don can be convinced to take care of the problem himself.* Harmon had never taken such an approach. What was required to persuade another human being to kill himself?

How do I inflict enough emotional abuse in the shortest amount of time to induce a state of hopelessness? Torture experts had figured this out. But they had days or months even. And some human beings managed to survive for years in spite of being tortured. Harmon had ten minutes. What would it take?

No one is unaffected by scorn, his mind answered as if it had been waiting to be asked. Harmon could use disdain to worm his way into Don's psyche. Seeding enough doubt and self-hate that Don would drive himself right off a bridge, of which there were four nearby, would solve everyone's problems.

Harmon arrived at this solution at the same moment he spotted Don leaning against his truck and smoking a cigarette in the recreation center's parking lot. Don's insolent posture alone was enough to convince Harmon his solution was the correct one.

Parking on the other side of the building as if they didn't know each other, Harmon sauntered toward Don like he was going to ask a stranger for directions even though their cars were the only two vehicles in the whole park. Someone could always be watching.

Harmon stopped an arm's length from Don. "Well, showing up at the bank was stupid. People could have seen you there. Now they'll think you came back to the bank to finish the job since the robbery failed. Everyone will see that you threatened me with physical violence if I didn't give you the money you weren't able to steal."

"No, man, nobody thinks that. You're the one who pushed me." Don's face went so pale it glowed in the moonlight.

Harmon tamped down a brief spurt of pity. "What do you imagine they think, then?"

Don scanned the asphalt parking lot. "I don't know."

"Have you heard from Charlie?"

"No. I have no idea where he is."

"I have to tell the police you guys stole my wife's car. It's the best I can do now."

Don's body jerked. "What? I had nothin' to do with the car. I was never even in her car. I didn't touch it. Anyways, that wasn't what happened. You—"

"I what?"

"You told us to take it. The car. You wrote down where to find it and where to drive to. You gave us the key and the instructions. We got proof."

Harmon swallowed. He'd forgotten about the incriminating piece of paper with his fingerprints and handwriting on it. "Do you have it, the instructions?"

"No. Charlie's got it."

In a blinding flash, Harmon pictured Charlie helping Trudy out of the trunk, showing her the paper. He imagined Trudy figuring out his plan. Who knew what her next move would be?

These two men were clearly a threat. Charlie could blackmail him for a long time with that little piece of paper even if Trudy weren't alive. The instructions demonstrated intent. Hopefully, Charlie was too dumb to figure that out on his own. But if he did, Harmon would deal with him also.

Harmon eyed Don. "So, *you've* got nothing to prove I put you up to it."

"Except the clothes. And your phone call."

"Who's to say you didn't steal the clothes when you kidnapped Trudy?"

Don balked. "Your fingerprints are all over the bag. Police will know you gave it to me."

"Of course, my prints are on the bag. You took it out of my house. My prints don't prove anything."

"You're crazy. I didn't take no bag out of your house. Why would I take your wife's clothes? Anyway, I've never been in your house."

"If you hand the clothes over now, I won't tell the police how you're involved in this."

"I told you, you give me five thousand dollars, and I give you the clothes."

Harmon leapt. "You give me those damn clothes right now, or I'll kill you." He grabbed Don by the throat and squeezed.

Stubble stabbed the pads of his thumbs as he pressed his fingers into Don's neck. The soft flesh below Don's whiskers gave way. He pressed against the tendons. A sensation unlike any Harmon had ever felt gripped him.

Don coughed and thrashed.

A surge of power ripped through Harmon the way it had when he'd held the pillow down over Trudy's face, but stronger this time. His fingers pressed deeper. His breath came faster. *The rush, my God, the rush.*

"Why don't you just die," Harmon whispered.

Don smashed Harmon's ribs, scratched his cheeks, and finally kneed him in the groin.

Harmon doubled over, fell to his knees, and groaned.

Don ran to his truck. "You'll be sorry," he yelled out the window as he sped away.

Harmon put a hand to his cheek and checked his palm. The guy had drawn blood. But it wasn't Don's wrath Harmon feared. It was the warning from those flowers on his doorstep that scared him. He had failed to keep a level head. Harmon inhaled the night air and promised his father he would do better.

CHAPTER 27

ETHEL'S Saturday open house for Harmon's property was packed from the moment she opened the door. In the weather lottery, she'd won a crisp, sunny October day with fall foliage at peak color, perfect for a drive in the country. Neighbors in the subdivision had decorated their front steps with festive yet understated arrangements of pumpkins, hay bales, and colorful mums.

She'd advertised the house in the Washington, DC, media, hoping wealthy urbanites with money to burn might decide they needed a weekend lodge an easy drive of sixty-five miles from the nation's capital.

From Harmon's living room, prospective buyers could gaze out over the green expanse of the well-landscaped course and picture themselves catching a round of golf, imagining they were breathing clean mountain air instead of automobile exhaust. Little did they know the air in West Virginia carried particulates from mountain-top mining and coal-burning power plants. Ethel did not intend to disturb their illusions.

Halfway through the four-hour event, Ethel flipped through the guest book she'd placed in the foyer and found ten pages filled with names and contact information. About a third of those entries would be useless. Looky-loos, curious neighbors, and competing agents would wander through an open house for reasons other than wanting to buy, leaving behind a trail of cookie crumbs, candy wrappers, and comments.

But today there was a good turnout of potential buyers, and Ethel was thrilled with her success, despite Harmon's terse handwritten note on the kitchen counter: *Be sure to clean up after the event. I detest messes.*

Ethel could hear the "or else" in his tone. She had crumpled the note and stuffed it in her bag, reminding herself that she was the kind of woman who could hold her own. After all, if she needed it, she still had the ampoule of poison tucked away. The man was offensive, but the crowd validated her decision to represent the property, not that she would have refused an opportunity to sell a chicken coop.

She'd worn her red pants suit, matching flats, and a bright red, white, and blue scarf so she could be spotted from across the room if a buyer couldn't see the brass name tag on her jacket lapel. In any case, it didn't hurt to wear one's best. Everyone else was more casually attired, but she had never succumbed to the modern bent for wearing jeans to every occasion. Like called to like, and she had her eye out for a couple wearing casual silk and cashmere weekend outfits. Those would be the people who bought this house, people who had their clothes dry-cleaned.

Ethel didn't meddle or harass anyone. She simply greeted visitors and made herself available for questions, handing out her card and the property brochure with the pertinent information listed on it. But she scrutinized every person who roamed through the rooms, checking, or unchecking her mental assessment of whether they could buy the house or not.

The opening notes of Beethoven's dreamy *Für Elise* drifted up the stairs from the family room. Instead of chasing the woman off the piano, Ethel made a mental note to hire a pianist for her next open house. Music created a welcoming mood, a sense that if you lived here, you'd be home now. A buyer might dream this was the place where her creative side would blossom.

One could never tell what would sell a house, what would make a person want to live in a particular place so badly he was willing to mortgage his life to have it. Unless, of course, the monthly bill on a nearly million-dollar house was a third of one's income, and then money wouldn't be a problem. Ethel sent up a small prayer for the buyer for whom price point didn't matter.

A couple with an agent in tow approached her. "Could we put in a pool?" asked the woman in gold capris topped by a crisp white blouse and a stunning amber necklace. Her hair was sculpted in waves around her perfectly made-up face.

Shivering with delight, Ethel studied the layered color job on the woman's platinum hair and shushed her internal debate about whether this woman was her reedy, balding companion's wife or mistress. From the indifferent look on his face, Ethel guessed the woman was soon to be a former whatever, but the man's money was as good as anyone's. If he wanted to stash his companion out here in the boonies far from his next, younger conquest, who was Ethel to judge?

"Unfortunately, no," Ethel said. "Not according to the neighborhood covenants. But the golf course is part of a country club which has a pool and tennis courts. Your annual homeowner dues include membership, so you would have access to the pool."

The woman twisted her lips. "With all those people." Her tone made "those people" sound like "vermin."

Ethel cleared her throat. "All club members own homes here," she said, gesturing broadly to the neighborhood, the mountains framing the river, the grand historic houses in nearby communities where she would happily reside.

"That's a deal-breaker, then," the woman said. "I must have my own pool for my daily morning dips."

Ethel guessed this was the way the woman resisted any pressure from her own agent to make an offer, and maybe a way to avoid being shuffled off to the hinterlands. "On your way home, you can stop off at the clubhouse and check out the amenities," she said. "They have a public restaurant and offer high tea every Saturday afternoon."

The woman said, "Hmmm," and the trio walked away.

Ethel had never understood what flipped a response from no to yes even though she'd taken a dozen classes on how to get to yes. There was always a point in the lecture when her eyes rolled up and her brain went to sleep as a protestor in her head yelled, "No means no" over and over.

At 3 P.M., the crowd thinned down to three couples who had been in the house for several hours. One couple had even driven away and come back. That was a good sign. Ethel's palms itched. She searched her memory for a checklist for how to manage a bidding war and hoped she wouldn't make a mistake. Did she need to see proof of funds, or a letter from a bank affirming financing, when they made an offer? She couldn't remember. No point in doing a mound of contract paperwork just to have a deal fall apart because buyers couldn't find the funds to close.

Ethel made a quick visual assessment of her possible buyers. An attractive middle-aged man stood stock still in the kitchen staring at the built-in grill and wine cooler while his partner, already at home, played Beatles tunes on the piano.

Another couple sat in the wicker chairs on the flagstone patio, their heads and knees nearly touching, probably doing the math of the monthly mortgage, taxes, and insurance against their combined incomes, and realizing it would be a tight squeeze.

In the second bedroom on the main floor, a woman stroked her pregnant belly, perhaps imagining how quickly she could run from the master bedroom to the baby's room in the middle of the night at the child's first whimper.

Three potential buyers would be enough; an agent might call her later with a full-price offer. Remembering her training, Ethel refrained from intrusive, pushy salesmanship tactics. The right buyer would figure it out, and she might have a contract for Harmon to sign by the end of the week. The sooner she was done with him, the better.

Feeling proud she had gotten this far without making any fatal errors and chasing every buyer away, she watched a lone woman enter the house followed by another a minute later. The women might be together, but Ethel didn't want to guess incorrectly. They greeted each other with the formality of new friends. They weren't a couple, but they clearly knew each other.

Neither of them appeared to be people who could afford this house— jeans, T-shirts, jean jackets, not a wrinkle on their faces. *Too young. Too carefree by half.* The woman with the wild, curly red hair and freckles might be twenty-two, although she was tall. *Must have played center on the basketball team.* The other woman, Ethel guessed, was in her early thirties.

Ethel kept her distance and surveyed them surreptitiously, planning to intervene the second they did something inappropriate. Rumors of open house looters frequently circulated on the real estate agent hotline. More frightening these days were the stories of shooters. She had no intention of allowing these two interlopers to spoil her perfect day or disrupt a possible sale with their shenanigans.

CHAPTER 28

THE intense fragrance wafting around Lena as Millie followed her into the house teleported the reporter to a Hawaiian beach—the crash of waves on the reef, the whoosh as the tide swept the shore, a body rolling up on the sand.

Whoa. Being on the crime beat sure can skew a person's imagination. Lena had nothing to do with Trudy's disappearance, unless she had kidnapped Trudy and was just going along to find out how much Millie knew. *That can't be true. Get a grip.*

A scowling Ethel Goodman, with whom Millie had assumed she'd created a good relationship during their phone interview, walked toward her. Maybe her jeans and a ratty jacket didn't make the cut for a real estate agent's idea of a prospective buyer.

Millie held out her hand. "Millie Overbee, reporter for the *Daily*. We talked on the phone the day you tackled the bank robber."

"Oh, right, of course, Ms. Overbee." Ethel squeezed her hand and dropped it. "That was a fun photoshoot."

Millie nodded. "The story looked great."

Ethel handed Millie a brochure. "If there are any questions about the house, please don't hesitate to ask me." She walked away without greeting Lena as if the woman were invisible.

Millie, eyebrow cocked, handed the brochure to Lena, who laughed. "I have that effect on some people."

Millie turned in a circle, trying to absorb the feel of the house for color in her future story.

Late afternoon sun streamed through the bank of windows in the living room as the sound of Beatles songs played on the piano floated up from downstairs. *Did Ethel hire a pianist to set the mood?*

Light from the foyer chandelier illuminated the large, colorful abstract painting on the wall. The house smelled like cinnamon, apple pie, and promises of Thanksgiving dinner. She shivered although she wasn't cold. The shiny allure of the place might hide a gruesome act. *Coming here could be a massively bad idea.* Any minute, Rutledge might sneak up behind her and growl, "Get out."

"Boy, this place is the whole *Architectural Digest* deal." Lena's amazement was clear in her voice.

"You've never been here before?"

Lena shook her head.

Millie took a second to adjust her idea about Trudy. *The good doctor kept her business—which is how she must have regarded her marriage—separate from her pleasure. Unless she hated this house.*

"Yeah, there's a definite upscale furniture showroom vibe." Millie had expected a doctor and a banker to have money, but she hadn't anticipated their wealth would be exhibited in quite this way. "The oriental rug looks like it might be real, unlike mine which came from a department store going-out-of-business sale. And the foyer chandelier looks like a Calder sculpture."

The glamour of the house distracted her. Her job was to find facts to back up her conjecture that there was more to the Trudy Davis disappearance than a runaway wife, or her shot at a prize-winning story would be over. The house had seemed like the likeliest place to find the relevant details. *But it turns out this is the very place where the truth might be the most thoroughly disguised.*

Hands jammed into her jacket pockets so she wouldn't accidentally break anything, Millie wandered into the living room and then the dining room. "Feels like I'm viewing museum dioramas of Earth's twenty-first century luxury residences."

Lena made a face and gazed around the living room. "I can't picture Trudy here. It's so . . . so—"

"Pretentious?" Millie rolled her eyes.

"I was going to say elegant, but yeah, that too," Lena said. "There's no room for an actual person to live here. You know, a human who burps and farts. Who gets colds and leaves snotty tissues lying around. I can't imagine anyone reclining on the sofa to read or slurping their soup at the dining room table. Dropping crumbs on the floor must be a crime."

"Yeah," Millie said. "Feels like it's a stage set, and real life happens somewhere else."

"You're right. I guess all properties for sale are staged these days."

"So, you've never been in this house before?" Millie fell into using her reporter's trick of asking the same question several times despite the fact that she wasn't interviewing Lena. *People lie.*

"Never. This house is nothing like Trudy." Lena's voice sounded as if someone were strangling her. "At least, the Trudy I know."

Millie glanced into the immaculate kitchen. Red apples gleamed from a bowl on the counter. *Are those poisoned?* "So if Trudy were going to leave him, would she have started packing up her things?"

"We could check." Lena consulted the house plan on the brochure and headed down the long hallway toward the master bedroom.

Millie made a quick assessment of whether anyone was observing them and, when the coast was clear, strolled down the hall. The whole point of being here was to find out what happened to Trudy. The pressure was on. Yesterday, the executive editor had warned her she'd better get the story, or she'd be relegated to covering county fairs and father-daughter dances. That was a fate worse than obits.

Lena stood in the doorway of the master bedroom staring at the king-sized bed. "I'm having a hard time imagining Trudy having sex with Harmon. In this room. On that bed." She put her hand over her stomach. "The idea makes me want to puke."

"Yecch." Millie shuddered. "I know what you mean. He's like the house. All show. I wouldn't want to share spit with him."

Lena laughed. "Oh my God, I can't believe you said that."

"Yeah, well. That's me. Brutally honest."

Lena strode across the room to a large walk-in closet with built-in dressers, a rotating shoe rack, and cubbies fitted with upper and lower rods from which hung jackets, blouses, skirts, dresses, and slacks set two inches apart. "Geez. This closet is the size of a bedroom in a normal house. It's even got its own window and recessed lighting."

Millie stopped in the closet doorway, although there was plenty of room for two of them to rattle around inside what should have been called a dressing room. "Based on the shoes and clothes, I'm guessing this closet is Trudy's. There's another closet on the other side of the bathroom."

"I'm not going through his things." Lena pulled open a drawer. "I don't want his smell on me."

"Ethel has a rule about not opening the drawers." Millie wasn't a great rule follower, so cautioning Lena sufficed to ease her conscience about invading someone's privacy.

"Too late," Lena said. "This stuff is definitely Trudy's. I recognize some of the panties."

For a split second, Millie was embarrassed, but her discomfort passed. She leaned over Lena's shoulder. "It's full, the drawer is full. The stuff in it isn't even mussed. She didn't take her underwear with her."

"Which means what?"

"It means she didn't intend to go anywhere. She didn't disappear willingly. She's not just missing. She was taken away. And suddenly."

"You're saying—"

"I'm saying what woman wouldn't grab at least a handful of under-wear to stuff in her bag if she were leaving her husband in a hurry or going on a brief vacation? There might be other stuff she didn't take." Millie headed for the bathroom while Lena pulled open drawer after drawer in the closet.

"She didn't take anything," Lena whispered as she followed Millie into the bathroom. "The drawers are full. All the clothes are perfectly folded. She's always so meticulous. It's a trait I love about her."

Millie opened the drawers in the bathroom vanity. "Hairbrush. Lip-stick. Oh, my God, she didn't take her birth control pills," she called out and then, realizing Ethel could hear her, clamped her hand over her mouth.

"She has birth control pills?" Lena's voice cracked. "Let me see." She grabbed the blue plastic container from Millie's hand. "She was lying about marrying him to get pregnant?" Lena took a ragged breath. "I can't . . . I guess I didn't . . ."

Ethel bustled into the bathroom. "What are you doing in here?" Face as red as her lipstick, she put her hands on her hips. "You have no right to go through their things. It's completely inappropriate. I want you to leave immediately."

CHAPTER 29

"SOMETHING bad has happened to Dr. Davis," Millie said, working hard to keep her voice low. "Don't you realize that?"

"We're trying to find out where she is," Lena said.

"Well, I certainly don't have any idea." Ethel looked at Lena. "Who are you, anyway?"

"I'm Trudy's friend and colleague. We work together at her medical practice. She's been missing for almost two weeks now. Something's wrong, and you're holding this open house like nothing's happened." Lena put her hand over her mouth and closed her eyes. Tears leaked from beneath her lids.

"It's not my fault she's missing. That has nothing to do with me." Ethel raised her chin. "She doesn't even own this house."

"Of course, it has something to do with you." Lena wiped her cheeks with her hands. "If she's the victim of a crime, and her husband did it, you're aiding the perpetrator."

Ethel fluffed her hair. "That's an absurd accusation. You don't know anything. The police haven't charged Mr. Rutledge with committing a crime. You need to leave now."

"What do you mean she doesn't own this house?" Millie asked.

"Just what I said. The title is in Rutledge's name alone." Ethel drew herself up to her full five-foot-three-inch height and raised her eyebrows. "He doesn't need Dr. Davis's permission to sell it."

Lena hovered over Ethel. "Doesn't it make you suspicious that he's selling the house while she's missing, that he's desperate to leave the area all of a sudden?"

Ethel's voice shrilled. "If he's so desperate, he would simply abandon the house, not sell it. It's not like selling a house happens overnight. This isn't Walmart. No one's going to hand me a million dollars in cash and walk out with a house under her arm."

Lena glared as if the words she wanted to say to Ethel were so hot they burned up the second sound emerged from her throat. Ethel glowered back at Lena. Millie imagined two black bears wrestling in the middle of a road, neither giving an inch.

"Geez. This is a waste of time." Millie linked her arm through Lena's. "Come on. We can't find out anything else here." When they were out of Ethel's earshot, she said, "Let's go out through the garage."

"The garage? Why?"

"Just come on." Millie pulled Lena through the kitchen and into the garage before Ethel could corral them and force them to leave by the front door.

The kitchen door lock clicked behind them. The garage had a painted drywall ceiling, recessed LED lights, built-in cabinets, and an epoxy floor. "Hard to believe anyone ever uses this garage," Millie said, allowing herself to open a cabinet door and peer inside. "Everything is so neat."

"What did you think we'd find in here?" Lena asked.

"The trash cans," Millie whispered, putting her finger to her lips. "Residents can't leave them out where people can see them from the street." She pointed to three gray resin trash bins with flip tops. "Let's check them."

"You're not going to go through his trash," Lena said. "That's gross. And maybe illegal."

Millie opened the top of the trashcan nearest to her. A mass grave of unspoiled white flowers gleamed at her. She recoiled as if the profusion of blooms were body parts. "What the hell?" She closed the lid and opened the next can.

A laptop lay on top of a green plastic garbage bag. "That's just too weird." She pulled her phone from her pocket and took a few snaps to show her editor.

Lena grabbed the laptop and set it on a rolling tool trolley. "Really weird."

"That computer might be broken, and Rutledge has no idea how to fix it," Millie said. "Or it's Trudy's, and he destroyed the hard disk. Otherwise, why throw it away? Unless he's hiding it in the trash, so the police don't find it."

"Or snooping open-house visitors." Lena, as if to demonstrate the danger, opened the computer.

Millie reached over Lena's shoulder and pressed the power button. The screen brightened. "It works."

"This is definitely illegal." Lena stepped back.

"So is killing someone. Can we get in?"

"Killing? Is that what you think happened? He killed her?"

Millie pressed her lips together. "You don't?"

Lena typed in numbers for the passcode, and the home screen appeared.

"How did you know her passcode?" Millie asked.

"I guessed."

"How could you guess it in one try? Do you have super psychic powers you haven't told me about?"

"It's the day of our first kiss."

"You know the date?"

Lena closed her eyes as her cheeks pinked.

Mildly rebuked, Millie said, "How did you figure the passcode would be that date?"

"It's what I use."

Oh, crap. I'm treating this like a treasure hunt and the experience is devastating for Lena. Trudy obviously remembers the kiss the way Lena does—as the key that unlocks her. And now Lena might have lost her. That was a lot, but Millie couldn't quite relate, never having experienced any moment she would consider using as a secret password.

"He must be pissed he can't crack the password and search Trudy's laptop." Lena's voice quavered. "That's why he's throwing out the device."

Millie lifted her hair and fanned her neck with her hand. "If he's throwing out the laptop, he knows she's gone permanently. Otherwise, she'd kill him when she got home. So to speak."

"Do you think there's a chance she's still alive?"

"I . . . Check the date of her last email."

"I don't need to," Lena said. "She never would have gone anywhere without her laptop. Her appointment schedule is on it, her access to patient records. Trudy was always working. Her dedication to her patients is another thing I love about her. The laptop being here means she didn't leave of her own volition. Just like we said. Rutledge is trying to cover something up. Maybe he's got her tied up somewhere while he sells the house."

"Would emails she wrote from her phone show up on the laptop if the devices are synched?" Millie asked.

"Yes. She can access patient info on her phone also. But she hasn't sent me any texts or emails."

Millie opened Trudy's email app and scrolled down the incoming list. The doctor hadn't opened or responded to any of her thousand unread emails in nearly two weeks. "A bad sign if we're still hoping she's alive," Millie's said and instantly regretted.

"You just gutted my heart."

Millie waited a second out of sympathy. "Should we take the laptop as evidence to give the police?"

"I don't think so," Lena said. "I think we should leave it where it was for the police to find, otherwise we could have found it anywhere. You have that photo you can show them. It'll be date stamped. Maybe you should take another picture that shows where we are. Harmon's fingerprints will be on the laptop, and now so are ours. If we try to wipe ours off, we'll remove his also."

"Shit. I forgot about not getting our prints on it." Millie imagined Sheriff Hammersmith's ire when she learned they'd been snooping in Rutledge's garbage. "By the time the police get here, he'll have destroyed the laptop. He hid it here because—"

The kitchen door flew open. Ethel stood in the doorway frowning, her face red, eyes bulging. "I knew I shouldn't have trusted you. This is the second time I've caught you touching his things."

Lena snapped the laptop closed and clasped it to her chest. "This laptop's not his."

"It's hers," Millie said. "The laptop, it's Trudy's. It was in the trash." She waited for her punishment like a kid caught sneaking out the window after curfew.

"What was?" Ethel looked bewildered.

Lena held up the computer. "This laptop. It's Trudy's."

"How do you know that?"

"The passcode and all the emails are to Trudy."

"She didn't leave here voluntarily," Millie said.

"She didn't take any of her stuff," Lena added. "She didn't just run away or go to a conference or any of the million other excuses he's told everyone."

Ethel walked toward them, her eyes in slits. Millie couldn't decide whether to run or stand her ground. Ethel had a history of unexpected action and might clobber her with one of the shovels hanging along the garage wall.

But Ethel stopped mid-stride. Her face grayed, and her lips turned down. "You think he killed her, don't you? He killed her, and now he's trying to get away with it."

"That's what I think," Millie said.

"But she could've died by accident, and he buried the body somewhere."

Lena gave Ethel the side eye. "Why would he do that? And why would he report her *missing* if she died?"

"Why would he kill her to begin with?" Ethel asked. "Seems like she was a nice person."

"Money, jealousy." Millie glanced at Lena. "Insanity. The usual motives."

"The thing that always traps women in thrillers is that they stop to pack." Ethel raised her eyes to Millie's. "Or they go back into the house for their purse. Maybe Trudy's smarter than that, and she got away in time by not taking anything. She's deliberately disappeared."

"Oh, God." Lena rubbed her forehead. "I can't stand not knowing."

"But if he did kill her, are we supposed to do something about it?" Ethel asked. "I feel like I dropped both canoe paddles in the lake and have no idea how to get back to shore."

"We? You said you didn't want to help," Lena said.

"I changed my mind."

"Why?"

"I found something odd. Just now."

"What?" Millie and Lena asked at the same time.

"A red cell phone, the color of her expensive lipstick. Definitely not the color phone a man would use. It was on the floor under the night table next to the bed like it fell there when . . ." She shook her body and grimaced. "I found it when I was checking to make sure you hadn't stolen anything from the bedroom. He must have missed it when he cleaned." Ethel held up the phone.

"One of your open house guests could have dropped the phone," Millie said, although she was instantly sure the phone belonged to Trudy.

Lena snatched the bright red phone from Ethel and typed in the same passcode she'd used on the laptop. Nothing happened. "Oh, wait. It's out of juice. Millie, do you have . . . ?"

"Yeah," Millie said, reaching into her voluminous bag and pulling out a portable charger. "I always carry one, just in case."

Lena plugged in the phone and the three women stood watching the screen until it brightened. She typed in the passcode and the home screen displayed Trudy with her arm around Lena, both of them grinning as if they'd died and gone to heaven. Lena ducked her head. "Oh, God. It is Trudy's. She'd never leave voluntarily without her phone. As if we needed more proof."

Millie reached over Lena and tapped the mail icon. "Check the emails, just in case the devices aren't synched."

Lena opened the Mailbox menu on the small screen and scanned the Inbox, VIP, and Flagged tallies. "Same number of incoming emails . . . Wait. There's an email in Drafts."

"Open it."

"It's to me. Trudy was sending me an email."

"For God's sake," Ethel sputtered. "Read it out loud."

"It says, 'I'm getting out of here tomorrow. He's being scary. Can't say much now, but is it okay if I stay . . .' That's all there is." Lena's voice cracked. "He must have interrupted her, so the email went to Drafts when she dropped the phone. And after a while the phone powered off, so it didn't beep when she got notifications."

"We have to call the police," Ethel said. "Harmon shouldn't get away with this."

Millie blinked. "I agree. We have to tell the sheriff. It might work better if you do it, Ethel. Hammersmith will think I'm just trying to gin up a story."

"Oh, I . . ." Ethel's courage appeared to falter. "She might . . . I don't think it can be me, because of Charlie. The sheriff might think I have a conflict of interest."

"We should tell the authorities right now," Lena said. "If we do it together it'll sound less like one nosy woman trying to insert herself into an investigation."

"Right. Three nosy women are better than one," Ethel said.

"I agree," Millie said. "But the fact that Trudy didn't take any of her stuff with her isn't proof that she was killed. She's rich enough to buy a whole new wardrobe and all the devices she wants. If she's running away, it would be better for her to get a new phone and change her email address."

"But she wouldn't do that," Lena said. "She's not a hasty person."

"The sheriff's going to beat us up for sticking our noses where we shouldn't and getting our fingerprints on everything," Millie said. "She'll remind me it's the police who investigate crimes, and my job is to report what they find. Maybe we need more proof before we talk to her."

Ethel slipped the phone into her jacket pocket. "We're wasting time. The open house is over. Everyone's gone but you. Harmon will be back at any minute, and I don't think he should find you here." She opened the side door and scanned the road beyond the driveway. "Who knows what he'll do."

Lena put the laptop back on the garbage bag and closed the trash can lid. "So that's it? We think he killed or abducted Trudy, and we don't do anything about it?"

"Okay, okay. I'm calling." Millie clicked the number for Hammersmith's office and put the phone on speaker. "But don't expect the sheriff to do anything except yell at us." She put her hand on Lena's arm to soften the blow of what she was saying.

"Tell her I have Trudy's phone," Ethel said. "Maybe it's enough evidence to get her to do something."

They were quiet while the phone rang. A clerk answered and explained that Hammersmith wasn't in the office, her calls were being forwarded to the department, and she wasn't expected back until tomorrow.

Millie asked for Hammersmith's voice mail. "This is Millie Overbee from the *Daily*," she said to the sheriff's message system. "I've got information about the Trudy Davis case. Rutledge is selling his house and he's throwing out Trudy's laptop. Also, we found her cell phone with an unsent email and some other things she didn't take. She wouldn't have left of her own accord without her phone and laptop. I'm at the house now. Call me back as soon as you can."

Millie clicked off the call and regarded the disappointed faces of her fellow sleuths.

Ethel huffed. "This must be how Miss Marple felt every time she tried to tell the police what she knew, and they ignored her."

"We can't give up now, but I don't know what to do." Lena walked to her green Volkswagen bug and opened the driver's door. "I'll call you if I think of something," she shouted.

Millie waved goodbye.

"I'm still selling this house." Ethel's face was set.

"I understand. I'll let you know if the sheriff calls me back," Millie said. "Call me if you find anything else weird. And, be careful."

Ethel walked back into the house. Millie hurried to her car.

Trudy's laptop in the trash, the birth control pills, the cell phone, the unsent email, and the fact that the doctor didn't take any clothes on her supposed trip might be enough for the sheriff to get a search warrant for the house. Still, none of that was proof Harmon did anything to his wife. But if the police didn't act fast, he would get rid of everything incriminating.

This day hadn't been wasted, though. Millie had confirmed her suspicions, and even if she couldn't write about them, she had another data point in the story. She needed to bring her editor up to speed.

A quiver ran through her. After the bungled bank robbery, she'd interviewed Harmon, written about him, had him photographed and lionized without realizing he was a killer. She felt like an idiot. The paper, her editor, the whole community would be mortified for applauding him if he turned out to be a murderer. On the other hand, if he wasn't a murderer, she might be sued for libel, lose her job, and have to move home with her parents, which was way worse than writing obits or covering father-daughter dances.

CHAPTER 30

SIX sleeps, a dozen British baking shows, and sixteen hours of playing Royal Match on his phone later, Charlie still hadn't figured out his next move. He couldn't just hang around in Emmitsburg for another week without going crazy. He slid off the bed in the cheap motel room, opened the orange plastic notebook lying on the small round table, and flipped through menus from nearby eateries. He had nothing else to do; he might as well eat.

Running his finger down the menu items from Pat's Burgers, he chose the two franks and beans meal with french fries and coleslaw, added a soda, and a piece of chocolate layer cake for dessert. Using Trudy's credit card to pay for his meal didn't bother him. It had worked so far.

The chirpy voice on the other end of the call took the card number without a qualm and said Charlie's order would be delivered to his room in thirty minutes or less. He experienced a swell of satisfaction. At least he could feed himself, an accomplishment of sorts.

It was Sunday, a week since he'd made the colossal mistake of dumping Trudy Davis's dead body in a golf course parking lot and stealing her car. Before that moment, he'd been following orders, using the car as directed. Since then, he'd taken ten showers, bought new clothes, gotten his hair cut, had the car detailed twice, and clipped his nose hairs, but the stink still clung to him. Then again, that might just be his conscience.

There was no coming back from that mess. Even though being picked up by the police for skipping town while on parole and disposing of a dead body would be bad, if his stepmother ever found out, she'd never speak to him again. And if Ethel didn't, who would pay for his room and board? He'd be homeless again. Unless the state planned on giving him room and board for the foreseeable future.

Lying back in the motel bed with his hands under his head, Charlie stared at the water-stained dropped ceiling. Canned television show laughter came through the wall from the next room. Being on the run was dead boring. How did criminals manage it? Drinking and smoking gave them the illusion of doing something. They must work out and play cards.

He had switched motels again yesterday without knowing why except he thought that was what a bad guy on the run would do. Good thing he'd kept Trudy's driver's license. The name on the license matched the name on the credit card, and he told the motel clerks his mother was in the car asleep. They always bought it. He got off the bed and peered into the mirror. It was possible he had one of those innocent faces.

Eventually he would have to leave Emmitsburg, get out of Maryland, and go far away from West Virginia, like to Wyoming. He needed a plan, though, and planning was his weak suit, which was why he always put off doing it as long as possible. He had gotten as far as consulting a map on his phone. That was a start; he was taking initiative. Pennsylvania was the closest state to this motel, minutes away if he drove north on Route 15. Gettysburg was practically over the next hill. He chided himself for not having paid enough attention in fifth grade geography class or he would've known this fact at the beginning of his getaway.

He sat on the bed and studied the map. Pennsylvania was a big state. A man could get lost in it, but not if he was driving a white Volvo the police were searching for, as Charlie assumed they were. There was one thing to do: he had to ditch the car, and that meant he had to find another way to run.

Maybe he could buy a used car—an old Jeep, nothing flashy—with Trudy's credit card and trade in the Volvo. Except he couldn't prove he owned the car without his name on the title or registration, so not. His best option for getting rid of the vehicle was to leave it on the street with the keys in it. After a few days, an enterprising kid would snag it.

Charging a high-dollar item on Trudy's card was an iffy proposition. So far, Charlie had had no difficulty buying motel rooms, clothes, food, and even the outrageously expensive funeral bouquet he'd sent to Harmon just to tweak the bastard for forcing him into this tough spot.

Strange how stealing a dead woman's money didn't bother him. It wasn't like she'd ever miss it. He also didn't worry about who would pay the credit card bill, and he got deep pleasure from imagining an infuriated Harmon forking over real dollars to cover the bill, which was a small bonus for doing that miserable job of disposing of a body by himself.

What was Trudy's credit limit, anyway? She was a doctor, raking in the bucks. He imagined her limit was fairly high. Maybe he could figure out how to buy a used car online and have the vehicle delivered to the motel. Identity thieves did this all the time without getting caught. How hard could it be?

If he went to a car lot in person, he would get the one salesman who picked up the phone to check the limit on the card and whether Charlie was authorized to use it. He pictured the place besieged by police, blue lights flashing, men leaping out of their vehicles with guns pointed at him. Charlie shook his head. No point in risking it.

A better option would be to find a log cabin off a dirt road that backed to the Susquehannock State Forest where he might hide out for a year or five. He'd have to ask Google about the statute of limitations on prosecuting someone for disposing of a dead body and stealing a car, so he'd know how long to stay there. But he could imagine the cabin, which meant it must exist somewhere. It would be dusty inside, inhabited by a few mice and a fair number of spiders, and dark at night because there'd be no electricity. There'd be a wood stove, a useable outhouse, and a hand pump for water in the front yard.

Charlie imagined himself sitting on the porch, tilted back in a wooden chair, watching the sun going down in the valley. He could get a guitar, not that he knew how to play, but he'd have five years to figure it out. Nobody would find him there. The cabin would have to have been abandoned by its owner so that no one else showed up unexpectedly.

He'd stock up on supplies he'd need, like an ax to chop wood, toilet paper, canned food, and maybe a couple books because his phone would run out of juice. He'd be good to go, at least until Trudy's cards were canceled.

Charlie assumed the police would eventually have better things to do than hunt for him. No one would guess he had taken Trudy's car, except Harmon and Don. What could they do about it without incriminating themselves? He did experience some minor discomfort, like an itch in the middle of his back, that his escape plan depended on his co-conspirators being bad people.

Charlie flopped onto his side and remembered how he'd felt like a jerk standing at the locked gate of the landfill. He knew the plan was whacked the minute Don said they had to meet a guy behind the rec center to get instructions. And then the guy turned out to be the vice president of the bank they'd tried to rob. How many alarm bells did he need?

The better angel on his shoulder was shrinking, her voice getting thinner and thinner until she couldn't even squeak. Which made him think of his lawyer, Angela, and what she would say about his stealing a car and leaving the state, not to mention dumping a dead body for money and using someone's credit card without their permission. Which was sort of like robbing a bank. The deal Angela had worked out with the prosecutor was probably blown. She'd be mad at him and wouldn't like him anymore, and that sucked, because for days Charlie had been fantasizing about her hand on his arm and the soft look in her eyes.

He got off the bed and stared out the window at the motel parking lot, seeing not the few cars parked there but the tall pine trees fronting the landfill and the paved road curving around like he was going to end up somewhere beautiful instead of a dump.

And then it hit him. Harmon knew the dump would be closed and deliberately didn't tell them. He wanted them to get caught. Charlie paced the small room. *That sonofabitch is going to get away with murdering his wife.* And he was going to point the finger at Don and Charlie. He stopped pacing. *What if I return the car to Harmon's house and leave it in the driveway?*

That move would drive the monster crazy. If the car was in his own driveway, Harmon wouldn't be able to report Charlie for having taken it. He could hitch back to the motel in Charles Town like nothing had ever happened. He'd be there for the court date, etcetera, etcetera. This idea was a cool breeze wafting over his sweaty body on a hot beach. Maybe for once, he could outsmart someone.

Someone knocked on the door. Charlie whirled around, and without thinking opened the door. The food delivery person was putting a plastic bag on the doorstep. Charlie thanked the kid, handed him two bucks for a tip, and surveyed the parking lot. Three women were getting out of an unfamiliar car. He could swear one of them was Ethel. He froze.

Forgetting to close the door, Charlie spun around, gathered up everything he'd brought into the room, and shoved it all into the plastic bags. So what if he was leaving a mess of food wrappers and receipts on the floor. The maids were paid to clean up the mess, weren't they? He pulled on his sneakers, dropped the bags out of the bathroom window and climbed after them, falling onto the grass behind the building.

Sliding along the back wall of the motel, Charlie rounded the corner and spied on the manager's office. Trudy's car was parked behind the motel out of sight, fifty feet from him. Charlie clicked open the doors with the remote key fob and dashed to the car. He threw himself into the driver's seat and swerved out of the lot.

CHAPTER 31

THE bell on the door tinkled. Millie, Ethel, and Lena entered the small motel office, their third stop in Emmitsburg since they'd agreed to check out Lena's hunch that Trudy had taken refuge in the B&B where they'd stayed before.

"I won't believe she's dead," Lena had said over the phone the night of the open house. "I think Ethel's conjecture that she fled and is hiding from Harmon is correct. If she went anywhere of her own volition, it's there. We should check it out."

"Sheriff Hammersmith did say Trudy's credit card was used in Emmitsburg," Millie said. "That's fifty miles from Charles Town. She had to stay somewhere."

After their first disappointment, they continued to search for Trudy based on that assumption but with increasing dismay.

Millie's editor had laughed when she checked with him about the road trip. "You get points for digging through his trash and finding the laptop," he'd said. "But you need real proof he did something to his wife, not guesses. I'd follow the trail the sheriff identified."

She took that as an okay and included Ethel on the jaunt. Ethel might know things about Rutledge that no one else knew. She'd spent more time in his creepy house and might stumble upon the one fact that made the pieces of Trudy Davis's disappearance fit together.

"They attempted quaint," Millie said, glancing at the knotty pine paneling and wooden blinds in the motel office. A mild mildew smell alternated with whiffs of floral air freshener. She scrutinized the image inlaid on the countertop through its protective plastic sheath, then bounced her palm on the bell. "This place is a throwback to 1950s movie sets."

"Yeah, like *Dial M for Murder*," Lena said.

Ethel rubbed the leathery leaves of three listing rubber tree plants in matching white pots lined up on the floor in front of a grimy picture window. "These aren't getting enough light." She stared out the window and pointed. "Wait. Look. Do you see that car?"

Millie turned toward Ethel. "What car?"

"The one that just blew by here," Ethel said. "The white one."

"I'll bet she's not here either," Lena said. When Trudy hadn't been registered at the Ramble Inn and no one at the desk recognized the woman in the photo Lena showed them, her positive mood had turned morose.

"I didn't see a car." Millie shrugged one shoulder. She was now sure Trudy was dead, and this trip was a mistake. But Lena was better off living with foolish hope than certain knowledge, and Millie didn't mind being a happy idiot. She should have just called Sheriff Hammersmith again, told her their conjectures, and left the sleuthing to the police. It was that damn curiosity gene that got her into these situations.

"I've got a weird feeling about this place," Ethel said. "Lena, did you see that white car?"

Lena raised her eyebrows but said nothing.

"Can I help you?" A young girl emerged from a back room and stepped behind the counter. No makeup, brown hair in braids, a sparkle in her eyes, and what Millie thought of as the dew of optimism still blooming on her cheeks. Millie guessed she was a university student clerking at the motel part-time who envisioned a future far from this wood-paneled box.

"Is Trudy Davis a guest here?" Millie asked. "We're supposed to meet her, but I forgot her room number."

Ethel whipped around to gape at Millie. Lena smiled, already accustomed to Millie's methods, and put her finger on her mouth to stifle Ethel's comment. "She's trying a new tactic," she whispered in Ethel's ear.

The girl pressed the keys on her computer and stared at the screen. "I don't see her listed as one of our guests."

Lena held up her phone and a photo of Trudy beamed from the screen. "Have you seen this woman?"

"No. I would remember if we had any guests that old because of special accommodations."

"You think she's old?" Lena gasped.

Ethel rolled her eyes. "I'm old. That woman is in the prime of her life."

Millie stifled a giggle. "Maybe her husband registered for them," she said. "He might have used her credit card. Could you check the credit card information you have for the last, uh, five days?"

Lena tilted her head and widened her eyes, an expression Millie took to mean, *where'd you get that idea?*

"I can't give you credit card information. One person registered in the last five days and he's a man. He came in yesterday. So cute." She sighed and looked past them. "He said he was the son of the lady whose credit card he used. He lost his ID, so he showed me hers." The receptionist stared into the distance as if lost in a dream.

"Remind me to cut up all my credit cards," Ethel muttered.

"Cute?" Lena's mouth twisted.

Millie cleared her throat. "That's it. He's her son. What room are they in?"

"Room 110 on the street level. Go left out of the office, ten doors down."

"Thanks so much," Millie said.

"But—" Ethel's eyes were full of questions.

Lena bumped Ethel with her elbow. "Not now."

"Come on," Millie said, signaling with her hand for them to keep up. She loped out of the office toward the room.

Ethel, scurrying behind Millie and Lena, called out, "It's not possible Harmon is with her. I just spoke with him this morning about an offer for the house. Anyway, he told the police he didn't know where she was. I can't believe he stashed her up here while he sold the house. Did he drug her? Why would he say she's missing if he knew where she was? It was in the paper. This doesn't make any sense . . ."

"I don't believe Harmon brought her to this motel." Lena's voice faltered. She turned in a circle. "Trudy would never have stayed in a place like this no-tell motel if it were up to her. Maybe he's keeping her prisoner while he sells the house."

"I don't think it's Harmon," Millie said. "No one would call him cute and swoon like that."

Ethel stared at Millie. "Did anyone see the car I saw right when we went into the office? Wasn't a description of that car in the newspaper?"

"Are you still talking about the car?" Millie tried to peer through the drawn plastic blackout curtains on room number 110. It was impossible to see inside the room. She knocked and they waited.

"Now you're being too polite." Lena pushed the door, and it swung inward. They huddled in the doorway of the dark room, their eyes adjusting from the bright sunlight outside.

"Hello," Millie said.

No answer, and no Trudy, no Harmon, no suitcase, nobody. But someone had slept in the bed. The room smelled of fast food and potato chips. Ethel rushed into the bathroom. "There's nothing here," she called out. "But the window is open."

Lena pushed open the closet's faux wood accordion door. "Nothing. If she was ever here, she already left."

Millie checked under the bed and opened the drawer in the nightstand. "This is a futile enterprise. I don't know what I expected to find, or what we'd do if we found it. But I sure don't think either Harmon or Trudy was ever here. Let's go home."

Lena's eyes filled with tears. "You're just giving up?"

"There's nothing left to do here. Trudy isn't in Emmitsburg. The sheriff got it wrong. We can stop at the farmers' market off Route 15 so the day won't be a total loss. I heard they have great homemade strawberry-rhubarb pie."

"How can you eat at a time like this?" Lena started out the door.

"I can eat at any time." Millie smiled, hoping to elicit one from Lena.

Ethel glanced around the room one final time. "Some people are disgusting." She scooped a piece of paper off the floor, smoothed it out, and stared at the contents. "Wait a minute. I recognize this handwriting."

Millie leaned over Ethel's shoulder at a handwritten list of addresses and a license plate number for a white Volvo. "Wasn't it a white Volvo you spotted five minutes ago?"

"Yes." Ethel said. "I remember it distinctly."

"Did it have West Virginia plates?" Millie asked.

Ethel blinked. "Well, I saw it from the front, and West Virginia cars don't have a license plate on the front. Lena do you recognize the license plate 'one W-V-D-O-C'?"

"Yes," Lena said. "It's Trudy's vanity plate. She was so proud of being a doctor." Her lower lip trembled.

"What kind of car does she drive?"

"A white Volvo."

"Well," Millie said, "either Trudy is alive or someone else is driving her car, just like the sheriff said."

"What do you mean?" Lena asked.

Ethel held the paper in both hands and read aloud.

White Volvo, license plate 1WV_DOC

Spot 105, Green, BWI airport long-term parking lot B, 7161 Aviation Boulevard, Ferndale, Maryland

Alpha Ridge Landfill, 2350 Marriottsville Road, Marriottsville, Maryland (in Howard County)

Turf Valley Golf Club, 2700 Turf Valley Road, Ellicott City, Maryland

"THAT had to be Trudy's car I saw."

Millie pulled up the map app on her phone and typed in the addresses listed on the paper one at a time. She stared at the tiny map on her screen, zooming in and out. "Did the person who was in this room drive Trudy's car seventy-six miles from her home to the airport in southeast Baltimore and then turn around and go northwest to a dump and then a golf course before they drove another fifty-five miles to Emmitsburg?"

"For that matter," Ethel said, "why would Trudy go to a landfill in a different state? This is a bizarre to-do list."

Millie rubbed her eyes. "I don't think it was Trudy who made any of these trips. Not driving, anyway."

Lena held her hand out for the paper. "You're right. This couldn't be Trudy's list. If she needed to throw something away, she would have gone to Leetown, twenty minutes from her house. Why would she write down her own license plate number? And why on earth would she go to a golf course? She doesn't play golf. Anyway, this isn't her handwriting."

"That printing is Harmon's. I saw it on the nasty note he left me yesterday," Ethel said. "And, it was a man, not a woman, driving that car just now."

Millie paced the room. "Then it had to be Harmon driving the car. Unless Trudy gave her car to someone else who drove her here. But then, where is she?" She shook her head. "I can't put these pieces together."

"You have to tell the sheriff about the note," Lena said.

Millie sat in the one chair in the room and called Sheriff Hammersmith to tell her where they were and what they'd found. She was immediately shunted to voice mail.

"Hey," she recorded, "This is Millie Overbee. I've been trying to reach you. This is important. We're in Emmitsburg, Maryland, and I think we've found a clue in the Trudy Davis case, but I don't know what to do next. If you could call me back right now, I'd appreciate it."

Millie clicked off the call feeling downright ineffectual. "I think maybe we shouldn't hang out in the room, in case we're messing up evidence the police will need." She ran her hand along the shelf in the closet and pulled down a clear plastic laundry bag. "I'll put this note in the bag so we don't get any more of our prints on it."

"I agree. Let's sit in the car and see if the sheriff calls you back." Lena headed out of the room.

Ten minutes later, Millie's phone rang. Without preamble, Sheriff Hammersmith said, "You can stop looking for Trudy Davis."

CHAPTER 32

THE memory of spending the midnight hour at a private golf course disposing of a dead body ran on an endless loop in Charlie's mind. As he'd climbed out of the car that night, a fox had screamed, scaring him out of his skin. House lights had twinkled between trees in the distance, but the clubhouse and parking lot had been dark. He'd waited, standing there, hoping a fairy godmother would save him. But he'd had only his own counsel to advise him, and that never worked out.

Galvanized by simmering rage for having been duped by Harmon Rutledge and abandoned by Don, Charlie had popped the Volvo's trunk. Stink enveloped him. He staggered away from the car. His eyes burned; he gagged. He pulled his T-shirt over his nose. Telling himself to breathe through his mouth, he flipped on his phone's flashlight app to see what he was dealing with.

A woman in a pale, shiny nightgown had been folded into the trunk. Her skin was slimy. Her mouth gaped open as if she were surprised to see him. At least her eyes were closed. Charlie closed his also and imagined pulling the body out of the car the way he'd seen soldiers carry wounded comrades in movies.

He yanked the hood of his sweatshirt over his head, pulled it tight under his chin, and tied it. Glad he'd remembered to wear gloves, he put his hands under her arms, grasped her body, and tried to make her sit. She was unbelievably heavy. Her arms flopped. Her head plopped against his chest. He shuddered and dropped her.

She fell back into the trunk with a thud. He took three deep breaths and tried again. Hoping he could pull the body out of the trunk without getting her slimy skin on him, Charlie yanked the corpse's arms. The body rose four inches, and something popped as if her arms had come out of the shoulder sockets. He dropped her again and walked in circles for a minute, taking huge gulps of clean air.

Determined to win this struggle, Charlie turned his face away from the body, held his breath, and wrapped his arms around her waist, shifting the body so he couldn't see her face. Then he pulled her left leg over the lip of the trunk. When the leg stayed where he'd placed it, he grabbed the right leg and yanked it over the edge. He stepped back and assessed. Both legs were sticking out of the trunk, her bare feet dangling a foot beyond the car. So far, so good. Charlie stepped between her legs, reached into the car and grabbed her hips, tugging until the body balanced on the lip of the trunk. With one final yank, he hauled her out of the car and dropped her. She gaped at him from the ground. He gagged.

This is the total worst.

Looking around in all directions to make sure no one was watching, Charlie listened for any sound—a rustling in the leaves, the click of a gun. Nothing. He imagined his father standing there, shaking his head in disgust. *Just get it done.*

Charlie grasped her ankles, hoping no part of her would come loose and dragged the body onto the grass at the edge of the asphalt parking lot. Her head bobbed as he pulled her across the uneven surface. He looked away.

When he'd maneuvered the body onto the grassy embankment at the edge of the parking lot, Charlie tugged the nightgown down over her knees and placed her hands at her sides so she'd be more presentable when someone found her in the morning. Thinking she was still too exposed, he covered the body with a thermal blanket he found in the trunk.

"Sorry about this," he whispered. "Hope no critters nibble on you before the police find you." To make double sure nothing would get at her, but staying arm's length away with his head turned, he tucked the blanket under the side of her body closest to him.

Charlie tossed the gloves and hoodie in the trunk, but the putrid smell clung to him. It would never come off. He'd have to get rid of his clothes, take a shower, shave his head, and pluck his nose hairs. And get the car cleaned twice.

He removed the driver's license for Trudy Davis, the checkbook, credit cards, and a couple hundred in cash from her wallet to repay himself for having to do this job alone and went to place the handbag next to the body. Except the body was no longer where he'd left it.

His breath stopped in his throat. *Where the hell is she? She can't have gotten up and stalked off. The last thing I need is a vengeful zombie.*

His heart banged away in his chest like it was trying to escape. Working hard to collect his wits, Charlie took a deep breath and looked around. The parking lot's grassy verge bordered a ravine. *She must've rolled down there.*

Slowly, anxious about what he might find, he stepped sideways down the steep embankment until he saw the body, now cocooned in the blanket, jammed against a tree trunk halfway down the hill. *That works for me.* Breathing hard, he tossed the bag in the general direction of her body and scrambled up to the lot. By the time he got back to the Volvo, he was shaking so hard he had to wait a minute to start the vehicle.

I am now an accessory to murder. Anywhere on earth was safer than Charles Town. He'd headed north on the highway with no idea where he was going until he landed in Emmittsburg. A week and three motels later, he was still clueless and on the run. He'd never be free of his fear that he'd be caught and jailed. To make matters worse, Ethel had just pointed her finger right at him and yelled as he skidded out of the motel parking lot.

After driving aimlessly around town for an hour, eating the hotdog and fries he'd had delivered to his room, his heart still pounded. *Does Ethel know what I did? Is she looking for me?* Finding himself at the university on the west side of Route 15 ten miles from the motel, he pulled into a visitor's parking spot, and sat in the car, trembling and unsure what to do next, which, like the lingering dead-body stink in the Volvo, summed up the problem with his entire life.

It might be safe here. It was unlikely he'd be spotted by anyone who knew him in a state where he'd never lived or gone to school. Staring at the blazing red, gold, and orange trees massed along the mountain ridge, Charlie realized he'd forgotten it was autumn. A shaft of sunlight illuminated the head of a huge gold-leafed statue rising above the tree line, its hand out in an offering of benediction to the entire campus below. After staring at the statue for ten seconds, Charlie recognized the iconic image of the Virgin Mary his mother had talked about and remembered she'd said there was a sacred grotto here.

Charlie had no particular religious connection to the statue, but with two hours of daylight to kill before he was willing to get back on the road, he had to do something. Sitting in the car all that time would be suspicious. While he was thinking that, a student walking to her car shot him curious looks. Charlie's heart rate accelerated. *She's going to report me!*

He raced out of the university lot and made a right onto St. Anthony's Road, following the signs to a much smaller gravel parking lot where he pulled the car into a marked spot. This felt safer; police were unlikely to search for Trudy's car here. To make sure no one who spotted the Volvo associated him with it, he got out of the car. The single option left was to walk to the shrine. At least, Ethel would never look for him in the woods.

The hike would settle his jitters and help him figure out what was supposed to happen next. Anyway, if he was going to live in a cabin in the woods, he'd better build up his outdoor skills. Maybe walking in the fresh air would yield a course of action that got him farther than from one parking lot to another but deciding anything was his weak suit. The last time he'd felt safe making any decision was before his mom died in a car accident when he was nine.

Ethel had come too damn close to finding him. What else besides the fact that she was looking for him explained her presence in Emmitsburg? And how did she know where he was? His stepmother didn't trust him to do anything. It wasn't like he was ten years old anymore. He hated being checked on, particularly when he was doing something he'd been told not to do.

That irritation was enough emotional thrust to get him away from the car. Charlie stomped over to the visitors center's welcome sign. The mountain path was still open, and he could visit the grotto. The brochure suggested the spring had healing powers. He was thirsty anyway after those fries, so he might as well drink the water in case it would take away his pain.

He found the well-trod path and trudged along the mountain, thinking about the gruesome task he'd completed for a measly one hundred bucks. Harmon, Charlie thought as he walked, had wanted his wife's body to be found. *He gave us the job because he knew we'd screw it up and get caught, and no one would believe we didn't kill her.*

Charlie stopped on the grotto path and listened for footsteps. What if Ethel had spotted the car in the university lot? Maybe she was following him right now. A white Volvo on black asphalt would stick out like Ethel's red geraniums in front of her white clapboard house. Charlie shrugged. *Too late now.*

A rushing sound, like rain pouring from a downspout, came from nearby. He walked toward it. The path opened to a cement and flagstone walkway that led him to a row of benches in the center of four stone nooks containing various religious statues and racks of flickering votive candles. Charlie lowered his internal voice to be polite.

A sign identified this place as the grotto. Three people were praying by the wall of a man-made cave. It struck Charlie that what made a place sacred was the belief of the people who prayed there. *All that faith must have a special energy.*

As he turned around to walk away, a small girl in rainbow-colored tights, a pink T-shirt, lilac hoodie, orange shorts, and pink Crocs spoke to him. "Would you help me reach the water?"

Charlie looked around for her parents or guardians. Child molester was the last thing he needed to add to his criminal resume. "Uh, where's your mom?"

"She died." The child said the words so simply, Charlie didn't register their meaning for a second. Instead, he concentrated on the shine of her dark curls.

"Well, you're not here alone, right? Someone had to bring you."

"My grannie brought me, but she's busy helping Grandad with his chair." The child pointed to a white-haired man seated in a wheelchair and a woman fussing at the blanket in his lap.

Charlie wondered why the kid had picked him. More reliable adults than he must have been available, like the ones who were praying. Praying had to be a testament to a person's character, didn't it? Maybe she picked him because he wasn't praying. She tugged on his hand and pointed. "The water's over there. It's too high for me. Can you lift me?"

He could feel himself caving, but before he did what the kid asked, he should ask her grandparents if it was okay. "What's your name?"

"Mia."

"How old are you?"

"Seven."

Charlie took Mia's offered hand and matched her unexpectedly swift pace over to the grandparents. "Excuse me," he said in his politest voice, "Mia says she'd like me to lift her up to drink the water. Is it okay?" Ennobled by the simple act of asking, regardless of what the old couple said, Charlie felt he was finally doing something the right way.

"Sure," her grandmother said. "Stay where I can see you."

The grandfather looked glum, reminding Charlie his own father was dead and he'd never gotten to say he was sorry for driving him crazy. Holding Mia's hand, which made him feel ridiculously necessary and strong, Charlie hit on the idea that he might have made a mess of his life to get even with his father. *Nah. That's too deep for me.*

He and Mia marched over to the brass plaque announcing, "Grotto Spring Water." The woman ahead of them was filling a gallon plastic jug from the faucet embedded in the rock. Charlie and Mia looked at each other. He could have sworn Mia was thinking the same word as he was—greedy. They giggled.

When the woman left, he gripped Mia around her waist, reminding himself to be gentle, and lifted her above the stone fountain so her hands could reach the water coming from the spout. She was surprisingly light and smelled like apples. The child cupped her hands, let the water fill them, and slurped it from her palms.

He tried to ignore the warm feeling in his gut. "Okay?" Charlie asked.

Mia's head bobbed. He lowered her gently until her feet were on the ground.

Mia wiped her hands on her shorts. "Your turn."

"You mean I should drink the water?"

She rolled her eyes. "Well, yeah. That's what you came here for, wasn't it?"

Charmed by their fellowship, Charlie imitated Mia, cupping his palm and leaning over to drink, slurping cold water that tasted mildly of moss and minerals into his mouth.

"Ta dah." He winked. "Am I magically different?"

Mia smiled. "I should think so."

After Charlie said his goodbyes, he knew what he needed to do next. Tomorrow he would do one more thing right. He would drive Trudy's car back to her house. Her address was on her license. He'd park the car in the driveway, leave the keys in the ignition, the credit cards and license on the seat, and walk the ten miles to his motel in Charles Town. He should have done it a week ago with the body in the car, but better late than never.

Maybe it was half a good thing, because he had no intention of telling the police he'd dumped the body at a golf course for a measly one-hundred dred dollars. He'd have to remember to wipe his prints off everything before he left the Volvo in Trudy's driveway.

The best thing about this plan was Harmon would have a lot of explaining to do, and Charlie would be where he was supposed to be when Ethel came to collect him for court. Finally, he would have a mark in the win column. Tonight, he'd get a room in the motel outside Frederick just to calm down. Fortunately, this new leaf didn't require him to stop using Trudy's credit card right away.

CHAPTER 33

"TRUDY Davis is dead."

With Millie's phone on speaker in the small car, Sheriff Hammersmith's voice reverberated like the sound of the last nail banged into a coffin.

A gasp came from Ethel in the back seat. Lena went pale.

"How do you know she's dead?" Millie's reporter brain zoomed into fifth gear, *Get the details on the record.*

I've got it, holy cow, I've got it! Pulling a notebook and pen from her bag, Millie scribbled as fast as she could, jotting down the date and time, who she was talking to, and what the sheriff said. The sheriff had called *her.* Everything she said was on the record and for attribution if she didn't specify otherwise. Millie had the scoop on the Trudy Davis disappearance, and it was a killer.

"Because I'm staring at her body in the state morgue in Baltimore," Hammersmith said.

"You mean, in Maryland?" Millie asked. "Not in a Howard County landfill or golf course?"

"That's some guess. How did you know about the golf course?" Hammersmith asked.

"From this piece of paper we found in a motel room in Emmitsburg that I just called to tell you about." Millie waved the plastic baggie in the air as if they were on FaceTime and Hammersmith could see her. "Are you sure it's Trudy?"

Hammersmith answered even though she sounded a bit miffed. "Aside from the fact that the corpse looks like her photograph, her practice manager identified her from a photo my deputy showed her. Also,

Davis's AMA card was in the purse next to the body, and we have her fingerprints," Hammersmith said.

"Trudy's prints are on file somewhere?"

"With the West Virginia Board of Medicine. It's required for their background check."

"You didn't ask Rutledge to identify his wife?"

"No."

Millie digested that fact. *Hammersmith suspects Rutledge; that's what she's not saying.* "Do the clothes she was wearing match the ones described in the BOLO?"

"No."

This process was like tiptoeing backwards in high heels over creek stones in high water. The sheriff would answer the questions Millie asked, but she wouldn't volunteer anything, even the most important information. *I need the color, beyond the basic who, what, where, when.* "What was she wearing when she was found?"

"A nightgown," Hammersmith said.

Millie wrote down *wearing nightgown not clothes* in her notes. "So she didn't drive away from home?"

"We don't know," Hammersmith said.

"Well, who drives around in a nightgown? What inference do you draw from that?"

"None. I'm waiting for the facts."

Millie heard the rebuke but plowed on. "How'd she get to Maryland in a nightgown if she wasn't driving?"

"You've hit the million dollar question," Hammersmith said.

Lena pulled on Millie's arm and mouthed, "Ask when they found her."

"When did they find her?"

"Howard County deputies were called last Wednesday morning."

Lena moaned into her hands. "Trudy's been dead a whole week," she whispered.

"Who called the Howard County police?" Millie asked.

"Some kids found her and went running to their parents."

If Millie had been standing, she would've paced in circles. The car was too small for this feeling growing inside her. She took a swig from her water bottle, barely resisting the urge to leap out. *I've been looking for Trudy in the wrong places. My guesses were totally off-base. I'm a crap detective.*

"Ask her how she knew Trudy was in Howard County," Ethel said.

Before Millie could oblige, the sheriff said, "The Howard County sheriff called me. The body and AMA photo ID found with it seemed to match the description in our missing person's BOLO. Howard County notified me on Thursday about a possible match, but they were backed up and didn't get fingerprint confirmation until today."

"Where did they find her?"

"At a golf course. Where are *you*?"

"We're at a motel in Emmitsburg. So, you've known for three days?"

Hammersmith didn't answer her question. "Who's we? And why are you in Emmitsburg? Isn't that way off your beat?"

"Lena and Ethel are with me. Because you said . . . Never mind, long story."

"I've got time. I'm waiting for the state medical examiner's office to hand over the official autopsy report that cites cause of death. Spill."

Millie inhaled. "Well, you said Trudy's car was in Emmitsburg, and Lena, Trudy's friend from work—"

"Wait. The Lena Cruz from the clinic who Davis was having an affair with?"

"Yes."

"Shit."

"Anyway, Lena remembered a B&B where they used to stay in Emmittsburg, and we'd already found Trudy's laptop and her phone, and—"

"For all you know, Lena could have been the one who killed her."

Millie gasped as she glanced at Lena.

Turning pale, mouth open, eyes closed, Lena shook her head. "Oh, God. Never, I would never."

"Wait," Hammersmith said. "You found her phone?"

"Well, Ethel did."

"Ethel? Ethel Goodman, the wannabe superhero from the bank robbery?"

"Yes. I told you."

"What a friggin' nightmare. You messed with my probable crime scene, didn't you?"

"Yeah, well, you weren't doing anything and Ethel held an open house, so . . . Wait. You're saying Trudy was killed at home? Then who's driving her car?"

Lena rocked back and forth, a hand over her mouth. "I've been fooling myself that she was alive all this time," she mumbled.

Hammersmith rolled over Millie's question. "So you three numbnuts tromped through Rutledge's house messing with possible evidence? Ethel held an open house? For the public? Damn. We'll never sort out those prints and fibers, not to mention DNA. Everything's contaminated. Rutledge is a genius. I should charge you with conspiracy to interfere with an investigation."

"It wasn't, we didn't intend . . ." Millie, impressed by the array of inventive curses the sheriff uttered, waited for her to finish. "But besides us spotting a white Volvo, the motel clerk here says Rutledge registered, so we went to his room and—"

"What? You what? Is that the Hideaway Hotel in Emmittsburg? You messed with a second crime scene? You're a one-woman wrecking ball."

"Geez. . . Well, three of us, a three-woman wrecking ball, to give credit where credit's due. Wait, how did you know the name of the hotel?"

"Dr. Davis's credit card was used there after the body was found."

"Oh, of course, you were tracking that. But are you saying Trudy was murdered at home? Can you confirm that? Is Rutledge now your primary suspect? Or was there a break-in and an abduction? How was she killed? And who transported her body to a Howard County golf club?"

"Whoa. Slow down. I did not say she was murdered at home. I specifically did not say she was killed."

Millie wrote *denying she said killed* in her notebook as muffled sounds of someone talking to the sheriff came from her phone. Millie no longer regretted her sloppy sleuthing methods. She'd been right. There was a story in Trudy's disappearance, and she'd be the first one to publish it. She had the scoop and needed to call her editor ASAP.

"What does she mean?" Lena's eyes were already red-rimmed and puffy.

"What's the address there?" Hammersmith asked.

Millie cringed at the sheriff's tone and gave her the motel's address. "What's happening?"

"We have the cause of death."

"What is it? How did Trudy die? When? Where?" Millie had to ask, even if the answers made Lena suffer.

Hammersmith inhaled. "Not natural or accidental. She died by suffocation. About two weeks ago. Obviously, the killer is still at large. Which could mean the three of you rubberneckers are in danger. I'm coming to where you are. Don't move. Don't go back in the room. Do not call Rutledge for a comment. And don't lose that friggin piece of paper. It's evidence. I'll be there in sixty minutes."

Before Millie could ask who suffocated Trudy, the sheriff disconnected.

Lena's face was blank with shock. Whatever Millie said next would ring in Lena's ears for years. The responsibility felt enormous; she wasn't ready to be this grown up. "I'm sorry." Millie closed her eyes so she wouldn't see Lena's face. "I'm so sorry."

Ethel leaned forward from the back seat and patted Lena's shoulder. "I knew it. I knew he killed her. Two weeks ago. She was already dead when the boys tried to rob the bank."

"Looks like it, at least according to the medical examiner," Millie said. "But the sheriff says she doesn't know who did it."

"Phooey. Trudy was dead when Harmon contracted with me to sell the house," Ethel said. "The sheriff is right. He used me to cover his tracks."

"How can you talk about it like this?" Lena wrenched open the car door. "He . . . that monster, of course he did it."

A sound like nothing Millie had ever heard escaped from Lena. She leaped out of the car, shrieks wrenched from her as if against her will, and in a wild frenzy she pounded on the hood, kicked the tires, and slammed her body against the vehicle. Her lament went on and on.

Millie's mouth twisted with the effort not to cry. She had never before had to comfort a grieving woman. The feeling of helplessness was overwhelming. She glanced at Ethel, whose face had gone pale. They shook their heads in unison. "I should never . . ."

"You couldn't know."

The motel clerk came out of the office and stared at Lena. Room doors opened. A man on the way to his car stopped in his tracks. Lena collapsed on the asphalt, her face in her hands, her body shaking. Millie and Ethel looked at each other, helpless.

"Should I . . . ?" Millie asked.

"I don't think so," Ethel said. "Let her do what she needs to do."

Millie got out of the car to watch over Lena anyway. When she finally stopped sobbing, Millie helped her stand and get in the car.

Lena fell onto the seat and closed her eyes. "I'm going to kill him," she whispered.

"I'll help you," Ethel said and rummaged in her huge bag until her fingers closed on the ampoule of poison she'd purchased to kill her husband. "I already have what we need."

"Sorry, I can't assist you with that," Millie said. "I don't even kill centipedes when they run across my apartment floor."

Ethel and Lena ignored her. She left them in the car to conspire about how to kill Rutledge. Taking multiple photos of the strange list sealed inside the plastic baggie and now considered evidence, Millie hoped one image would be clear enough for print. She also snapped photos of the motel and a close up of the door where they'd found the list.

Then Millie phoned her editor. "I got it," she said, the glee in her voice announcing her success even before she told him the story.

She didn't fault herself one tiny bit for her excitement. She had believed in the story, pitched it, pursued it, and gotten it before anyone else. The one missing piece was an on-the-record statement from the sheriff naming the suspect. If she could get Jo Hammersmith to say his name, she'd be golden. "AP wire," she whispered to herself, "here I come."

CHAPTER 34

As tall as Millie was, the sheriff had a good four inches on her. And if steam could come out of someone's ears, well then, Millie would be cooked. The lights on the police vehicle flashed, and a burly deputy stood four feet away with his hands resting on the gun and taser at his hips.

Millie swallowed her gum. She wasn't afraid the deputy would use his weapons, but the thought of being in the line of fire made her nervous.

"I should bring you up on obstruction of justice charges." Jo Hammersmith's voice was quiet, like the moment before people started throwing things.

Millie scanned the parking lot for exits. The word "should" meant the sheriff wouldn't charge her, but she could. Millie's heart thumped a little too forcefully. *She could do it anytime she wanted.*

Out of the corner of her eye, Millie noticed the motel clerk aim her phone camera at them. A maid sat down on a bench and lit a cigarette like she was settling in to watch her midday soap opera. On the second floor, a guest leaned on the railing, staring at the sheriff and the drama playing out in the parking lot.

Millie stood in the blast of the sheriff's eerily muted ire while Lena and Ethel cowered in the car. There was no point in defending herself. *Okay, I meddled. But . . .*

"We would have discovered the body without your snooping," Hammersmith said. "Now whatever evidence pointed to the killer has been contaminated by three witless women stomping around in my crime scenes."

"Not witless. We're not witless." Millie raised her chin, feeling more confident standing up for herself and her friends.

Hammersmith waved away Millie's interruption. "We'll have to take your fingerprints and DNA samples to eliminate you as suspects. You've made more work for us and slowed us down, maybe compromised our investigation."

Millie's head bobbed. "Yes, of course." She held out her hands and wiggled her fingers.

Hammersmith pursed her lips. "Very funny. Not now, obviously. Come to headquarters tomorrow."

Maybe the sheriff thought their actions were inexcusable, but Millie's byline would be under the headline story in tomorrow's paper: *Local Doctor Found Dead in Maryland.* The news had already gone out in a ticker on the newspaper's website and social media feeds, and her notifications were beeping like crazy. She'd have to write like the wind when she got back to town.

Best of all, her editor had said, "Guess your hunch was correct," his tone a pleasing mix of grudging respect and annoyance.

"Stay right here in the parking lot until we're done with our search of the room. I might have other questions for you." Hammersmith took possession of the plastic laundry bag in which Millie had placed the paper Ethel found on the motel room floor.

The sheriff scanned the paper. "How many of you touched this?"

"I guess all of us," Millie said and winced at the sheriff's glare.

"Christ." Hammersmith handed off the evidence to her deputy and strode into the motel office to question the clerk.

Millie hesitated for a second and followed. She still needed to know who had rented the room—*it couldn't have been Harmon Rutledge, could it?*—as well as who was driving the white car, and, of course, who killed Trudy Davis. A car door slammed; Ethel scurried after her.

"He said he was Harmon Rutledge," the clerk was telling Hammersmith. "He was about medium height, short sandy-colored hair, dark indigo eyes. Handsome in a Timothée Chalamet kind of way. You know, brooding and fragile. Mid-to-late-twenties?" She sighed.

"That's . . . that's . . . ," Ethel murmured.

"He's not Harmon Rutledge then," Millie blurted.

"Please be quiet, Miss Overbee," Hammersmith said. She addressed the clerk. "Did you take down the license number of the car he was driving?"

"Oh, yes, we always do it for insurance purposes in case someone claims damage to their vehicle in our parking lot, but they weren't our guest." The clerk paged through screens on her computer. "Here it is: one, W-V, underscore, D-O-C," she said, her face brightened by a smile.

Hammersmith made a note in her pad.

"That's Trudy's car," Ethel said. "Lena recognized the number written on that paper."

"Mrs. Goodman, please allow me to conduct this interview." Hammersmith shot Millie and Ethel a sit-down-and-shut-up look.

Millie pantomimed zipping her mouth. Ethel hmphed.

Turning back to the clerk, the sheriff asked, "Do you have a record of the credit card he used to pay for the room?"

The clerk printed out the reservation record and handed the paper to Hammersmith. Millie peeked over the sheriff's shoulder. The name on the card was Trudy Davis.

"Didn't you notice his name was different from the one on the card?"

The clerk shrugged. "He said she was his mother. He showed me her license."

Hammersmith gave her a skeptical look. "Pretty lax, don't you think?"

The clerk pouted prettily. "The card went through without a flag." She shrugged.

"That routine works for you, does it?" Hammersmith sighed. "When did he check in?"

"Yesterday. I put a hold of five hundred on the card—a week's worth."

Hammersmith showed the clerk a photograph of Trudy. "Have you ever seen this woman either alone or with the man who registered before this week?"

Millie frowned. *Why's she asking that? She already knew Trudy was dead a week ago.*

"No." The clerk bit her lip. "They asked me about her also." She pointed to Millie. "He came in here alone." The clerk shrugged and smiled at the same time.

Millie guessed that meant the young woman would have happily remedied his solitary situation for him.

"How long did he take the room for?" Hammersmith asked.

"Just day-to-day," the clerk said.

"If he comes back, or if you see the car in the lot, you call me immediately." Hammersmith handed the clerk a business card. "We're going to take the sheets and towels from his room. They're evidence. My deputy will give you a statement of what we collected."

"I guess that's okay," the clerk said.

Millie held the door open. "What do you think it means if Trudy never stayed at this motel, but her car did?" she asked as the sheriff walked out of the office.

"Unlike you, I don't make up theories before the facts are in," Hammersmith said.

"But the description she gave of the man, does it remind you of someone?"

Ethel grabbed Millie's jacket and tugged; Millie ignored her.

"Could be any teenage movie heart throb," Hammersmith said. "Witness identification is notoriously wrong."

"Could be anyone," Ethel said.

"But it's obviously not Rutledge," Millie pressed.

"Right," Hammersmith said. "We've been keeping tabs on Rutledge by tracking his phone. He hasn't left the county since he reported his wife missing. Unless someone else is carrying his phone, that wasn't him driving the car."

Millie sucked in her breath. *Hammersmith suspected Rutledge all along.* "What are you going to do now?"

Hammersmith stopped walking and confronted Millie. "I'm going to inform Mr. Rutledge of his wife's death before he reads about it in your newspaper, and I'm going to get a search warrant for his house. *You* are going to take those ladies home where they belong and stay out of my way."

"Wait. Do you think he has an accomplice? Because whoever was driving the car might have . . ."

Hammersmith glowered at Millie over her shoulder and kept walking.

Ethel tapped Millie's shoulder. "That's enough. She has enough information. We can go."

"But—"

"Let's go," Ethel said with a little too much urgency. "She's done with us."

They got into the car and buckled up in silence. Lena had her hand over her eyes. Millie took that as a signal not to say anything, but she couldn't help wondering what troubled Ethel, unless . . . *She knows who was driving the Volvo.*

CHAPTER 35

A T 7 P.M. on Sunday evening, two weeks after he believed he had
gotten rid of his wife forever, Harmon opened his front door to
Sheriff Hammersmith. Although he'd been hoping the authorities would
find Trudy's body, that horrific funeral bouquet had thrown him, and he
wasn't sure whether she was alive or dead.

An ominous feeling of doom had hung over him since his last contact with Don, making Harmon indignant and muddying his thinking.
Events had slipped out of his control; details had gotten away from
him, and he had no idea what would happen next. Nevertheless, he had
been rehearsing his grief in the mirror, confident his portrayal would
be convincing if needed. Although how he would deal with a living,
fire-breathing Trudy he had yet to figure out. She would never forgive
him, and she wouldn't keep quiet.

I'll just have to kill her again.

"Can we come in, Mr. Rutledge?" the sheriff asked, removing her
broad-brimmed campaign hat with a star pinned on the crown. She'd
brought a baseball-capped, brawny deputy along with her.

Harmon eyed the weapons on the deputy's belt and opened the door
wider. *The extra manpower is unnecessary.* "Of course." He took the sheriff's
formality as a good sign. Gesturing toward the living room, he reminded
himself to appear worried and mentally hummed the "Pomp and Cir-
cumstance" melody to keep the proper pace for this solemn occasion.

Sheriff Hammersmith faced him. "Mr. Rutledge, I'm sorry to inform
you that your wife is dead."

Harmon gasped, reared back, and fell onto the sofa. He put his
hand over his mouth. "Oh." He paused for what he considered the right

amount of time to regain his voice and hoped he wasn't overplaying his role. "Where did you find her?"

"Near the parking lot of a golf course in Howard County, Maryland."

"That doesn't make sense. You must be wrong. It can't be her."

"A lot of what we've found doesn't make sense, Mr. Rutledge."

"She's been missing for so long; I was still hoping she was alive. And you told me . . . the credit card . . ." Miraculously, a tear managed to fall. He wiped it off his cheek and congratulated himself on his artistry.

"She was wearing a nightgown when her body was found. Can you explain that?"

"No. I can't. I told you what she was wearing. Unless, as I've said before, someone kidnapped her from the motel where she was staying. Was that Emmitsburg? Or in the middle of the night someone broke into her room and killed her and left her in a parking lot. How horrible." Harmon covered his face with both hands. *Idiots. They didn't do anything right. I should have done it myself.*

"Stranger still, the body was covered by a blanket, as if the person who left her there felt bad about it. Do you have any idea who this person might be, Mr. Rutledge?"

"A blanket?" *Those bozos.* "No, no idea."

"We haven't yet found her car."

Harmon shrugged in a way he hoped the sheriff would take as brokenhearted. "Well, obviously, the killer fled in it. Maybe the person was someone Trudy knew. Didn't you say she was having an affair? I guess I should inform the insurance company that the car's been stolen, and I should call the credit card company . . ."

"I understand you're selling this house?"

Harmon grabbed a tissue from the box on a nearby table and blew his nose while he decided how to answer this line of questioning. "Yes. It's too big."

"And you listed it with Ethel Goodman a few days after your wife went missing?"

"Well, I meant it as a gesture of goodwill since Ethel thwarted the robbery at my bank."

"You know her stepson, Charles Goodman, was arrested for the robbery?"

"I do, yes, but as Ethel pointed out, the young man had no idea what he'd been dragged into, which was obvious from the way he behaved." Harmon felt like a child on a carousel, bright colored objects swirling around him, his arm outstretched to grab a brass ring he was moving too fast to see.

"Did you talk with your wife about selling the house before the bank robbery? Did she object? Is that why she left?"

"I don't see how what we argued about is any of your business." A huge chasm opened at Harmon's feet. *Another mistake. I made another stupid mistake. I shouldn't have listed the house so soon.* He took a deep breath and lowered his shoulders. *Keep a level head.*

"This is now a murder investigation, Mr. Rutledge. Nothing about your life is personal anymore." Hammersmith seemed to grow taller.

"Okay. Okay. We've been talking about having children. We agreed that if we weren't going to have them, the house would be too big. I was following through with our plans as if Trudy were here, thinking when she came back, she'd be happy that everything had been sorted out." He glanced up at Hammersmith to assess how the line was working. Her face was neutral. Then he remembered Trudy's pills in the bathroom drawer and sighed with relief. If the sheriff needed proof he was telling the truth, there it was.

"So, you held an open house here yesterday for people to wander around?"

"Yes. Ethel said it was the fastest way to generate an offer."

"Did it work?"

"I think so. A lot of people came through, and Ethel called me with an offer this morning. I'm considering taking it, but she advised me to wait twenty-four hours to see if another offer comes so we have a bidding war to push up the price."

"You'll have to put selling the house on hold. We're going to seal off the property and search it from top to bottom for clues as to what might have happened to your wife."

"Oh. No. You can't do that. Prospective buyers might want to take another tour before they sign a contract. I can't have police tape wrapped around the house."

"Yes, you can, and we will. I have the search warrant." Hammersmith glanced at the deputy who handed Harmon a copy. "I'll take you to my office and we'll chat while the forensics folks do their job." She signaled for Harmon to stand. "You can come in my vehicle. We'll be searching yours."

The laptop. Trudy's laptop is in the trash can. Harmon's mind raced around the house trying to ferret out what else might be taken as evidence that would implicate him in Trudy's death. His mind was blank. This was not going according to plan. *I should ask for my lawyer. Except it will appear I have something to hide. No, that's wrong. Smart people always get lawyers.*

Harmon knew the county prosecutor from Rotary but clearly couldn't ask him for a referral. Title attorneys he occasionally had a drink with wouldn't have a clue what to do with a criminal prosecution. Besides, he would be a pariah now. All that sympathy his wife's disappearance had engendered would turn to anger. People would be bitter that they'd been duped. He needed protection. Who had the biggest account at the bank? *Duchamp, he's the one. He does criminal work and has a reputation for getting people off.*

Harmon stood and summoned his dignity, as if he had been affronted by the sheriff's disrespect. *The nerve of this woman.* "I want to call my attorney first, if you don't mind. He can meet us at your office."

"Go ahead," Hammersmith said. "I'll wait."

In the bathroom near the front door, a place he doubted the sheriff would follow him out of courtesy, Harmon googled Duchamp' offices, clicked on the website, and then the phone number. He had no idea whether anyone would answer the phone on a Sunday night.

When a real person answered the call, a relieved Harmon explained who he was and that he needed the lawyer to meet him at the county sheriff's office right away. The woman on the other end of the call explained she would call Duchamp at once to give him the message.

When he exited the bathroom, the sheriff was standing in the hall. "I'll take your phone, Mr. Rutledge." She held out a small plastic bag. "It's covered under our search warrant."

Harmon handed over his phone, trying to mentally review what was on his call list. He drew a blank. Everything was coming apart.

"By the way, Mr. Rutledge, you never asked how your wife died. Why is that?"

"I assumed it was by gun, knife, or strangulation—the usual grue-some methods."

"She was suffocated. We found white linen fibers in her nose, the kind certain luxury sheets and pillowcases are made with, the kind of linens they don't use in motels. The kind we might find in *your* house."

A deep sense of dread spread out from Harmon's gut to his farthest extremities until even the hair on his head seemed to be uncurling.

CHAPTER 36

DON Whitley, never one to rise early if it could be helped, awoke at 5 A.M. on Monday after a nearly sleepless night on the couch in his mother's basement. He'd been haunted by nightmares of Harmon chasing him all night—the man's hands around his neck, the disgust on his scrunched-up face as if Don were a roach he was squashing.

By first light, Don was determined to take his revenge. Uncrimping himself from the sofa, Don staggered into the two-by-four bathroom, peed in the filthy toilet, and splashed water on his face from the hand-sized sink on top of the tank. He stared in the mirror and promised himself today would be the day he fought back.

He pictured himself in a movie, standing at the edge of a cliff as the cold wind whipped against his back. Without warning, his feet slipped, his arms whipped around like windmills. Below him the ground dropped away into darkness. Helpless to stop his fall, he heard Harmon say, "Why don't you just die?"

Don rotated his shoulders. "Shut the fuck up, man."

He picked up a T-shirt from the floor and sniffed it. *Not too bad.* He pulled on his jeans and tucked in the shirt. This was it. He wasn't taking anyone's shit anymore. He was tired of being pushed around by know-it-alls, including his mother, his lawyer, and Charlie. Everybody thought they were better than him. Someone had to pay for his years of misery. And that someone was Harmon Rutledge.

Harmon was the one who had cooked up the crazy plan to kill his own wife and dump her body in another state. Harmon was the one who had insisted her body could be moved without anyone noticing. What a joke. And now, because he didn't want to part with a few measly bucks, he was going to tell the police that Don was the murderer. What did five thousand dollars mean to Harmon? The edges of Don's fingers sizzled he was so mad.

Harmon can't prove that I killed her. I never got out of my truck. I never touched the body, never saw it. For all I know, there wasn't even a body in the trunk of that damn car. Well, except for the smell.

His fingerprints weren't on Trudy's vehicle. He had driven in his own vehicle. He was allowed to drive around; this was a free country. He could go anywhere he liked without anyone's permission. That jerk was trying to make him do something stupid.

Without wanting to, Don pictured his hand passing Trudy's car keys to Charlie and then handing over the deodorizers hanging from his rearview mirror. His fingerprints would be on the keys and the tiny cardboard pine trees. Charlie had worn those purple gloves. Don's stomach lurched. He smacked himself in the head.

"Fuck!" he yelled as loud as he could, not caring if he woke his mother. "Fuck!" He smashed his fist against the bare cinderblock wall. Shock ran up his arm. Don stared at his bleeding knuckles and collapsed on the couch, cradling his hand.

As with every other time in his life, he had already done something stupid. He had taken the job Harmon dangled like bait for a few measly bucks and become a criminal for life as a result.

I'm an idiot. I should've known right away that the vice president of the bank I tried to rob wasn't going to do me any favors.

There was one solution. Harmon needed to be taught a lesson and Don Whitley was the guy to do it. All the banker's hoity-toity ways, as Don's mother would say, would bring him down. All those fancy clothes and airs he put on for his bank customers. He was a con artist.

Don paced the basement floor, hands in his hair, wild with excitement like he'd hit upon an Oscar-winning movie idea. *Come to think of it, everyone's a con artist, pretending to be somebody they aren't just to get something from people who never would have given it to 'em if they'd known better.*

Now that he knew this, he could win a round, maybe the whole fight. He just had to figure out what to do. Thinking about himself like this made him feel smart. Don Whitley would show the world that Harmon was nothing, a bag of wind, a fancy suit. When Don Whitley was done, there would be nothing but smoke left to remind anyone of the greedy bastard.

He rewound the bank robbery screw-up in his mind. If Charlie had done what he'd been told to do, they would've been in and out of the bank before anyone caught them. He should never have asked Charlie to join him. And if he'd had a real gun, Charlie's stepmother, that busybody, would have backed down in a minute, no questions asked, and no struggle. She would've been the one on her back begging for mercy. He could've walked out of the bank a rich man.

Time to put things to rights. He needed to do what he needed to do. The hell with his mother. What did she ever do for him, anyway? He should go farther away than Texas. The farther away from here he was, the better off he would be. In movies people always went to Thailand. Don saw palm trees, open beaches, dirt roads, a place where he could disappear, and no one would be able to find him. Hell, he didn't even know where the country was, which meant most other people didn't either. It was the perfect place to hide.

A twinge of regret for sucking Charlie into this mess stuck in Don's throat for a second. They weren't friends anymore. Maybe they shouldn't have tried to pull off a bank robbery. They weren't ready for it. Because of Harmon, Don had lost everything.

All that was left was revenge. He climbed the stairs to the kitchen as quietly as possible and grabbed the box of Crunchy-Os from the kitchen table. Then, keeping the TV sound on mute, he searched for *The Count of Monte Cristo,* his mother's favorite movie, on the streaming movie channel to study how revenge was done.

CHAPTER 37

EARLY Monday morning Ethel received another offer by telephone for Harmon's house, ten-thousand dollars higher than the earlier full-price bid. That made it a million-dollar sale, and a seventy-thousand-dollar commission. Her heart danced the Flamenco as she assured the breathless buyer that she'd deliver the offer in person at once.

She called Harmon and left a message on his voice mail saying she was on her way over with a contract for him to sign. "This is the one!" Even if she hated the man, she had done her job and sold his house. Ethel hadn't felt this proud of herself since she won a blue ribbon in her second-grade spelling bee.

On the other hand, now that she was sure Harmon had killed his wife, the idea of being in the house alone with him caused a small earthquake in her stomach. But being there in person to secure his acceptance of the offer and his signature on the contract was necessary, according to all the real estate closing experts.

Anyway, she had a duty to tell him about the offer, and it was harder for people to say no to someone's face. Just in case, she checked her bag to make sure she had mace and the tiny ampoule of aconite still tucked away for an emergency.

Waiting for morning bridge traffic into Maryland to subside so she could turn left onto Shepherd Grade Road, Ethel pondered whether Harmon knew she knew he had murdered his wife. Would he still be calm and snooty now that he almost had what he wanted, or would he glower and loom over her the way he must have done to Trudy before he killed her?

Ethel shivered. What might he do to her if she foiled his plans? How easily he could squash her. The police would take weeks to find her body the way they did to locate his dead wife. Best to get this transaction done as soon as possible and be through with him.

Lena had said Harmon belonged in a special kind of hell, and Ethel agreed. But if a special kind of hell didn't wait for him, the original would do. For her part, she hoped knowing a killer had tuned up her observational skills. If she ever met another cold-hearted bastard, she would recognize the type immediately and not be sucked into a compromising business arrangement.

Ethel did not include herself in the category of callous killers. "I would never murder anyone for convenience," Ethel affirmed to her image in the rear-view mirror. "But I'm still going to get my commission for selling the house."

It was 8 A.M. when Ethel turned into Harmon's development, perhaps too early to pay a call on her client, but after yesterday, getting his signature on the contract had to be done before anything else happened. If Harmon weren't there, she could leave the offer on the kitchen counter for him to sign as soon as possible.

Ethel made a right onto Harmon's street. Motivated or not, she refused to go faster than the stated twenty-five miles an hour. The road curved twice before she would make another right onto his lane. At the entrance to his driveway, she was stopped by police tape.

Hammersmith must have arrested him. That's why he didn't answer his phone. She works fast.

She idled there for a second, trying to decide what to do, then parked her car up the street about twenty feet from the house. Other than the "DO NOT CROSS" tape across the front door, the house seemed untouched. Ethel left her car and walked to Harmon's door. Examining the police seal, Ethel worked her way through another legal conundrum. *I'm not the one under arrest, and if the police wanted to stop me, they'd be here. So, it's okay to break the seal and go inside.*

Even so, she rang the bell twice. Satisfied no one was there, she tapped in the code on the key box and got it wrong. She cursed and tried again. The red light came on, meaning she'd done it wrong again. She had three chances to get it right. "I hate these techno gizmos."

Ethel gritted her teeth and input the numbers. The light on the key box changed to green. She twisted the lid and extracted the front door key. The house was completely quiet. Through the wide living room windows, she saw a tiny figure teeing up on the golf course.

"Harmon, Harmon, hello, are you here?" Perhaps he had already gotten out on bail and entered the house through the garage. Leaves from the bushes and trees nestled near the front of the house rustled against the windows, but no Harmon appeared. "Okay. Just as well."

Ethel strode into the kitchen, pulled the contract documents out of her tote bag, and laid them on the white counter. In case a sudden breeze scooted the papers onto the floor, she placed a red apple from the wooden bowl on top as a paperweight. She was writing a note telling Harmon to call her ASAP, when a vehicle roared through the exquisitely landscaped plantings encircling the front of the house.

CHAPTER 38

A T 7:30 A.M. Don had thrown four plastic gasoline cans, a jumble of rags, and a pickax he found in his mother's junked-up garage into the back of his truck. Two of the gas cans leaked, but that didn't matter. He wouldn't be on the road for long and wasn't bringing them back with him. He stopped at the closest convenience store to put two gallons of gas in each can, and while he was there, he snagged a Coke and a Snicker's bar to eat on the way for nourishment.

Can't take revenge on an empty stomach.

To be extra prepared, Don grabbed a few BIC lighters from the counter while the attendant haltingly counted out change from the forty dollars Don had stolen from his mother's purse. He didn't feel bad about taking his mother's money. She owed him for making him sleep in the basement.

He also didn't feel bad about swiping the convenience store's lighters. They were already charging too much for the gas and could afford to let him have the lighters for free. He hopped back into the truck and drove fifteen miles to Harmon's fancy house without looking anywhere but the road ahead.

After Harmon had tried to strangle him in the rec center parking lot, Don had tailed him home. The bigshot's Range Rover was easy to keep in sight, and he'd stayed back one or two cars like the detectives in the TV cop shows. Harmon was so confident, he hadn't even noticed he was being followed.

Driving slowly past the house as Harmon pulled into his garage, Don had spotted the For Sale sign at the front of the property and wrote the address on his arm. He'd found the house listing online, proving he could be as techy as Charlie, and studied the layout diagram until he knew the placement of every room.

Now, idling his truck in front of Harmon's house, Don noticed the neighborhood was completely still. *They're all retired and don't have to wake up until noon.* Gunning his truck over the grass, and hoping Harmon was fast asleep in his bed, Don ploughed through the landscaped garden in front of the house and left the motor running.

He won't know what hit him until he's half fried, running screaming from the house with his body on fire. Don snickered.

He eased out of the cab and stood on the plantings under what he thought was Harmon's bedroom window. Staring out toward the east, Don imagined he could hear the river running. *Wish Mom could've lived in a place like this.* He lit a cigarette, took a deep drag, and counted his grievances.

No one had ever trusted him. The Frohlers had never given him a key to the funeral home in case he had to open the building early. Mr. Fancy Pants had tricked him and used him as a patsy. Charlie didn't trust him. Even his mother had never given him a key to his own home. He'd spent hours after school sitting on the porch waiting for her to get home.

No matter what he did, people didn't like him, even his own mother. It was like he started out less than zero and everything he did subtracted from that. He was just there to do the dirty work, the jobs other people didn't like to do, the running and fetching, setting out chairs and packing them up, taking out garbage, moving dead bodies.

Don twitched thinking of all the dead people he had touched while working at the funeral home. Today he would settle the score, all scores. He would get even. Today, everyone would finally know who they were dealing with. Don ran a hand through his hair and patted his belly. He liked himself at this moment, sure about what he was doing.

He took a few more tugs on his cigarette and threw the butt on the ground. Jumping up into the truck bed, he lined up the gas cans. Next, he stuffed the rags he'd brought from home down into the plastic, five-gallon containers until the bottom of each rag was submerged in gas with a six-inch cloth tail hanging from the top of the can.

This house is going to blow sky high.

Gas can in hand, Don balanced himself in the truck with one foot on the side rail. He lit the cloth and stood for a second, watching the fire chew up the rag like a hungry child with a candy bar. The bomb would blow out the entire floor, and when the fire got to the gas reserve for the fireplace, that would blow also. He had a minute to get the hell out of there before the boom and a whoosh. The house would be sucked into a bottomless sinkhole and Harmon with it.

He swung the lit can behind his head and flung it through the large corner window. The glass broke, and a satisfying thud came from inside the house. Then he lit the remaining Molotov cocktails. He wasn't taking any chances.

The cans weren't heavy. He could easily raise them up in the air and hurl them through the glass. No one in this fancy neighborhood would know what had happened until the house blew and flames shot out of the roof. By then, he'd be long gone.

Don listened for the expected boom from the first bomb. He didn't hear it, but he couldn't wait any longer. Out of the corner of his eye, he caught sight of Charlie's stepmother. She yelled something at him. Ignoring her, he hefted the next lit gas can back above his head and threw it with all the force he could muster at the large window.

The can fell short of the window, dropped like a heavy stone into the ground cover, and exploded in flames, catching the purple leaves of the plum tree and the still-green pachysandra.

Doesn't matter. I've got more.

Gas dripped on him from the third can as he raised his arm above his head. He leaned back and tossed it as hard as he could. Flames on the ground followed the line of gas from the can back to the truck bed, found the remaining container and its wick of cloth, and Don, who had enough time to say, "Oh, shit."

CHAPTER 39

PEERING out the front door to see what had made that racket in the driveway, Ethel's mind stitched together the strangest picture. A pickup truck was parked under Harmon's bedroom window. A man stood in the truck bed with a Molotov cocktail aimed at the house. Glass crashed. Stunned, Ethel looked toward Harmon's bedroom and then back out the door. Something exploded in Harmon's bathroom.

Then she recognized Don. "Hey! Cut that out," Ethel yelled.

Don Whitley glanced at her, snarled, and tossed another bomb at the house.

She watched it fall to the ground and light the bushes on fire. *Lord have mercy, that idiot has more!* Rooted to the spot, she stared as he threw another bomb.

The truck burst into flames. Screaming, he whirled around and around as fire licked his pants and shirt. Flames leapt from the house. The tree nearest the house broke into a blaze. A blast rocked her. Smoke alarms on both floors bleated. And Don hurtled onto the ground like a meteor.

My commission is going up in flames! "I have to save the house!"

There was no time to call 911. Ethel dashed back into the kitchen to find a fire extinguisher. Pulling open one cabinet after another, she found a small, red extinguisher in the pantry. She flipped it upside down and pulled the ring.

But the second she dashed back toward the bedroom, smoke enveloped her. Her eyes stung, her throat burned. Wrapping her scarf around her face, Ethel turned around, retreating to the kitchen. She grabbed her bag and ran toward the back door. Another huge boom rattled the house, knocking Ethel over backward. With a crack, a timber from the great room's cathedral ceiling dislodged and crashed to the floor. Engulfed by smoke and falling plaster, Ethel lay on the floor disoriented, arms protecting her face, imagining she was in her spinning car, and this time she wouldn't make it out.

CHAPTER 40

CHARLIE took in the scene at Harmon's house one frame at a time: the burning truck; flames leaping from the house; the open front door; the smoldering body on the grass; police tape flapping in the breeze, and Ethel's car parked up the street.

Fuck me, she's in there. Ethel's in the house.

He pulled Trudy's Volvo into Harmon's driveway. *Good thing I decided to bring the car back today.* Without hesitating, he flew out of the car and sprinted across the front lawn into the house. "Ethel," he yelled, standing in the foyer, "Ethel, where the hell are you?" Smoke stung his eyes and burned his throat. He pulled his shirt up over his nose and mouth.

She's trying to save that asshole banker.

Charlie had no idea how the house was arranged. Not finding his stepmother in the living and dining rooms, he dashed to the left and spotted her sneaker-clad feet, toes up, in the kitchen.

"Ethel, I'm coming."

Charlie reached her as she was trying to sit up. "Oh," Ethel murmured. "I didn't . . . get my bag . . ."

He lifted Ethel off the floor and half carried, half dragged her outside. His arm wrapped around her waist, they hustled away from the house and stopped at the curb to look back.

An ambulance, sirens blaring, pulled up on the street. Two men leaped out of the vehicle and ran toward them. "Get back, get away from the house."

Charlie and Ethel stumbled to the other side of the street where the emergency vehicle had stopped. While the medics hustled them inside the ambulance, Ethel asked, "How did you get here?" and then dissolved into a coughing fit.

Charlie pointed to the Volvo. His extreme relief that she was still alive made him giggle. "Good thing, huh?"

Ethel's head bobbed. "I wasn't going to make it." She coughed and gripped Charlie's hand. "I was so dizzy, I couldn't get up. Harmon isn't in there."

"Figures," Charlie said as the paramedic checked him over for burns, smoke inhalation, and shock. "The guy's Teflon."

He could have sworn Ethel winked but maybe she was trying to blink away ashes that were falling like snow around them. Anyway, he'd done what he set out to do. Whatever else was going on, the Volvo was now Harmon's problem, and therefore he wasn't a car thief.

When Charlie's head stopped spinning, he stared at the charred truck and body lying next to it and knew without a doubt who the dead man was. Shock and then relief washed over him—by staying in Emmitsburg, he had accidentally avoided being sucked into Don's final caper. *For sure, that would've been me.*

CHAPTER 41

THE first thing Sheriff Jo Hammersmith noted when she pulled up behind two fire trucks, besides the blazing truck, house, and smoldering body in Harmon Rutledge's yard, was the white Volvo with the plates 1WV_DOC parked at the top of the driveway.

She strode to Fire Chief Samson, who was standing with his hands in the pockets of his neon yellow vest. Pointing to the Volvo, she said, "Where did that car come from? It wasn't here yesterday evening when we taped off the house."

Samson shrugged. "It was here when we got here. Lots of vehicles on the street, for that matter. Residents are s'posed to leave us clear access."

Hammersmith grunted. Everyone always had their pet peeve. *Isn't that the license plate number of the vehicle that bumbling trio of amateur sleuths stumbled across yesterday?*

"But even with local traffic," Samson went on, "it took us seven minutes to get here from the time we got the alarm on the scanner. The house was already fully engulfed. From what's left of the truck, I'm guessing the gas tank exploded."

Flames devoured the house like a gourmet appetizer. A dozen people in neon yellow helmets and vests deployed hoses at full force to quell the blaze before it spread to the grove of trees next to the house. Two people draped a fire retardant blanket over the unrecognizable body.

"Didn't expect this mess," Hammersmith said. "The burglar alarm got us here."

She surveyed the scene and mentally noted that pesky reporter was talking to Ethel and Charlie Goodman, who was out on bail until his trial for that bungled bank robbery. Ethel was wrapped in a shiny silver blanket and hooked up to an oxygen tank. Hammersmith decided she could question the witnesses after the emergency had passed. Meanwhile she yelled to her deputies to set up a crime scene perimeter out to the stop sign.

"No one else gets on this street," she barked as they sprinted to do the task.

Neighbors in jogging outfits and golf clothes stood on their front porches with phones, birding binoculars, and coffee mugs clutched in their hands. Hammersmith spotted a gaggle of early morning golfers congregating in electric carts on the green about two hundred yards behind the house.

Photos of the fire and emergency services response would be all over town by now with ample rumors about every aspect of the spectacle on social media. There was no way to control the narrative these days. For her own purposes, the question was whether this fire was connected to the murder of Trudy Davis and the culpability of Harmon Rutledge.

While the fire was quelled, Hammersmith and the fire chief walked the property's perimeter trying to identify the sequence of events. Hammersmith pointed to the broken window. "This had to be the entry point, right? That must be what triggered the alarm alerting us."

"This was deliberate, but I don't think it went the way he wanted."

"Don't you think it was arson? The break-in alarm was the earliest indication something was wrong. That must be where he threw something into the house. Don't you think?"

"For sure." Samson nodded. "You can smell the gasoline. He might've thrown something through the window to start the fire. We'll know more when we get inside."

"You're sure that's a man?" she pointed to the unidentifiable body on the lawn.

Samson shrugged. "We'll know soon enough. Either way, someone did a thorough job even if they didn't know what they were doing."

"You think the perp was an amateur?"

"No doubt about that. Look what happened to him. I'm guessing he was thrown from the exploding truck," Samson said.

The sheriff glanced in the direction of the body and then looked away. Samson threw out his arm to stop her next step. "Back up. We're too close. See those shards of plastic and slivers of glass? They're strewn everywhere. They're from gas cans exploding and the windows being blown out of the truck."

Hammersmith covered her nose and mouth with a tissue and walked away from the house and toward her witnesses.

Samson kept pace with her. "This might've been the stupidest arsonist on the planet. It appears that in the course of setting the fire, he accidentally ignited himself."

"You don't think this could be one of those deliberate self-immolations?"

Samson raised his eyebrows. "Out here in the boonies? What would he have been protesting?"

"Greedy corporate practices? The coming environmental apocalypse? Economic inequities. Name your cause." Hammersmith rubbed her ripening pregnant belly as if she could conjure a genie who would whisk her off to a place where nothing like this would ever happen near her child.

Samson hooted. "Looks personal to me." He stroked his unshaved chin. "The person had a grudge against the owner of this house. I mean, he pulled his truck up onto the plantings. That's sacrilege in this neighborhood."

"Yeah. Like a protest," Hammersmith said. "But I agree with you. The person had a grudge against Rutledge. Do you think the arsonist had an accomplice, someone who got away?" She pointed to the Volvo at the end of Harmon's driveway.

The fire chief shrugged. "Don't know about that. At first glance, the car doesn't show any signs of having been here when the explosion occurred. Not even any carbon particulates on it."

"So, the vehicle got here after the truck blew up?" Hammersmith asked.

"That'd be my guess," the fire chief said.

A deputy ran up to them. "Sheriff, the fire crew has cleared the interior, and they say there's no bodies inside the house."

"I didn't expect any, but it's good to have it confirmed," Hammersmith said more to herself than to the fire chief.

"How's that?"

"I kept the owner of this house in one of our finest cells last night and inadvertently saved his life. The forensics team was supposed to go through the house today and now my crime scene is toast. Unless our quick search yesterday yielded anything incriminating, I've got no physical evidence."

"Evidence of what?" Samson asked.

"Murder. I'm pretty sure a woman was murdered here. But if my suspect sticks to his cockamamie story of her being kidnapped, without direct evidence or a witness or even decent circumstantial evidence to support a theory of means, motive, and opportunity, the case will never go to court. Especially after this mess, since it looks like someone was determined to ruin Rutledge and that person might be the smoldering body right there."

Samson stared pointedly at Hammersmith's pregnant belly. "Sometimes you got to let go of things you can't control. You got better fish to fry."

Hammersmith rubbed her face with her hand and then called the coroner's office to send a van to take the body to the morgue for an autopsy. Even though the cause of death was evident, they needed the official coroner's report and the right documents signed. They also needed to figure out who he or she was so they could find the next of kin to take charge of the burial.

On a hunch, the sheriff sent one deputy to Don Whitley's house to check on his whereabouts and another to locate the VIN on the truck doorjamb and run the number through DMV for ownership. If the truck wasn't stolen, the number might help them ID the dead guy. "Let me know right away."

Hammersmith then called for two tow trucks, one to remove the charred metal wreck and the other to haul the Volvo to the state police forensics depot. Just maybe the forensics techs could pull something out of the car to help her make sense of what was going on.

Next, she had to interview the witnesses to this fire when what she wanted to do was go back to her office, put up her swollen feet, and have a cup of coffee and a chocolate croissant. Hammersmith considered handing the questioning off to a deputy but changed her mind. Something odd was going on with Millie, Ethel, and Charlie Goodman, but she couldn't put her finger on it. She'd have to tease it out of them.

It didn't surprise her that Millie and Ethel were comfortable with each other since their sleuthing jaunt to Emmitsburg, but the last time she'd seen Ethel with her stepson was at Charlie's arraignment. Court formality hadn't allowed her to observe them closely, but she could have sworn they were chilly with each other then. They appeared to have thawed.

She walked over to the back of the ambulance where the three were assembled. "So, you got here when?" Hammersmith said to Millie.

"I was in the newsroom working up a second day piece on Dr. Davis when I heard the police scanner call for fire and ambulance at this address and ran to my car. Got here just as the fire engines were pulling into the subdivision. I followed them in."

Hammersmith turned to Ethel. "And you?"

Ethel removed the oxygen mask. "I got here earlier to give Mr. Rutledge an offer on the house. I was leaving him a note and the offer . . ." She took two deep breaths of oxygen. With a shaking finger, she pointed to the covered hump on the grass. "And this crazy guy pulls up onto the plantings and sets the fire, and then the house exploded, and I tried, but I fell down. And Charlie . . ." Ethel began to cry.

"I got her out." Charlie shrugged as if rescuing his estranged stepmother was no big deal.

Hammersmith stared at one face and then the other. "How did you get here, Mr. Goodman?"

Ethel blotted her face with a tissue Millie handed her, and then gave her stepson a look Hammersmith couldn't interpret. "Charlie was with me," Ethel said. "I had some errands to do after I talked to Harmon, and Charlie was going to help me."

The sheriff turned to Charlie. "Why didn't you stop the arsonist?"

"Me?" Charlie raised his eyebrows and pursed his lips.

Ethel huffed. "How could he have done that? That man was insane. Besides, it happened so fast."

Hammersmith could swear Charlie's entire body relaxed. "Do any of you know anything about the Volvo in the driveway?"

Before Charlie or Millie could open their mouths, Ethel said, "It's the car listed on that piece of paper we gave you yesterday."

"The car that drove by you at the motel in Emmitsburg?" Hammersmith asked.

"It flashed by, but I'd say yes," Ethel said.

"Lena said it's Trudy's car." Ethel pursed her lips. "So, it makes sense that it's here."

"Let me check," Charlie said and darted to the Volvo.

Hammersmith shouted, "No," and then watched helplessly as he opened the driver's door, put his hands on the steering wheel, sat in the seat, and opened the glove box.

He emerged from the car holding aloft the key, the car's registration card, a driver's license, and a credit card. "Says the car belongs to Trudy Davis," he yelled.

Hammersmith ground her teeth. He reminded her of a golden retriever who'd just caught a tennis ball. *And now the car's covered in his fingerprints and DNA detritus.* "Just leave the key and ID stuff on the seat and close the door," she called out.

On his way back to the ambulance, Charlie appeared to stumble on a paver. He caught himself by holding onto the trunk of the car.

"Christ," Hammersmith muttered. "Is there anything else you can tell me about this fire, like the name of the guy who set it?" She frowned at Millie and Ethel.

They glanced at each other. "No idea," Ethel said. "Certainly not Harmon. He was about to clear three-hundred-thousand dollars profit on the sale of his house."

"Do you know what happened here, Millie?" Hammersmith asked. "Any wild guesses?"

"I got here too late. But what about Rutledge? Was he in the house? Did he die in the fire?"

"No," Hammersmith said. "I have him in custody. I'll have a statement on the Trudy Davis case later today."

"But the arsonist was someone who hated Rutledge, right?"

"We don't know who the arsonist is yet," Hammersmith said. "Or what his motive might be. When we do, and after his family has been informed, either law enforcement or the fire marshal's office will put out a statement."

"That reminds me," Ethel said. "I have something for you, Sheriff. Charlie, give me my bag." She pointed to an oversized tote bag on the floor of the ambulance.

Ethel rooted around in the bag Charlie handed her and pulled out a red cell phone. "This is Trudy's. I found it on Saturday during the open house. It was on the floor under the nightstand by the bed. With everything going on yesterday, I forgot to give it to you."

Hammersmith pulled a glove out of her pocket and took the phone from Ethel's hand.

"Look at that color; it must be Trudy's. A woman would never leave home without her phone, I don't think," Ethel rattled on. "Not voluntarily. Unless she's a flibbertigibbet like me, which I don't think Trudy was. I confess I leave mine at home from time to time, and then I worry I'll die of a heart attack in the car and not be able to call anyone."

Hammersmith closed her eyes and bowed her head. *You just never know. Evidence, with provenance, and a witness to confirm where, when, and how it was found.* She could almost hug Ethel for being such a busy body. Her next thought was that a defense attorney would question the chain of evidence, suggest the phone had been tampered with, and the sheriff's office was derelict. She sighed.

"There might be an important text on it, I think," Ethel said. "The last one she typed. I forgot the passcode to unlock the phone, but Lena knows it. The text was something like, 'He's coming. I'll pretend to be asleep. Talk in a bit.' But she never sent it."

Hammersmith made a note on her pad. "Thank you. I'll talk to Lena. You should go home and rest now."

Ethel closed her eyes. "Good idea. Let's go home, Charlie. You drive."

Charlie helped his stepmother into her car. Ethel said something to him. Charlie smiled and ran a hand over the top of his head. He slipped behind the wheel and started the car.

Hammersmith turned to Millie. "Do they seem different to you, like suddenly they like each other?"

Millie shrugged as if to say she had no idea one way or another, but Hammersmith could have sworn the reporter knew something she should know.

CHAPTER 42

"YOU'LL look good in gray," Sheriff Hammersmith said when Harmon was seated in her interview room four hours later. His clothes were rumpled, and the dark bags under his eyes indicated he might be tired from his night in her cell.

"Mr. Rutledge, before I begin this interview, I want you to know you have the right to remain silent. You have right to a lawyer to be with you during questioning, but"—she looked pointedly at Harmon's lawyer—"you should know that anything you do say may be held against you in court."

"I advise you not to say anything, Mr. Rutledge," his lawyer, John Duchamp, said.

Harmon stared at the sheriff and the man in an off-the-rack navy-blue suit seated next to her. "What are you talking about? When do I get out of here?"

Hammersmith smiled. "I'm talking about what you'll be wearing while you're waiting in the regional jail for the grand jury to indict you and then a while longer until your trial in our historic courthouse. Oh, and by the way, your fancy suits burned up in the fire. But it doesn't matter. Your lawyer can get you something from Kohl's for court appearances. After the trial, you'll be wearing penitentiary orange for a very long time. Not your color, I think."

"I'm not charged with anything," Harmon sputtered. "It's an outrage that you're holding me in this disgusting facility and speaking to me in this way."

"I can hold you for seventy-two hours without a charge," Hammersmith said, "but I promise you it won't be that long."

"For the record, I would never wear anything from Kohl's," Harmon said. "And what fire are you talking about?"

Hammersmith leaned back in the chair. "I'm about to make everything crystal clear. By the way, this is the county prosecutor, Mr. Ruffino. He wanted to sit in on our conversation to make sure I don't mangle your Constitutional rights."

"What fire?" Harmon turned to his lawyer. "Do you know anything about a fire?"

His lawyer looked startled by the question and shook his head.

"Didn't you hear through the prison grapevine? The fire at your house destroyed everything. Although insurance will pay since the arson was likely perpetrated by one of your frenemies."

Harmon paled. "What the hell are you talking about? What frenemy?"

Satisfied she had him off-kilter, Hammersmith pressed on. "As the story lays out for me, based on the medical examiner's report and the report we just got from forensics on her Volvo, you suffocated your wife with a pillow, stuffed her dead body in the trunk of her own car, and disposed of her in a strange, roundabout way."

Harmon stiffened. "Ridiculous. What happened to my house?"

"We have Dr. Davis's body. We have her car. We recovered hair, fibers, and DNA from the trunk of the Volvo that was parked in your driveway. No woman voluntarily rides in the trunk of her car. And no matter how much you paid for professional cleaning, you can't get rid of all the evidence from a body."

"I don't know what you're talking about. I never cleaned her car." His face mottled. "What do you mean you have her car?"

"I urge you not to respond, Mr. Rutledge," Duchamp said. "We can discuss the charges later in private."

Harmon gave Duchamp a look that would have seared the whiskers off any other lawyer. But her suspect's confusion was so sincere, Hammersmith paused for a second, wondering if she had the wrong perp. *Nah. This is part of his misdirection routine.*

"Yesterday, we recovered your instructions to your accomplice, in your handwriting and covered with your fingerprints. On this piece of paper, you identified Trudy's car and license plate and helpfully listed the addresses of various locations, including the place where her body was found." She slid a piece of paper inside a transparent holder toward Harmon.

"I never wrote any instructions." Harmon squished his lips together.

"Mr. Rutledge," Duchamp whispered. "It's best not to respond. She's trying to bait you."

Harmon twisted his head to glare at his attorney. "Innocent people always proclaim their innocence."

Hammersmith noted Harmon's tell. He pressed his lips together to stifle what he wanted to say. She pressed. "One of your accomplices is dead. He died trying to blow up your house. Did you fail to keep your end of the deal?"

"None of this is true. You're lying to get a rise out of me. I don't know what you're talking about."

"Your house burned to the ground." Hammersmith slid a photograph of the charred carcass of a house across the table. "The botched bank robbery and perhaps the arson were obviously distractions meant to obscure your real crime. You hired them to do it."

Harmon's body lurched as he gaped at the photo of what had been his house. "You're out of your mind. I didn't know the robbers. I certainly didn't hire anyone to blow up my house. Someone is out to destroy me. First, they try to rob my bank, then they kidnap and kill my wife, and finally they try to burn me alive! I'm the victim." He put a hand over his mouth and closed his eyes. "When did this happen?"

"This morning. One of them certainly knew where you lived."

"What do you mean?"

"Remember Don Whitley? He tried to rob your bank with his finger and an old lady stopped him."

"What about him?"

"He torched your house."

"Not possible."

"I have the preliminary report from the fire chief right here." Hammersmith slid a piece of paper across the table.

Harmon stared at it, gasped, and put his head in his hands. "You're trying to confuse me."

"Whitley's mother has identified her son's remains. He always wore a St. Christopher medal his grandmother gave him. We also have DNA." She didn't have to tell Harmon it would take weeks before she knew whose DNA it was.

222 × Ginny Fite

"This is insane. I haven't done anything to Don Whitley. All I've done for the last twelve hours is suffer the ignominy of being incarcerated in this shithole and being harassed by you."

"This is the time to exercise your right to remain silent," Mr. Duchamp whispered.

Harmon ignored his attorney. "Are you charging me with something? Because if you aren't I'd like to go home now."

Sheriff Hammersmith leaned across the table. "We know Trudy was dead two weeks before her body was found. She was wearing her night-gown when they found her."

Harmon shook off his lawyer's restraining hand on his arm. "Not possible."

"We know she was afraid of you and was planning to leave you and live with her lover."

"She did not have a lover," he said through clenched teeth.

"But she did. Her lover will confirm Trudy was planning to leave you, giving you motive."

Harmon closed his eyes. "A motive for what?"

"We also have Trudy's cell phone with her last text to her lover on it. It pinpoints the time of her death."

Harmon had the look of a young boy facing a brace of bullies. His eyes reddened, his mouth opened.

Got him. Hammersmith gave herself a moment to gloat.

"We have Don Whitley's prints and yours on the same piece of paper with her car's license plate number and the location where she was found. We have Whitley's prints on two hanging deodorizers we found in Trudy's car and on her car keys. How do you think they got there, Mr. Rutledge?"

"I have no idea."

"Mr. Rutledge," Hammersmith said, tamping down her glee as much as possible, "I'm charging you with the premeditated murder of your wife. In a few minutes, we will transport you to the regional jail for intake. Whatever you plead at the arraignment, Mr. Ruffino will be asking for remand."

Harmon stared at the wall as his lawyer murmured something in his ear.

CHAPTER 43

SIX months after his arrest, Harmon Rutledge went to trial on an expedited calendar due to what Harmon's lawyer, John Duchamp, claimed was undue hardship for his client.

Millie had badgered her editor into assigning her to cover the trial, but by the middle of the second week of testimony, the thrill of seeing her byline on the front page above the fold every morning was offset by growing unease. In her opinion, which she couldn't include in her daily pieces, the prosecutor, Mr. Ruffino, had lost control of the story, and all she could do was watch and report what happened in the courtroom.

Millie read the jury members' doubt and disapproval in their raised eyebrows, slight shakes of the heads, and compassionate looks at the defendant, who sat at his table with a supercilious scowl on his impeccably clean-shaven face, scribbling on a pad as if this entire procedure held no interest for him.

Ruffino had questioned Sheriff Hammersmith, as well as the Howard County police officer first on the scene where the body was found, the medical examiner, a handwriting expert, and the state's forensic expert. Hammersmith presented a chart showing the investigation's chronology and what evidence had been collected at each turn and by whom.

In Millie's mind, Ruffino had developed a picture for the jury that pointed to one conclusion—Harmon Rutledge murdered his wife. But during each cross-examination, Harmon's attorney raised just enough doubt about each of the findings that a small whirlwind of panic had started in Millie's gut and grew larger each day of the trial.

Charlie, Lena, and Ethel had all been called to testify for the prosecution on the same day. Ruffino had promised in his opening statement that these three witnesses would establish without a doubt Harmon Rutledge's motive, means, and opportunity and show that he had methodically planned and executed his wife's murder and the disposal of her body with the intent of scapegoating people he believed to be disposable.

Without stammering or getting lost in his thoughts, Charlie responded to Ruffino's questions, telling the jury how he was picked up by Don Whitley, conned into helping him do a job for Harmon Rutledge, dumping the body, and how he returned Trudy's car to Harmon's driveway just after the house blew up.

"Please tell us in greater detail about the day you accepted this job for Mr. Rutledge," Ruffino said.

"We met him behind the county rec center, the one with the playground with big yellow ducks, you know, the kind you ride on," Charlie said. "Harmon had instructions written on a white piece of paper, and he handed them to Don with a bulging plastic bag and the keys to the Volvo. He told us to use the clothes in the bag to dress the body that was in the trunk of the car. Then, he said to dump the body in the woods near a golf course in Howard County and that the address was on that paper, and he gave each of us cash money."

"How much money did Mr. Rutledge give you?" Ruffino asked.

"One hundred twenty dollars," Charlie answered.

A murmur rolled through the gallery. Millie couldn't tell if the spectators thought that amount was a lot or too little for the job.

"And how did you come into possession of the instructions?" Ruffino asked.

"Don handed them to me when we were driving to the airport parking lot because I was the one who was going to drive Dr. Davis's car with the body in it."

"And when was the last time you had the instructions?"

"I threw them away in the motel where I was staying in Emmitsburg."

The county prosecutor thanked Charlie, and Duchamp stood to cross-examine him. "Mr. Goodman," Duchamp intoned from behind his table. "Isn't it true you're an incorrigible drunk and were homeless for some time?"

The prosecutor jumped out of his chair. "Objection, Your Honor." Ruffino pointed to Duchamp. "He is slandering the witness."

"Overruled," Judge Giacometti said.

Charlie flushed. "What? I . . . Yes, but—"

"Answer yes or no, please," Duchamp said.

"Okay." Charlie sucked in his breath. "No."

Duchamp faced the jury. "Weren't you fired from your job because while in a drunken haze *you* slandered the company where you worked?"

"I didn't slander them, I—"

Ruffino stood. "Objection, Judge. The witness is not on trial here."

"Overruled."

Duchamp whirled around and pointed his finger at Charlie. "Didn't your inebriated mistake precipitate the layoff of four hundred people?"

"I . . . not, but—"

Ruffino stood. "Judge."

Giacometti waved his hand. "Sustained."

Duchamp twirled like a dancer toward the jury. "Weren't you recently charged with robbing the First Charles Town Bank?"

Charlie gazed into the gallery. His lawyer, Ms. Markey, smiled and nodded. "The charges were dropped," he said.

"But you were in the bank that day. Correct?"

"Yes."

"You had a mask over your face. Is that right?"

"Yes, but—"

"And if you had succeeded, you would have run off with the money. Right?"

Charlie looked dumbfounded. Ms. Markey raised her hand in the stop position.

"Objection, Your Honor, to this whole line of questioning," Ruffino said. "I repeat, the witness is not on trial."

"Goes to credibility, Your Honor," Duchamp said.

"Sustained," the judge said. "Move it along, Mr. Duchamp."

Duchamp waved his arm as if the prior question could be erased from the jurors' memories. "Did Mr. Rutledge tell you that the body in the trunk of the Volvo was his wife?"

Charlie scratched his head. "I think so?"

"Yes or no, Mr. Goodman."

"Yes. No. I can't remember his exact words. Wait. Yes. He said we had to put the clothes in the bag on Dr. Trudy Davis."

"And did you?"

"Well, no. Things happened. So, I didn't."

"Things happened. What an interesting take, Mr. Goodman." Duchamp looked over his shoulder at the jury. "Did Mr. Rutledge tell you he had killed his wife?"

"How else would he know she was in the trunk of a car at the airport in another state?"

"Yes, or no?"

"No, he didn't say he killed his wife. But he gave us money to move the body. He gave us the keys to her car."

The judge leaned over and said, "Answer the questions Mr. Duchamp puts to you, Mr. Goodman. Don't embellish."

Charlie hung his head.

"Had you ever met Dr. Trudy Davis before?" Duchamp asked.

"No."

"Then how do you know it was her body in the trunk of the Volvo?"

"Are you saying he killed someone else?"

A chuckle rippled across the standing-room-only crowd in the courtroom.

Duchamp glowered. "Was Don Whitley your friend?"

"Yes."

"Did you conspire with Don Whitley to kidnap Trudy Davis, kill her, dump her body, and steal her car?" Duchamp's voice rose to a crescendo.

"No. Of course not."

"We have to take your word for that, don't we, Mr. Goodman? Did you take Dr. Davis's car after you dumped her body?"

Charlie wiped his face with a trembling hand. "Yes."

"Is it true the county prosecutor gave you immunity from any charges related to this case in exchange for your testimony against Mr. Rutledge?"

Charlie glanced at Ms. Markey, who nodded. "Yes."

Duchamp gestured to the jury, his arms out in supplication. "I have no more questions for this unreliable and obviously compromised witness."

"Move to strike, Your Honor," the prosecutor shouted.

"The jury will disregard," the judge said.

Charlie stumbled out of the courtroom with as much dignity as he could muster.

When it was Lena's turn in the witness box, she testified that Trudy had been afraid of her husband and planned to leave him. Prompted by Ruffino, she explained how they found Trudy's laptop and phone and that she'd been able to identify them because they used the same passcode. She was calm until Duchamp opened his cross-examination.

"Weren't you and Trudy Davis lovers?" Duchamp's bottom lip curled.

"Yes." Lena straightened her back.

"Even though you knew she was married?"

"Yes."

Duchamp glanced at the jury. "I guess we'll have to believe you that Dr. Davis said she was leaving Harmon Rutledge since there's no one to corroborate your assertion. Isn't your testimony based on your own fantasy of a life with a wealthy doctor?"

"Objection, Your Honor," Ruffino said.

"What? That's absurd," Lena said. "Are you saying she didn't intend to leave a man she thought might harm her? Who did, in fact, kill her?"

"Withdrawn," Duchamp said.

In the end, although Lena tried to hold her own against Duchamp's barrage of inuendo and insult, she left the court in tears.

Already upset when she took the stand, Ethel's white curls stood up like an angry porcupine's quills. Responding to the prosecutor's questioning, she calmly recited the facts of her interactions with Harmon, how he had contracted with her to sell his house soon after the failed bank robbery, and what she had discovered in his house—the lipstick, the birth control pills, the phone. She identified the piece of paper with his handwritten instructions on it as the one she'd found in an Emmitsburg motel and subsequently turned over to the sheriff.

"How long did you have the phone in your possession, Mrs. Goodman?" Duchamp asked her.

Ethel's face turned red. "Well, I found it during the open house, so that was a Saturday, and I meant to give it to the sheriff right away, but I forgot about it when we went to Emmitsburg the next day and found the note, and then the sheriff told us Trudy was dead, and I didn't remember I had it until that Monday after the house blew up."

"So, you had the phone for three days. Did you use it?"

"No, of course not. Anyway, it was out of juice."

Duchamp raised his eyebrows. "And how did you know that?"

"Well, when I found it, we had to plug it in to find out whose phone it was, didn't we?"

"You're saying several of you handled the phone? Did someone know the passcode to unlock it?"

"Lena did."

"You're saying that Lena, Trudy Davis's lover, took the phone from you and unlocked it and scrolled through its contents before you gave it to the sheriff?"

"Yes."

"And where did the phone go after that?"

Ethel looked at Duchamp as if he were a fire-breathing dragon about to scorch her with his next exhalation. "It was in my bag."

"And the same is true of that list of what you're calling instructions, right? All of you handled the piece of paper and could have added something, or maybe even forged the entire document. Is that correct?"

"What? No. That's absurd. We would never do anything like that."

Duchamp smiled the way a shark does before it bites. "So, you're claiming you didn't plant incriminating information on the phone?"

"No, we didn't!" She pointed at Rutledge. "He's the one who killed her. That monster killed her with the missing pillow, the square white one that matched the other white pillows. That's what he smothered her with."

"What on earth are you talking about, Mrs. Goodman?" Duchamp, eyebrows elevated, turned to the jury. "No such pillow has been entered into evidence." He smirked.

"I'm talking about how a man like that," Ethel's voice shook, "wouldn't have three white pillows and one gray one on his bed. He just wouldn't. The matching white pillow had to be the murder weapon. He must have gotten rid of it."

"This, of course, is another of your senile fantasies, is it not, Mrs. Goodman? Since no one but you ever saw these killer pillows."

Ethel sputtered, "I am not senile." Harmon looked up from his doodling and grinned.

Duchamp called Harmon to testify as his third and final defense witness the next day. Harmon insisted on his innocence. He cried and fumed, reminding Millie of a certain Supreme Court candidate responding to allegations of sexual predation during his Senate hearing.

"Mr. Rutledge," Duchamp said, facing the jury instead of his client. "When was the first time you met Don Whitley?"

Harmon sat up straighter. "When he tried to rob my bank."

"Have you ever had any other dealings with him?"

"He accosted me twice after the attempted bank robbery." Harmon glared at the jury. "When Trudy went missing, I was sure Whitley had something to do with that. I tried to tell the sheriff I thought she'd been kidnapped."

Duchamp nodded. "Did you give Don Whitley instructions for what to do with your wife's body?"

"I did not. Trudy left the house in a huff after we had a fight. But she snapped me the location of her parking spot at the airport. We've always done that as a precaution. I wrote the location down on a piece of paper because, as you know, snap chat doesn't retain messages. I must have left the paper lying on the desk in the kitchen, and Whitley stole it during the open house."

"Clearly, the perpetrator of these heinous crimes against you," Duchamp said, "was none other than Don Whitley, who harbored a venomous hatred for you as proved by his inane assault on the bank, repeated public confrontations, and his subsequent bombing and utter destruction of your house. Isn't that right, Mr. Rutledge?"

Mr. Ruffino had jumped to his feet. "The defense attorney is testifying, Your Honor."

"Overruled," the judge said.

Ruffino began his cross-examination from behind the prosecution's table. "Let's talk about what your wife was wearing when her body was found almost two weeks after you reported her missing. You told Sheriff Hammersmith that she was wearing a white T-shirt, jeans, green sweater, and flip flops. Is that right?"

Harmon darted a glance at his lawyer. "Yes, that's right."

"But when the police found Trudy, she was in her nightgown."

"That's what I was told. I didn't see her."

"How do you account for that?" Ruffino asked.

"I don't know." Harmon's mouth twitched. "As I said, I wasn't there. They never let me see or say goodbye to my dead wife." He ran the tip of his forefinger under his right eye.

"Didn't you in fact give a bag of clothes to Don Whitley and tell him to dress your wife in them?"

"No. I didn't."

"Why did you lie to the sheriff about what she was wearing?"

"I didn't lie. I thought that's what she was wearing. I told you; she ran out of the house in a huff. I didn't see her leave."

"How could you be so specific about the color of the sweater, then?"

"Green was her favorite color." Harmon had ducked his head and wiped the corners of his eyes.

THE case went to the jury for deliberation after closing arguments the next day, and Millie took the morning to drive out to the Whitley home in Bridleburg with the *Daily*'s photographer. Her instincts for a story competed with her distaste for sensationalism, but her editor insisted that a bereaved mother was always good copy.

Standing at the door of the Whitley's tumbledown home, Millie asked, "Did you hear what Harmon Rutledge's attorney said about Don in court yesterday?"

Marge stared at the bearded photographer behind Millie as if she'd never seen anyone like him in her life. Her stringy hair was matted together, and she was wearing a soiled turquoise sweatsuit that she appeared to have been sleeping in for weeks. Swaying, she clung to the door. "I'm not . . . I don't . . . that man . . . the news is . . . it's lies, all lies."

Millie glanced over Marge's shoulder into the living room. A rind of dust and grime covered everything. Ashtrays overflowed. Empty whiskey bottles and food wrappers lay on the floor. "Mrs. Whitley, Rutledge's defense attorney is saying Don abducted and killed Trudy Davis. Do you think that's true?"

Marge's hand trembled as she brought her fingers to her lips. Her nails were chewed down to the nub. "No, he didn't. He couldn't. He wouldn't know how. Not my boy. He was a sweet boy who just didn't know much. He made mistakes, but he would never hurt anyone."

"He did blow up Harmon Rutledge's house with Molotov cocktails."

"No. No, no, no. This ain't right. He couldn't have done that. No." Marge doubled over. A moan escaped her as she sank to the porch floor and hid her face against her knees.

The camera shutter whirred behind her. Millie backed away from the door. "Don't," she said to the photographer. Turning back to Marge, she stammered, "I'm sorry, I won't write this—I'm so sorry."

Millie dragged the photographer to her car. Unable to get the look of shock and despair on Marge Whitley's face out of her head, Millie never jotted a word in her notebook. Her story reported that Mrs. Whitley denied the defense attorney's assertion.

At lunch with Lena and Ethel in a café opposite the courthouse the next day, in case the jury quickly decided Harmon's fate and Millie had to run back to cover the verdict, she couldn't shake the feeling that everything was going downhill.

"Bottom line, I've got a feeling Rutledge might get off," Millie said as she sat down.

"The jury is snowed," she explained. "You can see it on their faces. Duchamp might have confused them into thinking the evidence pointing to Rutledge's guilt is circumstantial and therefore doesn't count as proof he killed her."

"What? That can't be." Lena put her hands in her hair and closed her eyes. "All the incriminating stuff we found. The paper with her license plate number on it has his fingerprints. That's not circumstantial. The handwriting expert said it was his writing. We told them about finding Trudy's laptop in the trash at his house before he'd been told she was dead. Her phone had the text to me with a time stamp."

"And if her phone was at home and automatically shut off because the battery was down to zero, then she couldn't have messaged him from the airport," Ethel bellowed.

"It's infuriating," Millie agreed. "The prosecutor tried to knock Harmon off his lies. But Harmon said she must have bought a burner phone because she forgot hers and that's why she got money out of the ATM."

Ethel raised her eyebrows and scrunched up her mouth. "What about whatever evidence they found in the trunk of Trudy's car?"

"The defense witness said Rutledge's hair and fingerprints in her car could be explained by the fact that he also used the car. Same with Trudy's DNA. A hair might have dropped off her head or skin cells flaked off when she put grocery bags in the trunk."

"But the pillow," Ethel said. "Hammersmith testified about the white fiber they found in Trudy's nose. That was in one of your reports for the paper."

"Yes, she did," Millie said. "And so did the medical examiner. They have the linen fiber but no pillow to match it to. The other pillows I saw on the bed in the open house burned up in the fire so the fiber couldn't be matched to them. I don't know why Ruffino didn't call a rebuttal witness to prove the pillows existed. Everyone at the open house would have seen them."

Ethel raised her arms and shook her hands like someone testifying in church. "But Hammersmith connected the dots for the jury, didn't she? She had a timeline and everything."

"And that business about Don stealing the piece of paper during the open house is crazy," Lena sputtered. "Why would anyone believe Don would go to an open house? Besides, Ethel would have taken one look at him and thrown him out. Wouldn't you, Ethel?"

"There's also the possibility that Judge Giacometti may be in the defense attorney's pocket," Millie said. "He kept denying the prosecution's objections and ruling against him."

"Are Giacometti and Duchamp buddies?" Ethel asked.

"I did some checking," Millie said. "They were in the same fraternity at Yale. And now they're in Rotary together."

"Yale frat brothers. That figures," Lena muttered.

Ethel rubbed her temples. "My blood pressure's going through the roof. Didn't the prosecutor score any points?"

"I thought he might have shifted the jury when he started questioning Harmon about what Trudy was wearing," Millie said. "He started out strong enough but fizzled quickly. The fact is, the jury might think the defense's alternate version of the crime is more likely than that a man of substance like Harmon killed his wife.

"Duchamp made it sound like the police were theorizing without proof. No one saw him kill his wife or drive her car to the airport. Not a single person can swear Rutledge was near Trudy or her car after the date she disappeared. No bag of clothes turned up anywhere the police searched. Any traces of Harmon's DNA on her body can be attributed to the fact that they lived together and slept in the same bed, which of course burned up in the fire."

"So, Don did him a favor?" Ethel put her face in her hands. "What about the cell phone?"

"Duchamp explained away the phone by saying Trudy didn't realize she'd forgotten it until she'd already left the house. Rutledge's fingerprints weren't on it, but ours and Trudy's were. It doesn't prove he killed her, even if she was afraid of him. And there was that whole thing about preserving the chain of custody for evidence, which made Hammersmith look incompetent."

"So, he gets away with murder?" Lena paled. "That can't be what happens. If the law isn't going to handle this, we have to do something."

CHAPTER 44

AFTER five days of deliberations, the jury found Harmon Rutledge not guilty. Millie called Ethel and Lena right after the verdict was delivered.

"Infuriating," Ethel sputtered. "We'll have to take care of this ourselves."

She stormed around her house yelling, "How could twelve people believe that monster? I mean, look at him. He reeks of evil. That smirk, the awful way he leers at people. I can't believe I stood next to him to have my picture taken." She shook her body to rid herself of any lingering DNA.

"They didn't necessarily believe him," Millie said. "Not guilty doesn't mean innocent. It just means that the jury thought the state didn't prove its case. The verdict has to be unanimous. One determined person can hold out and stymie a guilty verdict."

"Then they should've found him guilty of something else," Ethel sputtered. "Even bad penmanship or failing to send his mother birthday cards would be a start."

Millie choked on her soda. "The charge was first degree murder."

"We have to kill him," Lena said through gritted teeth. She had taken a leave of absence from work after being found sobbing in the supply closet by the office administrator. "I can't continue to live if he's alive."

Lena was grieving so hard that Ethel despaired of her ever recovering. "I want to whack him to death with my purse," Ethel said, "but that's too good for him."

Lena snorted. "That poor Don Whitley had the right idea. Burn the bastard."

"Sorry. I can't help you," Millie said. "Killing Rutledge interferes with my journalistic neutrality."

"You're still neutral?" Ethel gawped as if Millie had turned purple.

"No, but I'm sort of against killing people."

Harmon had skedaddled the minute the judge said he was dismissed. He was beyond their reach, but the poison in Ethel's bag tempted her like the ice cream sundae she shouldn't have when she was five pounds from her goal weight. She pondered mailing the aconite to him with instructions to add it to his tea as a flavor enhancer. *A little gift from your friendly neighborhood real estate agent,* she would write on the gift card.

Desperate to find a solution that restored their equilibrium, Ethel drove Lena to Herbs & Remedies, the shop where a year ago she'd bought the poison she hoped would end her dreadful marriage to George. The minute she introduced her friend to the white-haired owner of the shop, they began chattering together in Spanish as if they'd known each other forever. Ethel stood back to watch.

Heads bobbing in unison, Lena's and Hannah's fingers flitted like birds, touching each other's hands and arms, smiling, and laughing. They behaved like old friends who hadn't seen each other in decades. Everything around them glowed. Lena's face shed ten years. Through the haze of smoke from the sage Hannah burned to cleanse Lena's aura, Ethel imagined she saw her friend's sorrow lift off her shoulders.

Feeling left out and old, Ethel fingered paper packets of sachet stacked in a small basket on the counter. This place was her discovery, after all. *Place under your pillow,* one wrapper instructed, *for sweet dreams.* She sniffed it. "Huh. It's just lavender." The magic of the shop dissipated like fog chased away by the afternoon sun.

After a few minutes of breathing burnt sage, though, Ethel's anger also lightened. Her shoulders, bunched up around her ears for weeks, slowly lowered. The furrows in her forehead smoothed out, and her hands tingled as if she'd let go of a rope she'd been clinging to for dear life.

If there was one thing the last six months had taught Ethel, it was that nothing ever went the way she expected. Nothing. The big commission she'd hoped for from the sale of Harmon's house had literally gone up in smoke. Anything left of the house after the explosion and fire had been razed to the ground along with her hopes of being a successful real estate agent. The hardest part had been telling those hopeful buyers that their dream home had vanished.

"Nearly a million in property value lost, and that commission," she mumbled to herself. The young man whose own fury had killed him came to mind. If she hadn't unmasked him in the bank, if she'd realized what he was doing five minutes earlier, maybe . . . But maybe not.

In the next second, Ethel realized she didn't need a million-dollar sale to have a successful life. Life was about bearing up under disappointment and grabbing whatever happiness came to hand in the moment. She'd already won her competition with George: he was dead, she was alive, and she had Charlie, who had come through when she needed him.

"So, there, George." She jiggled her shoulders. "Life's just messy. But I can deal with that."

"Ethel, did you say something? Hannah wants to talk to you," Lena called out.

Ethel, pretending to read a pamphlet, kept her back to them.

"Ethel," Lena held out her hand. "Hannah wants to see your palm."

"Oh. Right." A tiny rebellion held Ethel in place another minute. *I'm being a silly old poop.* She pushed the pamphlet back into the rack and smiled at Lena. *This meeting isn't about me; it's about getting justice for Trudy.*

Ethel held her hand out for Hannah to hold, not expecting her original experience to repeat. But in seconds, she was floating. The feeling of her feet hitting the floor when Hannah let go of her hand startled her.

"You've come a long way," Hannah said.

"About sixty miles," Ethel said.

Hannah giggled. "You don't need to do anything right now. You're where you need to be. And you can return the aconite to me for a refund."

Ethel's cheeks heated. *How does she know I kept it?* She scrambled through her pocketbook and pulled out the tiny ampoule still in the original bag and put it on the counter.

Hannah laid her hand on top of Ethel's. Warmth seeped from her skin and spread up Ethel's arm. "Don't worry about this. You've done everything you were supposed to do."

"But he's the scum of the earth," Ethel mumbled. "He killed his wife, tried to destroy Charlie, and unless we do something, he's going to get away with it."

"No one gets away with anything," Hannah said. "You've done everything you're supposed to do."

"I think I understand," Lena said. "You're saying this isn't our task. We did what we could." She placed her hand on top of Hannah's so the three of them were linked together. "The universe will take care of him."

"Correct," Hannah said. "He will get what's coming to him. Your task now is to enjoy your life, bask in the earth's beauty, and love some people. That's the best revenge."

Ethel squinted at Lena and Hannah. "You're saying go play Mahjong and leave him to fate? Is that all there is to it?"

Hannah tilted her head. "Yes. Focus on what *you* want. You too, Lena. See it in your mind, see it happening, let the joy of everything you already have fill you."

Lena closed her eyes and smiled.

Ethel clasped Lena's and Hannah's hands and focused on what she wanted. She pictured Harmon Rutledge at this exact moment driving from Vancouver to a five-star hotel in Whistler, maneuvering a four-wheel-drive rental car at ninety-five kilometers an hour around a hairpin turn on snow-covered Highway 99.

She saw him in vivid detail down to his red nose hairs, the dimple in his chin, and the red hairs on his fingers curling as he gripped the steering wheel. He smiled at himself in the rearview mirror, admiring his masterful control of the vehicle.

Acquitted, Harmon was free to go anywhere with the fifty-thousand dollars he had stashed in a competitor's safety deposit box, plus Trudy's trust fund and her life insurance. Murder might be messy, but his reputation was legally intact, and, as Ethel had witnessed during the trial, he was happily unencumbered by guilt of any kind.

Ethel's trance-like state deepened, and she could hear Harmon whistling the *Star Trek* opening theme. She concentrated on what she wanted to happen as Harmon's car zoomed around the second bend in an S curve. It was as if she were sitting next to Harmon, seeing what he saw, hearing his thoughts.

A huge brown bear lumbered into the middle of the road. The bear stopped, turned its head, and glared at the oncoming car. For three seconds as the car ate up twenty feet of snow-covered road, Harmon didn't brake. He leaned on the horn, rolled down the window, and shook his fist.

"Get the hell out of there," he yelled.

He might have been terrified of the bear that had blocked the highway when he was four years old, but this beast was not going to get the best of him. Not after everything he'd been through. He'd had enough of small-minded people trying to thwart him.

The bear rose to its hind legs and roared. Harmon automatically jammed his foot on the brake; the car swerved and skidded out of control. He grabbed the wheel with both hands. The vehicle hit a boulder hidden in the snow piled on the shoulder, launched itself airborne, and flipped.

Harmon slammed his palms against the roof of the car. Briefly, he hung upside down while stars danced before his eyes and his breath caught in his throat as the car pinwheeled and then, in slow motion, slammed into the trunk of a two-hundred-year-old cedar and burst into flames.

The bear rose to its hind legs and roared, a bloodcurdling, triumphant bellow. No one crawled out of the burning wreck. Dropping onto all fours, the bear shook its body and rambled into the woods.

Ethel opened her eyes and sighed. Hannah's advice certainly worked. For an entire minute, she had felt like the number one best thing since buttered bread.

THE END

Acknowledgments

Mrs. Goodman's First Murder began life a decade ago as four separate short stories detailing the travails of Don, Charlie, Harmon, and Ethel who, in those incarnations, never met. These four characters haunted me while I wrote other novels, taunting me from the sidelines with assurances that they had more to say and do. The doing part was important.

Their startling and sometimes annoying persistence as they popped up in other stories completely out of place, waving their arms and yelling, "Hey, I'm still here" like out-of-work actors auditioning for roles that haven't yet been written, finally got my full-time attention.

After finishing the collaborative novel *Thoughts & Prayers* with Catherine Baldau, Tara Bell, and K.P. Robbins, which taught me how four minds together might stir the cauldron of invention, I thought, "What if I put these guys together?" The result was like crossing the streams in *Ghostbuster*.

Feeling their way through the maze of this experiment with me were critique partners to whom I owe a debt of perpetual gratitude: award-winning mystery novelists Saralyn Richard, Susan Baker, and Phyllis Moore; The Holey Roaders Maryland-DC-Virginia writers group, each with his or her own distinctive genius, Frank Joseph, Solveig Eggerz, Katherine Lorr, Linda Morefield, Catherine Flanagan, Leslie Rollins, Bob Gibson, Stanley Whatley, and the late Phil Harvey; and the brilliant writers in the International Thriller Writers "Delta" critique group, Jen Dozier, Jeff Soloway, Kathleen Barber, Michael Rothrock, and John Thibault. I wouldn't have made it through all the rewrites and killed darlings without their succinct observations and invaluable feedback.

A special note of thanks goes to my developmental editor Barbara Goffman, who saw what I was trying to do and helped me do it, which

I think is the highest praise possible. And many thanks to the wonderful team at Sunbury Press who have deftly supported my quest to turn words into books, a fairytale feat often similar to turning straw into gold.

I thank my family for granting me the space to ramble around in my own world for long periods of time without interruption. It's possible they worry about me when I ask them strange questions, like what online game could you play for hours, or whether someone would run into a burning house, or should the bad guy get it in the end or not. (The vote on that was split fifty/fifty, and interestingly the women were a lot more bloodthirsty.)

One of my favorite things in the world is watching my children jump into a story and play with its possibilities, carefully assessing at the same time whether their mother has gone off the deep end this time and how to bring her safely to the shore. In the end, they are my best story.

About the Author

GINNY FITE is the author of nine previous novels, three books of poetry, and a collection of humorous essays about aging. A graduate of Rutgers University, Johns Hopkins University, and the Novel Year program at The Writer's Center, her forty-year career in communications included roles in newspapers and magazines, universities, politics, and a robotics R&D company. She lives in beautiful Harpers Ferry with a pair of querulous ghosts. For more information, go to https://ginnyfite.com.

www.ingramcontent.com/pod-product-compliance
Lightning Source LLC
Chambersburg PA
CBHW011342010726
47493CB00009B/2916